Afraid to Breathe

by

Debra Jupe

The Donavon Sister Series

Afraid to Breathe

Cover Art by *Diana Carlile*

The Wild Rose Press, Inc.
PO Box 708
Adams Basin, NY 14410-0708
Visit us at www.thewildrosepress.com

Publishing History
First Crimson Rose Edition, 2019
Print ISBN 978-1-5092-2396-1
Digital ISBN 978-1-5092-2397-8

The Donavon Sister Series
Published in the United States of America

Teddie strained to focus,
adjusting her vision to the dimness. Her gaze swept the moonlit room. Everything seemed normal, nothing disturbed. She stepped to the bed and stared at layers of grubby blankets. Something seemed off. She leaned closer and squinted.

An object rested in the center.

She inched nearer, gaping at the entity. A scream burned the back of her throat. Backpedaling, she hurried outside, fleeing down the staircase. She sped to the foyer and threw the door open.

An elongated shadow obstructed the doorframe. Teddie shrieked again.

"Teddie, it's me." Drew surfaced out of the shadows. Grasping her arm, he guided her to the sofa, and gently eased her to sit. "Hold on, let me turn on a light." He clumped across the hardwoods, his boots ringing in the blackness. A click snapped. A dim glow flooded the room.

Drew strolled to the couch and lowered next to her. He turned to study her, worry etched across his face. "What happened? Another bad dream?"

Her shaky hand swiped at the wetness, moistening her cheeks. "The gun, the one that he—Daddy, used…" Her voice wobbled. "I saw it, just now. Lying on their bed."

Other Titles by Debra Jupe
Available from The Wild Rose Press, Inc.

Echoes in the Wind
Tomorrow Doesn't Matter Tonight
Toxic
Echoes in the Storm

Dedication

To my cousins, Clifford, and Kathy.
You have my heartfelt gratitude for all you've done.
Thanks for reading, the feedback,
and the steadfast support.
Oh yeah, and the wine.
You both rock!
Love you,
Deb

Prologue

Seventeen years earlier

"I'm sorry, Drew." Theodora "Teddie" Donavan inched across the seat toward the pickup's opened door. Hips lifted, she slid off heated, cracked vinyl, allowing her bare feet to sink into the velvet grass below.

She snatched her shoes and clutched the outer handle as she peered into the cab. Her boyfriend, Drew Millard, sat motionless behind the wheel and stared straight ahead.

"Drew?" she whispered.

His head snapped to face her. His angry, pained expression ripped her heart in pieces. She hated to be the cause of his agony.

"I don't get it, Teddie. This is supposed to be about us. Our goal, our dream. We talked about this since we met; hell, we could see it. In a mere blink, it's all changed. Now *our* dream has turned into just *yours.*"

"You're the one who's making this into a *me* situation. I'm trying to offer a solution, but you won't pay attention."

Teddie eased the truck's door shut. Spinning around, she scampered to the front porch of her family home, while fighting to keep in the tears flooding her eyes. She reached toward the screen door.

A slam startled her, and she paused. Drew's

footsteps pounded on the ground, then the sound altered when he stomped onto the porch.

Teddie returned to him as he halted near the edge.

One fist went to his hip, and his nostrils flared. "Go ahead. Say what you need to. I'm listening."

Teddie swallowed and spoke in a wobbly voice. "We can still chase our dream, only we have to redirect to attain our goals."

"How?"

"Come to Nashville with me. I'll meet people"—a hiccup escaped—"the right people. We'll put together a list of contacts, and then we can start to network you."

He aimed his left forefinger and stabbed the air. "Again, how? You're an unknown. You can't just waltz into bigwigs' offices and say, here's my boyfriend, listen to him play."

"I'm aware, Drew. We'll have to plan."

"No point, unless you make it big. No guarantee that's gonna happen, no matter what they tell you. You might land in the middle of the pack or take a flying leap and flop. Wherever you are career wise, your influence will be nothing in the beginning. Your professional decisions will be left to whichever conglomerates you're tied to," he declared with a foreboding edge in his tone. "Besides. I refuse to let anyone say my success—if I happen to find success—came on the hems of my girlfriend's coattails."

"I don't understand what difference it makes if I help. The plan's always been to share credit."

"Different scenario. We were equal partners. Except now you changed the rules."

"Okay, say you're right about a rough road ahead. Things still won't be so bad." She hesitated as he shot her a "you've lost your mind" look. "If you come with me," she finished nervously.

"And do what? I'm not exactly useful, am I?" He held up his right arm. A plaster cast encompassed his hand and wrist. "What'll I do? Follow you around while you travel cross country? Or maybe you'll hire me as your errand boy. Or worse, I'll be labeled the slacker boyfriend, who lives the highlife while his girl works her butt off." His head shook. "I don't think so."

"You could venture out on your own. Pound the pavement, hit the circuits and—"

"Not the plan, Teddie."

"We have to deviate if we can't make our original idea work. Tons of musicians make the rounds before they become famous."

"I don't intend to be one of them. I've already paid my dues."

Teddie gnawed her bottom lip, stumped how to revise his turmoil into tranquility.

She hoped he'd act reasonably once he calmed down.

She tossed a glance his way.

More accurate, when he calmed down. The man had a stubborn streak times ten.

"I should be more supportive," he uttered. "But I'm having a tough time dealing with your moving on without me."

"Okay, Drew, what do you want me to do? Turn them down? I will if it makes you feel better."

"You're talking crazy."

"I want you happy."

"Passing up a recording deal with a major record company won't make me happy."

"I haven't signed anything. I'll tell them no. We can go on performing at clubs and fairs once your cast is off."

"Doc's not sure I'll keep my dexterity after I heal. Might've damaged the tendons in my fingers."

"You'll recover completely," she stated with more conviction than she felt.

"Too late to go backward, anyway. You'll resent or blame me if we fail. It'll be my fault if you don't make it, and I can't live with that responsibility."

"Failure isn't an option." She strolled to where he stood and flanked his hand between hers. "Come on, let's keep our act together. We're so close, we can practically touch our dreams."

"You mean, *you* can." He jerked his hand away as if her touch burned his skin. "You're already there."

"Okay, Drew." She spun away. "I pleaded with them. I tried to convince them to take you too. I explained we're a team. They wouldn't budge."

"Great. The entire industry will view me as a pity case. No one will ever listen to my songs or care to hear me perform."

Her mind screamed. She couldn't win. "Broken bones certainly make you unreasonable," she half joked.

"The music business isn't a big one. Insiders do talk," he continued his argument. "Trust me. Word will get out my girlfriend pled to get me into their inner circle and was told no. I'll be nothing more than a joke."

"Rumors will also circulate you punched a hole in the wall and broke your hand." Her lips leveled into an even line. "After you realized the record company only wanted to sign me."

"Thanks. I wanted to hear a play-by-play again. Like it's not on my mind enough."

"I've apologized repeatedly, but this is the last time I'm saying I'm sorry. I shouldn't have to ask forgiveness for something that isn't my fault."

"Then stop," he snapped.

A strained silence stretched between them. Drew perched a shoulder against a slim pillar; his unimpaired fist had returned to his hip. He stared out onto the cove and studied a pair of cranes, searching to find a late afternoon snack.

He pushed off the pole and jerkily checked his watch. "I gotta get to work."

"How are you going to do your job?" She motioned at his cast. "You have a major fracture."

"I'll figure a way."

She did a mental shrug. His trade involved using his hands. Teddie didn't know how he'd perform with shattered bones, but she was through debating. No use wasting her efforts when his attitude remained so disagreeable.

Drew pivoted toward his truck, then paused as if he had more to say.

Teddie walked up behind him. "We're on for later, right? Jake's barbeque and swim party?"

"I'm not in a party mood." He raised his arm to exhibit his cast, again. "Nor swimming."

"Mmm, better. We'll hang out by ourselves." She grinned. "Interested in sneaking to the woods for a little one-on-one time?"

He frowned, his concentration still centered on the water-filled cove. He didn't speak.

Teddie stepped closer and placed a gentle palm on his shoulder. He tensed, his frame rigid from her light stroke. "Drew? You don't want to go?"

He waited before he answered. "I'm thinking we shouldn't see each other anymore."

Teddie gasped as her hand fell off his shoulder. "You're breaking up with me?" Her expression elevated to a high squeak. "This isn't fair. I didn't do anything wrong."

His disappointment was expected, yet she never imagined their relationship would end. He turned to face her. The natural warmth in his dark eyes had dissolved and was replaced by an emotionless blank.

"You're right. You didn't. Still, I can't see us having a future if you're moving to Nashville, and I'm staying in Jacob's Cove. We'll be hundreds of miles apart. How can we be a couple living that far away?"

"Many couples live in separate cities and are successful."

"I don't do long distance."

"You won't even consider moving with me?"

"No point. I don't need a recap of my failure every day."

Teddie gripped onto a pillar to steady herself. Their bond was strong and would withstand whatever life threw at them. Or so she believed. But a peek at his cold, unyielding profile told her otherwise.

"You've wanted to leave Jacob's Cove since your family transferred here. We decided to go after our dream a long time ago, and now you're giving up because we need to change directions? You're stronger than this, Drew."

"You'll do better if I'm not in your way."

Drew circled away. Without another word, he walked to his pickup while she watched, wounded and speechless. She wanted to argue more, but he didn't leave her anything else to fight about. He had made his decision, and they were done.

Teddie whipped around and ran into the house. Tossing her shoes on the floor, she scaled the staircase and hurried down a long hallway, her paces ricocheting off the walls as they struck the hardwood floors.

"Mom," she sobbed.

She stopped at her parents' bedroom door. A fist raised, but she held up before she knocked. Enraged voices yelled from behind the walls. Her parents were in a fiery argument? Unusual. They normally displayed the portrayal of happiness and were deemed a perfect couple by others.

And a chime chirruped in between short, quiet spaces. Her mother's music box. Why was it playing?

Using the topside of her hand, she brushed the wetness off her cheek and leaned forward to eavesdrop. Their screeching words weren't clear. The animated conversation lasted another two or three minutes, then their disagreement abruptly ended, tinkles from the music box the only sound.

An eerie stillness shrouded the corridor as if a heaviness filled the air and squeezed.

A frightened shout erupted from behind the secured walls.

Pop. Pop.

Hair on the back of Teddie's neck stood straight up. Panicked, she tripped over her feet and stumbled to the floor. Creeping onto her knees, she edged toward the doorway and positioned her ear to listen.

An odd stench seeped past the doorframe. The odor resembled bundles of lit firecrackers. A brief mind-flit made her curious over the strange smell, but she was too confused to analyze the peculiar scent.

She crawled to her feet. Trembling fingertips tapped the doorknob. Her jittery hand grasped the handle, rotated, and flung the access ajar.

Dashing inside, she skidded to a halt, just beyond the threshold. Her body braced. Waves of shock bolted as a cry wedged in her throat, blocking her screams. Grotesque smells intensified. She slapped a palm across her mouth, giving the gruesome sight another glimpse, and willed her feet to tread backward into the hall.

A warm hand encircled her arm as she reentered the hallway and whirled her the opposite way. "Teddie, what's wrong?"

"Drew," she wailed, pointing to the bloodshed.

Drew sidestepped her and hastened to the entrance, curving past the doorway. He stopped, then bicycled his legs, backpedaling until he smacked into the far wall.

His eyes were open wide and filled with fear. "Teddie, what the…"

"I don't know, but I have to do something," she shrieked, rushing toward the bedroom. "Help me, please."

Drew peeled his body off the wallpaper, curved his healthy arm around her waist, and tugged her back to him. He cradled her against his chest.

"It's too late, baby." His declaration was grim. "It's too late to help them."

8

Chapter 1

Present Day

"You made me your assistant for a reason."

Teddie Donavan craned her neck, her cell phone clasped between her shoulder and ear. She wrestled with the steering wheel, ready to make a third stab at squeezing parallel into a compact parking space.

"I'm not standing in your way, Aubrey," Teddie snapped. "You should be able to perform your duties without my input."

She struggled to straighten her vehicle. Once the sedan was even, she drove forward to align her car's nose next to the pickup parked ahead of her. Shifting into reverse, her foot tapped the accelerator as she orbited the wheel, far right. Slowly, the car backed, veering within a pair of monster-size trucks. Trucks purchased to overcompensate for something their presumed male owners lacked, evidently.

Her car rolled until the rear tires bumped a curb and came to an abrupt stop. Blowing out a frustrated breath, she threw the gear into drive and mentally regrouped, prepared to attempt round four.

"I can't do my work effectively if you refuse to cooperate," her elder sibling pestered. "Your feedback's required."

Teddie fought to reel in her aggravation. "You've

overseen my agenda since my beginnings. You're more familiar with my routine than I am."

"Not the point, Teddie. We have quite a few details to discuss concerning your current itinerary."

"I'm on sabbatical. That's as detailed as my schedule gets."

She repositioned the car, primed to restart the parking process. This time, she smoothly manipulated into Main Street's last open spot. An arm raised, executing a muted fist pump. She killed the engine and unbuckled her seatbelt, happy to abandon the torturous drill.

Next on the list. End this call. Aubrey wouldn't lay off, and Teddie was way past tired of her constant debate.

"Your calendar is still full. You need to tell me which events are postponements and what we can cancel."

"I'm aware, Aubrey."

"Good. Also know I didn't make the flight here because Jacob's Cove is a great vacation destination. Nor did Raven."

"No one asked you or Raven to tag along. In fact, I'm not clear why you're here. This work could've been done electronically."

"We're worried, Teddie. Your last few months were rough. Personally and career wise. You have to keep your guard up and watch every movement."

Teddie pocketed the car's remote and snatched a credit card lying in the center of the console, then exited, using her rear to slam the door. "Right. Since we'd rather avoid the press jumping in to speculate why I'm revisiting my hometown after a seventeen-year absence."

"No, we don't want them to know. Our job is to protect you, and you're not cooperating."

"They can always research archives."

"True. Even so, your personal life's been under a microscope. Are you set to suffer more when the unknown is divulged and dissected?"

"I'll manage any new leaks the same as I did the old ones." Teddie rested against a warm fender. Legs crossed at the ankles, she surveyed the neighborhood. "Might as well get past the hard part."

"Which is why you decided to make a trip into town?"

"Pantry's bare. I prefer my nourishment closer than fifteen miles. A journey into the Cove's jungle is warranted."

"You should check into a hotel. Ease into ancient memories instead of delving in full throttle." Aubrey hesitated. "Or better yet, come to Cerulean Beach, and stay with us a while."

"I'm fine where I am."

"We've ordered room service. Lobster Bisque and homemade bread."

"Sounds yummy, but I'll pass."

"The old house must be a total disaster."

"Yeah, but I didn't anticipate finding it in good shape after so many years of vacancy. The crew we pay to do upkeep does a decent enough job on the exterior, but the inside's a mess. I plan on bringing in professional cleaners."

"Then tonight you'll sleep in dust, dirt, and whatever." Aubrey stopped. "A bunch of creepy crawlers may invade your space once lights are turned off."

"I'll manage."

A span of silence ensued. Teddie hoped the pause meant their exchange was about to wind down.

"Did you walk through the whole house?" Aubrey questioned, foiling Teddie's wishes.

"Not yet."

"You didn't check upstairs?"

"Not the section you mean."

"The door's locked, right?"

"I assume." Teddie's grip squeezed, almost crushing the phone. "I can't find the nerve to step into the hallway. You know my nightmare still haunts me."

"Exactly. Which is why you shouldn't live in that house. Especially by yourself."

"I have to tackle whatever this is so I can put it to rest."

"What if this memory refuses to fade?"

"Not sure yet."

"Well, I am. Let's place the property on the market." Aubrey's demanding tone became coaxing, serene. "I've thought a lot about it, and Raven agrees."

Teddie didn't speak. Her opinion didn't match her siblings, which they already knew. Yes, she must confront her demons, but once she put history in perspective, the necessity to sell the family home may not seem as urgent. She preferred not to casually file away Donavan lineage, since younger generations waited in the wings.

"Our great-great grandparents left Ireland and immigrated to the states. They built the home from the ground up. Historical principles mean a lot to me, and you're suggesting we cash in on the Donavan dynasty."

"A tragedy happened inside that house," Aubrey almost shouted. "You experienced the catastrophe firsthand. I can't make myself return." Her demeanor calmed. "Drop this, Teddie. Forget everything in Jacob's Cove; forget Jacob's Cove."

"You expect me to ignore my youth. A big part of who I am is attributed to where I grew up. Savannah…"

"Is fine with her life," Aubrey interrupted. "Teddie, I'm begging you. You're not well. Let's pack our stuff and go home to Tennessee. We can care for you while you rest, like doctors have prescribed."

Teddie's jaw clenched so tightly it ached. Neither sister got it. This journey belonged to her. Specific life-altering events demanded reexamination before she laid them to rest. Her revisiting the past opened the possibilities of a tranquil future.

"Doctors diagnosed you with exhaustion due to your working too much, and your tiredness contributed to a terrible spill off stage. You're supposed to relax and recuperate."

Teddie smiled into her phone. Aubrey refused to sacrifice an inch.

"This argument is a repeat. Correction. Countless repeats." Teddie paused. "I'm doing this. Accept it. End of story."

"Fine. Then let us join you. We're forty miles away. We can be there in less than an hour."

"First, I prefer to do this alone, and second, you and Raven avoided our old home like it's possessed."

"We'll sacrifice if that's what you need."

"I'm fine." Teddie's eyes rolled. They couldn't fathom how this stay was a huge part of her healing. Emotional healing. "I'll make you a deal. Let me do this. I'll bring in a company to clean, to make the house livable. A few major repairs are needed too; therefore renovations are also necessary. Once those are done, both of you can join me."

"Whoa, wait, renovations?" Aubrey's speech mounted to an elevated squeak. "If you're thinking what I think you're thinking—let's just say, not a good idea."

"You're talking riddles," Teddie responded lightly.

"No, I'm not. You know what I'm referring to." She hacked a fake cough. "Or shall I say, whom."

"You're overreacting. Tons of restoration businesses are located nearby."

"Oh, Teddie. You're plunging off a high dive and into more heartache."

She ignored her sister's prediction. "Why don't I meet you for lunch later this week. After I'm settled in."

"Your way or no way. You should've been the first born instead of last." Aubrey performed a slick subject change. "How are you feeling? Are you taking your prescriptions?"

Teddie also preferred to avoid this conversation. "I'm fine. I told you no pills. I won't even open the packages. My vitamins are enough."

"You're too tired to notice how exhausted you are. Take your meds, Teddie."

"I'm hanging up now, Aubrey. Stores may close early, and I want to find food. We'll touch base soon. Tell Raven hello. Love you." She swiped the off icon, before her older sister had an opportunity to reply.

Cell tucked into her rear pocket, Teddie deposited the conversation, her overprotective sibling's advice, and warnings aside.

She strolled the vacant bricked roads in search of sustenance. Her interest drifted to her surroundings. Dusk set in as a blue moon soared. A salty breeze blew off the water. Streetlamps pooled circles of golden light over the walkways as midsummer foliage lined the sidewalk and created a perfumed mixture to scent the air.

She marveled how the community revolutionized. Much of the town square had been refurbished, yet a sameness also lingered. Cottage-like buildings painted in beachy colors endured, but as an alternative to selling of coastal goods, the updated storefronts sold whatever trended.

This evening, stores were closed, including the eateries. Teddie might be forced to settle and eat convenience store cuisine. If a drive by meal was her only choice, she'd go hungry.

She walked the streets, bordering on waving a white flag and surrendering to hunger, when she came upon an opened café nestled among the unopened shops. The outdoor chalked sign promised upscale, delicious food in a relaxed environment.

She wandered through the entryway and found the eatery almost empty.

"Just one?"

She turned to the hostess and grinned. The girl's expression conveyed her opinion on dining solo. The young woman's attitude didn't bother her. Single didn't include complications as opposed to a happily ever after not panning out.

"Inside or outside?"

Teddie peered into a wide uncluttered space,

leading to an inviting patio. "Let's do the terrace."

She smiled, delighted at the prospect of dining outdoors sans a crowd bombarding her. Wonderful folks helped her afford the ability to live a comfortable life and do what she loved to do. She didn't mind when fans recognized her and desired to connect. Much.

Occasionally, she craved anonymity. One of the reasons she chose Jacob's Cove to recover. People knew her. They'd leave her in peace after they realized she returned.

Seated next to a three-foot decorative iron fence, she disregarded the menu in front of her and gazed across the street. She smiled to herself.

The Phoenix Opera House.

An elegant ballroom located in the center of town. Once an old warehouse, the overhauled building was a premier entertainment venue and used to hold large gatherings. Nothing different there. Remembrances widened her grin. Parties, proms, her first paid performance floated amid her thoughts.

Perhaps she should've invited her sisters to accompany her rather than insist they lodge a town away. They'd get a kick out of seeing the place again. Maybe she'd sway them to make the trip after she resolved her conundrums. She might even drag them onstage and sing a song or two. The trio singing together again would add a bit of fun to this jaunt.

"You decided?"

Teddie flinched. A willowy woman had put a glass of ice water on the table and lingered nearby.

"What do you recommend?" Teddie squinted to see her nametag. "Darby? Unusual, but pretty. A name you don't hear often."

"I come from unusual circumstances. My name kinda works."

"Do you live in Jacob's Cove?"

"Not really. I'm a drifter, of sorts." A shoulder lifted. "Or I was until the money ran out. Now I'm biding my time and padding my wallet. I intend to hit the road once I'm flush again."

Teddie gave a non-committal nod.

Darby trained her pencil at the meal selections. "Know what you want?"

Teddie handed the menu to her, not bothering to check inside. "I'll take the special."

Darby ambled toward the building. She stopped midway, spun to Teddie, and gestured toward a small group dining inside. "They say you're famous?"

Teddie's head shook. "I'm just Theodora."

"Thought so. I'll turn your order in. Shouldn't take long."

Teddie slackened in her seat. Her interest reverted to the Opera House. Expensive automobiles flocked around the circular driveway. Valets welcomed the well-attired visitors as they exited their rides. The party seemed in full swing. The uncovered floor-to-ceiling windows permitted a peek inside, although the hordes of guests obstructed her view.

A basket of heated, homemade bread materialized and diverted her attention. Teddie found a knife and buttered a slice. She took a loving bite, humming a sigh. She didn't consume carbs often. and this tasted like heaven.

Her attention was redrawn to the event across the street. A shift in the moonlight sparked her curiosity and guided her away from interior activities to an attached open-air pavilion situated over the water.

A faint outline—yes, two people stood almost nose to nose, their identities concealed by murky shadows.

The silhouettes looked as if they were in a heated argument. Heads bobbed and hands fluttered. Voices elevated and vibrated, indistinct across the bay. The taller of the two spun away and paced across moon-beamed splotches spilling onto the deck, while the other person leaned against a wooden rail.

Teddie's focus stayed glued to the near inaudible scene; she stretched her neck to catch a clearer view.

They reconvened at midpoint and circled in a frantic war dance. Heads continued to bobble as arms flailed in the air. The taller gave the shorter a hard shove. The shorter staggered in reverse and stumbled, collapsing into a gate. It released and opened to a set of stairs, leading to a miniature dock underneath.

The person tumbled downward, bouncing off the staircase as if in slow motion. A faraway boom suggested they struck the dark pier below. A soft splash resonated.

Teddie hitched a breath.

The remaining party curved over the wall.

"Call an ambulance," Teddie whispered.

Rather than heeding Teddie's soundless pleas, they shut the entry, dusted their palms, and disappeared into the darkness.

A scream caught in Teddie's throat as her heartbeat raced. She bounded from her chair and onto her feet. The seat toppled and crashed to the cement.

"What's wrong?" Darby deposited Teddie's dinner in front of her. She twisted in the direction Teddie's finger aimed.

"A murder," Teddie cried. "I just witnessed a murder."

Debra Jupe

Chapter 2

"Call the police," Teddie shouted to Darby as she hiked a leg above the small fence. "I'm going to see if I can help." She twisted over the barrier and made an effortless dash to the other side of the road.

Boots clicking on the driveway, she hurled her hands into the air and reversed to dodge an onslaught of incoming cars. Honks and beeps encouraged her to move quicker. Once she engineered the treacherous drive, she tore past a pair of beveled glass doors and charged inside the Phoenix.

The ballroom's tranquil atmosphere brought her to a standstill.

Spherical tables shrouded in navy tablecloths dotted the space. A miniature peach and white floral design and flickering tea candles were centerpieces. Low-lit chandeliers dangled from uncovered beams and glowing sconces ornamented exposed, red-brick walls. Centered in the rear sat a massive brick fireplace. The hearth and mantel were adorned with multitudes of silver candles, completing the dreamlike climate.

This ambiance didn't suggest a hint of criminal action.

Except she saw someone pushed to their alleged death.

Now she had to confirm it.

She ducked into the shadows, backed into a far

20

wall, and studied the scenery to formulate a plan.

Guests appeared engaged. Men congregated near the bar, while women clustered around tables and chatted. Other attendees cruised a lavish buffet, their fares piled upon refined bone china. A Vivaldi String Quartet accompanied the low background chatter.

Everyone was occupied.

She could seize the advantage and slip out the back, unseen. The destination was a set of double doors across the polished wood floor, almost in alignment from her current spot. Traveling direct wasn't an option, but the gap around the walls remained unencumbered and dark.

Teddie began a steady progression, keeping a keen eye on the invitees to ensure no one detected her. Achieving midpoint, she entered a section where the radiance intensified and lights beamed much brighter.

Carefully, she slinked over the visible stretch, her attention alerted to any abnormal activity, maintaining her even pace. A few more feet and she had this. She was within inches of her destination when she heard it.

A soft utter, almost inaudible, yet the words were distinct. "Isn't that Teddie Donavan?"

An instant hush captured the room. Heads swiveled.

Suddenly, she became sensitive to how her faded jeans and laced top didn't blend in with the partygoers posh attire. Why her current wardrobe popped into her head as her chief worry wasn't sane; what she wore didn't matter.

A crowd gathered. Each person's face silently posed the same question.

Why was she here?

Stage smile in place, she waved an arm overhead as she crept toward her escape. "Sorry to crash your bash. I'm on my way to the deck." She walked in reverse, toward an etched doorway. "I'll be out of your hair in a jiff."

The curious group closed in. Questions peppered from every side.

"When did you get into town?"

"How are you? Have you recovered?"

"Do you remember me? I'm Mandy. We both went to Camp Calypso in sixth grade, and we were assigned to the same cabin. Our beds were next to each other."

"Are you home for good?"

Her bottom bumped the door's handle. Intrusions and delays hindered her. She sought to break away, but she also had to sustain discretion. Due to recent media speculations, she couldn't reveal the reason for her disruption. Not till authorities obtained hard evidence to support her.

She swung both arms above her head, once more. "Thank you. Your concern is touching. I intend to stay in Jacob's Cove for a long holiday. I'm excited to reconnect with my old friends and anticipate making some new ones, as well."

"Can you sing us a song?"

She peeked at the quartet in the corner. "I won't hone in on another entertainer's performance." Her butt nudged the door as she backstepped, nearing her escape. "Enjoy your evening."

"How dare you attend this benefit uninvited? Leave the building, *NOW.*"

A bewildered quietness spread. A slender woman in a clingy, red dress and gold high heels barreled among the mayhem until she materialized ahead of the throng.

She halted, standing toe to toe with Teddie, fists planted on her waist, her eyes blazing. "You're not welcome. Not tonight or any other night. No one wants you in Jacob's Cove."

Teddie's lips curved. Her old friend Evie St. John. Correction. Ex-friend, whose enraged demeanor hadn't diminished over time.

"Nice to see you, Evie."

"Don't act coy, Teddie," Evie spouted through gritted teeth. "You ran away from Jacob's Cove and never bothered to look back. Not once in your illustrious career have you credited us for supporting you early on. You don't rate a smidgen of admiration." She aimed a forefinger at the exit. "It's time for you to take a final bow and leave. No encore's required."

Teddie planted her feet, refusing to move. She wasn't about to let Evie St. John order her around or make her feel guilty.

Their initial encounter arose on the playground in first grade. Each claimed the last swing on the schoolyard swing set, which evolved into a fistfight. Teddie verged on pommeling the girl when a teacher intervened and hauled them to the principal's office. Their troubled moment bonded them into their later teens until an amorous conflict dissolved their alliance.

Evie confronted the shocked audience. "I'll say this to her face, the same as I'd tell anyone who's impressed that Jacob's Cove is the great Teddie Donavan's hometown." She turned a seething glare on Teddie, pausing for effect. "You're ashamed of this town and the residents who live here."

Mutters sprinkled among the gathering.

"What Evie says is true." The prattle stopped. "To a point." Teddie ambled into the cluster's core. "I don't talk about my place of birth. But I do not"—she rotated an inch to stare Evie down—"harbor any shame against this wonderful city or the fine citizens who live in it."

Evie snorted.

"Her parents, Evie. Sad, sad incident." A mature gentleman near the front shook his head. "Can't blame Teddie or her sisters for avoiding Jacob's Cove."

"We understand, Teddie," another supporter offered.

"Thank you." Teddie smiled. "There are reasons for my silence. And those reasons should be respected."

Evie did an exaggerated eye roll and applauded a loud, gradual clap. "Spoken like a true performer. You got the shtick down, don't you, girlfriend?"

"If you bother to read my music covers, I give recognition and send love to my extended family members in JC. I just don't state JC's identity."

"You include the initials because mystery sells your songs. I'm not a bigwig in your world, but I'm familiar with marketing tactics. Clandestineness makes people curious. They crave to discover your secrets. Jacob's Cove residents are nothing more than pawns you use to heighten your career."

"This discussion has ended," Teddie announced in an understated tone.

She spun around, unwilling to give Evie the satisfaction of continuing the argument. The woman was toxic. Teddie didn't realize the extent of Evie's resentment until way too late.

Evie clapped her hands and steered everyone back

to the event. "Party's this way, people."

Teddie utilized the opportunity and fled outside, hurrying to the edge of the dock. Her shaking hands grasped the handrail.

Evie rattled her. She'd forgotten the nasty sting her venom inflicted. She squinted and looked inside one of the huge windows. Festivities had resumed in full force. Evie stood next to the entrance, safeguarding the exit, to guarantee her fundraising buddies remained indoors.

Her interest in Evie and crew deviated, and her attention returned to the squally sea. Someone went over the side. With help. Since no one around required aid, she assumed the victim suffered their fate amid frothing whitecaps below.

Police should've shown up by now. She checked the diner, wondering if Darby followed her directive and phoned them. Her stomach lurched as a surge of nausea struck her.

Lights were extinguished, indicating the bistro had shut down for the night. Darby must not've believed Teddie and disregarded her pleas to call help.

So now what? Phone the sheriff's office? An investigation was warranted, and officials needed to recover the poor soul.

She just didn't want to be the one to report it.

A shiver ran through her. The night air possessed a frosty edge, and breezes blowing off the water amplified the chill. She chaffed her bare arms, then reluctantly stretched a hand to her rear pocket to retrieve her cell.

"Teddie?"

Teddie's whole body braced. Her breaths shortened as her heart battered her ribs. Seventeen years had gone by, yet she'd recognize that raspy, deep voice anywhere. She had made this jaunt to tackle ghosts and put ancient history behind her, but she was unprepared to stumble upon her past this soon.

"Teddie Donavan? Is that you?"

She swallowed and did a slow pivot. "How are you, Drew?" Her vocal cords sounded faint and drained.

Drew looked as stunned as she felt. Dark, calculating eyes trailed her up and down, absorbing every detail. He finally zeroed in on her face. "I'm well. Better, I think. Or I will be eventually." He released a tense chuckle. "I can't believe you're in town."

"I'm having trouble imagining it myself."

He walked toward her but stopped five feet away. They'd known each other since they were kids. Together, they journeyed into hell and back, yet neither tried to embrace.

"What you've done, wow, your talent didn't surprise me—you're one of the biggest stars in country music and held the honor a long time."

She smiled. "I can say I made it."

"What brings you to Jacob's Cove?"

"I overdid my workload. Can't sleep, I mean, I do, but only an hour or two. I also fell off a platform a few weeks ago. I'm forced to take time off and rest." A brief pause ensued. "Doctor's orders."

"You're rich and can travel to any place in the world. Why Jacob's Cove, and why visit now?"

Her mouth dried. Their conversation shouldn't continue in this direction. She did a U-turn in dialog. "What about you? What are you up to?"

"Still at Millard's Restoration."

"Your business crossed my mind after I arrived. The old house needs a major overhaul. I'll contact your father in a day or two."

"Dad semi-retired eleven years ago. He and Mom moved home to East Texas, and he has a smaller business there. My cousin and I run the place, now."

"Oh. Good for you," was all she managed.

She gulped more air, fighting her brain to preserve lucidity. She'd mentally gone blank. Too many memories stood in front of her. She sang before millions, performed for presidents, kings, and queens, and shared the spotlight with the most famous people in the world, and never broke a sweat. Nothing she aspired to presented as much anxiety as facing Drew Millard this second.

Searching her thoughts, she struggled to find something else to say. "How's your hand? Can you play? Do you still perform?"

"Yes, to all of the above. I'm healed, I play, and I'm in a band. We've been together about ten years. We do local clubs and bars. Lots of the places we used to…" He stopped and cleared his throat.

"Well, well," came a voice from behind.

Teddie and Drew swiveled toward the newcomer. Both visibly tensed. Evie emerged out of the ballroom and strolled between them, arms folded over her middle.

An eyebrow arched as she glared at Drew. "I wondered where you were, but I should've guessed. You knew about her arrival?"

"No. I just found out."

"Evie, he couldn't've. Only my manager and my sisters are aware of my location."

"I bet. I just bet."

An enormous swell pitched above the pavilion and interrupted their exchange. A fleeting reprieve was granted to relocate and avoid getting soaked.

The water's motion jogged Teddie's memory and reminded her why she invaded the Phoenix. "I don't have time to join in your silly games, Evie. A horrible incident occurred here, and someone's dead because of it."

Drew displayed confusion. "What are you talking about, Teddie?"

"Somebody went over the side a while ago."

"You mean they jumped?"

"Not exactly." She preferred not to go into details, but feared she was left without a choice. "I dined at the café across the street. Two people were out here. They argued. One shoved the other into the water. As far as I know, that person hasn't surfaced."

Drew sprinted to the rail. "Where?"

Teddie indicated at the gateway. "Gate's unlatched. They fell into the opening, down the stairs, and hit the wharf before falling into the water."

Evie walked to the banister and peered at the churning surfs. "I don't see anyone." A satisfied smile flashed at Teddie. "Hmm…reports are right on, aren't they? Addiction to prescription drugs, is it?"

Teddie refused to be drawn in. She already responded to ample inquires relating to her tumble and health issues. If Evie desired to go there, she could take the trip by herself. Teddie would have none of it.

Drew jiggled the gate. It wouldn't budge. His mouth hardened as he glanced at her. "Locked."

"Maybe the killer bolted it."

He slipped the latch and raced down the staircase to the boat ramp. "Nothing," he yelled over the waves. "Too dark and too wet to tell if there are blood splatters."

Teddie focused on the lapping breakers beneath the pier. Her heart plummeted, sure whoever was propelled into those cold sprays would never see another day.

Drew climbed upstairs, refastening the clasp to the entrance. "Did you phone the sheriff?"

"I doubt it," Evie interjected. "This is a product of Teddie's drug-induced imagination or"—she wagged a finger in front of Teddie's face, then pointed at Drew—"a lie you two concocted so you could meet."

Fatigue unexpectedly inundated Teddie, snapping her patience. "You're as ridiculous as ever."

"Seriously, Evie." Drew's hands rested on his hips. "I get you think I'm on the right side of stupid, but you and I scheduled a talk. Why would I invite Teddie?"

"You tell me." Her brows expanded up her forehead. She reverted to Teddie. "You witnessed this so-called murder. Why isn't a homicide team here to examine the scene? First thing I'd do is dial 911 if I saw a person killed."

"I told Darby, the waitress, to phone them." Teddie turned her head to verify the eatery was still dark. "I guess she ignored me."

Teddie's emotions were being dragged away from the perilous situation. The victim had to be found. Without a body, she couldn't verify a murder happened, and proof was required.

Tabloids had distorted her plunge off stage and her illness into a more ominous problem, alluding to substance abuse because of a meltdown which stemmed from a personal disappointment. The assumptions weren't true, yet rumors swelled like a raging wildfire. If law enforcement heard of her negative accounts, they may conclude she hallucinated the entire episode.

Had she? Was she so tired her mind tricked her?

"Your server undoubtedly heard you're crazy." Evie's jaw clenched. "Truthfully, I don't care about your private struggles. You deserve whatever karma's wrath doles. However, I do care about Drew, and I demand answers." Evie slanted closer. "And I want them now. What's going on between you and my husband?"

Chapter 3

A hand flew over Teddie's mouth to cover a noisy gasp. She couldn't think of a satisfactory retort to curb Evie's paranoia, and by the look on Drew's face, he was at a loss too.

No one said a word.

After a long stretch, Drew shattered the uneasy quiet. "Your accusations border on hysterics, Evie."

Evie whipped around and glared at her husband. Her chin stubbornly jutted as crimson tinted her cheeks. "You're trying to manipulate me and make me wonder if I'm the problem. I'm not falling for your tricks, Drew. I'm clued in on your every deceit."

"What are you talking about?"

Her eyes narrowed. "You don't know?"

"How would I?"

"Allow me to elaborate. I was naïve when we married, but I'm not now. You never got over your true love. Hell, how could you? She fled town and *you* two months before we walked down the aisle."

Drew gave a sarcastic chuckle. "I'll give you a gold star for creativity."

"You're saying tonight's a coincidence?" She marched to an electrical box and flipped a switch. Light flooded nearly half the landing. "Jacob's Cove's favorite daughter reappeared on the same night we…" the corners of Evie's lips boosted, "let's just say her timing's a little too perfect."

"Is this necessary?" Teddie abandoned the dock's edge and paced near the quarreling couple. "Someone tossed another into the ocean, and now they're dead. Recovery should be our first concern."

Drew's brow furrowed. "Did you phone the sheriff?"

"Not yet."

"Why the delay?" Evie shouted. "Are you too worried reporters will realize your claims are outlandish? I'm sure you'd rather your fans not find out you're hallucinating, along with all your other problems. Certainly would wreck your sales, wouldn't it?"

"Enough, Evie."

Evie's face reddened as she spun toward Drew. "Of course, you'd defend her."

Teddie hurried away from the pair, withdrew her cell-phone, and punched in the emergency number. She received an immediate response. After she disconnected, she wandered to the far side and rested against the banister.

Evie stood on the opposite end of the pier, scowling at her husband.

He tugged a jittery hand through his hair. "I get what this must look like, but I swear," his voice faltered. "I didn't know she was in town."

"Psst." Evie sneered. "Like you'd tell me. You just want me to suffer."

Drew's intonation grew softer. "Just offering you the same joyfulness you gave me over the years."

"You're such a bitter man."

"Had nothing to do with living with you, did it?"

"I've kept us afloat, remember?" Her face flushed again, and her temper visibly soared. "I shouldn't have to remind you, I am the breadwinner in this household."

"Thanks for the recap, Evie. Direct hit, as always."

Evie glowered at Drew. Her skirt billowed in the strong gust but she made no move to adjust it. Drew equaled his wife's tenseness. His expression was tight and displayed his angry emotions.

Teddie swallowed as tension grew thicker than the fog rolling in. The disharmony between the two was heartbreaking. She hoped to avoid observing a second physical clash within hours. Although she didn't expect six-foot-plus Drew to sail over the banister by means of his smaller wife.

Yet, stranger things happened.

Drew's lips pressed into a straight line. "If your high society compadres could see the true you, oh wait, doesn't matter. You're alike, aren't you? You thrive in sucking the life out of those you claim to care about." He gave Teddie a sad grin. "Quite a homecoming, huh?" He turned and stomped around the building, into the darkness.

"I bet you took pleasure viewing that."

"The scene made me uncomfortable." Teddie re-settled next to the rail, closing her eyes. Waves cavorted beneath as icy droplets sprinkled over her bare skin. She fought the urge to shiver.

"Why didn't you leave if you felt awkward? Oh, wait, you can't go anywhere. You're anticipating the sheriff finding your so-called murder victim." Evie's voice carried a gloating tone. "You are some kind of crazy."

"Am I?" Teddie opened her eyelids and met Evie's

gaze. "How does crazy stack up to stinking paranoid?"

Evie's sneer faded. She clenched her fists and stepped toward Teddie. "Don't mess with me. I'll make you sorry if you do."

"Threats, Evie?" Teddie chuckled quietly. "Who saw that coming."

Deep laughter roared behind and interrupted their building scrape. Both spun toward the merriment. Shaded outlines materialized from around the building's side.

Teddie's insides quivered.

Had Drew returned with friends? Part of her plans included her addressing an issue with him, but after observing his and Evie's discord, were her intentions even sensible? Maybe not. Perhaps Aubrey's opinion was spot on. Should she abort her idea and fly back to Tennessee? After all, she managed okay by allowing history to remain dormant.

One man separated from the cluster and strolled from the dimness. Scents of tobacco melded amid a thick breeze. Teddie sniffed the air. Cigar. Her dad's brand. The aroma always brought back bittersweet memories. She inhaled another satisfied breath and smiled.

"We heard a lot of screams and yells over here," declared the newcomer with the cigar. "Is there a problem?"

"Nash." Evie glowed, extending her hands to welcome their latest guest. "I'm thrilled you came this evening."

"Evie." Nash Sewell pitched his cigar across the side, trekked to her, and accepted her greeting. "I'm glad I attended, too. You do such wonderful work and this lovely party is a joy. The center will greatly benefit because of your efforts. Congratulations on a well-done inauguration." He skimmed the region. "Were you entangled in the boisterous altercation I heard?"

Evie glanced at the colleagues accompanying Nash. Her façade altered to a combination of suffrage and innocence. "Drew again."

"You're such a saint for all the sacrifices you make, my dear. Our friends agree, you go above and beyond. I hope you stood your ground."

"He's a fine man, but he's resentful. I wish his life would've been easier. I just want his happiness. That's why I do what I do."

Teddie almost gagged, unable to tolerate the phoniness after witnessing such open animosity.

"We create our own fortunes." His eyes bored into Evie. "Your husband can blame others only so long, but after a while, responsibility falls upon him."

"Nash Sewell?"

"Yes." He rotated toward Teddie; his eyes tapered as he focused on her. His lips curved. "Teddie." He squirmed out of Evie's clutches to embrace her. "Welcome home."

A much younger Doctor Nash Sewell was Teddie's father's colleague and weekend golf buddy. They met when Nash interned at the local hospital, and later they shared a medical practice until her dad's death.

Nash had been a true friend to Teddie and her siblings. He was incredibly supportive when her parents passed, going as far as to speak at their memorial, offering a heartfelt tribute. Her family would always be indebted to him.

"I'm visiting a short period."

"Long enough to ruin my marriage," Evie put in.

Nash cast a stern glimpse at Evie and reverted to Teddie. "Now, I understand."

"I don't think you do."

He snapped up a palm. "I'm not judging *you*, Teddie. Everyone's familiar with Drew's antics."

Teddie chewed her bottom lip. Yes, Drew had his obstinate moments, but she could not imagine the man she once knew so well behaving horribly. He may dig in his heels, but he always manned up and selected to do right in the end.

"I've followed your career." Nash nodded approvingly. "Your accomplishments are impressive. I'm sorry you didn't feel comfortable enough to come home and share your accolades with the people who treasured and championed you early on."

Remorse swept through Teddie. She loved her hometown, but she couldn't make herself reappear until now. This journey hadn't been easy. She trembled the whole flight, and her stomach was twisted in knots. Numerous times she resisted the impulse to tell her pilot to turn around or continue flying and head to Europe. Aubrey and Raven's echoed cautions remained at the forefront of her mind. She dreaded the forthcoming, "I told you so" they'd each dole later.

"I do love everyone here." Words caught in her throat. Teddie stopped to inhale the salty air.

"I empathize with your objections to visit." Nash shook his head, adding a tsk. "The Donavan girls suffered a great deal. Neither of your sisters returned, as I'm sure you're aware." He hesitated. "What brings you to the Cove now?"

"I needed to see my home again." She rubbed her

arms. "You may recall, I packed and moved to Nashville right after I signed with Sony. Never looked back."

She almost retracted her statement. She didn't forget yesterday, the cost of leaving her old life behind, nor the regret she endured. To say she didn't remember her years in Jacob's Cove wasn't the truth. Luckily, Nash understood her well enough not to call her on the remark.

"Your parents died near the same time you left." The sorrow in his expression was evident. Her mother's and father's death haunted him as much as it did her. He eyed her intently. "You chose a tough time to return."

She blinked away a sea of mist, clouding her eyes. "I don't believe any time would be easy, but I have questions and have to find answers."

"You've yet to deal with your parents' death or the way they died?"

"I choose not to live in the past, but I must make peace with it. As in every traumatic loss, I'll never understand why it happened, but I've accepted their passing." A melancholy smile touched her lips. "I'm referring to a different ghost."

"Oh, I can tell you the ghost she came to bust."

Nash scowled. "Everybody is conscious of Drew's connection to Teddie, Evie. This isn't the appropriate time to air your personal grievances. It makes you appear small."

Evie frowned and shrunk away, surging into the far barrier.

Nash gave Teddie a kind smile. "You're strong. I trust you'll win the war against any ghoul who dares to cross you."

Teddie's face darkened. Ninety-nine percent of the time, she prevailed in her internal battles, but in this case, the certainty of triumph dangled.

Nash's curiosity shifted to worry. "Press releases refer to your struggle with health matters. Is a revisit to times gone by a wise idea?"

"My life has been a whirlwind since I released my first single. Because of my packed schedule, a spare second has been scarce. I didn't have a lot of time to devote to my previous life. Now"—she browsed the area's perimeters and sighed—"I do."

"Reports claim you're exhausted. You also fell off the stage during a performance. Doctor's orders are to take things easy, correct? You aren't supposed to tackle ancient history."

"I need to keep busy. I'm not good idle."

"But you are good at inventing stories." Evie shoved off the barrier. "She says she spotted somebody fall off the pier into the water." She ambled to where Teddie and Nash stood. "As in they were pushed."

"This happened here?" Nash raised his brows. "Tonight?"

"Close to an hour ago."

"We need to notify authorities," Nash instructed, once she gave him the incident's facts.

"I called already." Teddie scanned the street paralleling the Phoenix. "I expected them to've arrived."

"They drag their feet and will move even slower if you called during dinner hour."

"Seriously, you're not buying into this outrageousness, are you?" Evie's vocal sound held a

38

skeptical tenor. "Jacob's Cove is one of the safest places in the country. Murders don't happen here." She smirked at Teddie. "At least not in a while."

"Evie," Nash admonished. "You're standing on a very thin line. You can't dispute Teddie's account if you weren't here. Let Breena and her men solve this mystery."

"Fine. Bring in the cops. Why it took so long to inform them is beyond me." Evie pointed at the ballroom window. "Lots of people attended this function. The deck's visible from each angle. Strange, none of them spotted this so-called death when it occurred."

"Actually, I did detect someone." Nash's gaze settled on Evie. His expression was grave. "The timeline coincides with Teddie's."

"Who did you see?" Evie questioned.

Nash's mouth leveled before his lips curled into a forced smile. "Drew. Drew was on the pavilion."

Chapter 4

"Thanks for your statement, Ms. Donavon." The policeman who took Teddie's information wiggled his notepad face-high, then snapped the top shut, and tucked it into his shirt pocket. "Sheriff Dover will want to do a more extensive interview later."

Teddie backstepped and separated from the officer, ready to disappear. "She has my number."

"Yes, ma'am. Thank you, Ms. Donavon."

She flicked a glance toward the exit. Phoenix staff had switched on additional lights and a bright glow beamed across countless unfamiliar faces. Most guests had drifted outside and lined behind a ribboned barrier, watching the commotion at a distance. Shouts hailed her way as soon as she and the officer parted.

While she'd rather not come off as a spoiled diva, she neglected the audience's pleas. She couldn't handle the cop's stanch interrogation and hordes of the way too curious in one night.

Scanning the pavilion, she searched to find an alternate getaway. Every passage was barricaded. She checked across the street. More Cove citizens lingered, surrounding the Phoenix. Unmarked cars and vans were now parked.

Damn. Reporters. The nasty kind.

She'd been outed. Someone leaked her whereabouts to tabloids. The vehicles' occupants tried to blend in among the growing mob, but she'd been around long enough to spot them.

She whirled in the opposite direction, toward the packed crowd, and hiked the other way. Evie stood by a cluster of her friends, the same clique she ran with while in high school. They huddled, their arms crisscrossed to protect themselves from the frosty breeze propelling off the water.

Evie glared, a glare icier than the wind. She motioned at Teddie. "Her mind's totally scrambled."

Heads swiveled. "I read she's high most of the time," a bestie announced. "The latest National Probe says she's hooked on amphetamines."

Teddie struggled to not stop and explain. Any efforts to clarify would make her seem more pathetic.

Let police investigate. She glanced at the agents swirling around. A body would submerge to confirm and exonerate her. And after she was absolved and her issues were settled, she'd haul ass and escape this small-town nonsense.

"Teddie Donavan, wait."

She swung around. Evie wriggled from her inner sanctum, storming Teddie's way.

"I want you to leave, *now*," she demanded as she advanced.

"Excuse me? You can't tell me what to do."

"But I am. Pack your stuff and fly back home to Nashville. The quicker the better."

"Better for you."

"For you too."

"What I do doesn't concern you, Evie. I don't understand why you're interested."

"This won't end like you think. Your fans are

aware of your problems. They're already questioning your sanity. I mean seriously, can you stand more bad press?"

"Your worry over my livelihood is touching, but I'm staying in Jacob's Cove until I'm finished doing what I came to do." She shoved her windblown tresses off her face to give Evie a full view of her smile. "You'll just have to deal with me living in Jacob's Cove."

Evie stepped in closer. "Go back to Tennessee, now." Her intonation lowered as she added a peal of doom. "Or I'll make your life miserable."

"Again with the threats? Do your worst; you don't scare me. I've fought a lot worse than you, Evie St. John. And won."

"My last name is *Millard*."

"Not for long after what I observed."

"Stay away from my husband."

"As long as he's your husband, I will."

Hating that she'd stooped to Evie's level, Teddie pivoted on her heel and marched to the clearest outlet. She wished she could retract her statement, but her reactions were out there, and she couldn't take them back.

A young, uniformed man stood by the egress. He grinned. "Evening, Ms. Donavan. Would you like an escort out of the building?"

"Not so much." She rose to her tiptoes to inspect the expanding flock. "Unless you know a shortcut where no one will see me. I'd rather skip bumping into paparazzi."

"I do know a secret route." He walked to her side. "If you're ready, I can show you the way."

"You're a lifesaver."

He signaled to indicate for people to part and let them pass. She squinted over her shoulder, meeting Nash Sewell's watchful eyes.

"Teddie, don't go just yet." He bolted across the wooden planks, clasping his lit cigar between two fingers. He glanced toward the deputy when he caught up to them. "May I?"

He didn't pause to let the cop answer. He grasped her forearm, gently spinning her to him, then he tugged her aside. He leveled, so their noses almost met. "Are you okay? I can write you a prescription, either for Xanax or Klonopin. Both are calming medications and will help you sleep. A good night's rest will make everything much better."

She analyzed the man in front of her. He appeared compassionate, but his eyes said something else. He didn't believe her.

Teddie paced backward toward the waiting cop. "I'm fine. My physician prescribed sedatives. Aubrey filled it, but I've yet to take any, nor do I intend to."

Nash straightened and puffed on his cigar. A trail of smoke wafted upward and evaporated into the night. He scrutinized her; his face held a trace of empathy. "Perhaps you should reconsider. You'll find those medications are beneficial."

She sighed, sick of doubts. Yes, she experienced an upsetting episode. Plus, she had overextended herself by taking on too many projects. She was exhausted and a little sore from her fall, but she didn't require anything but rest.

"Except for witnessing a killing earlier, I'm okay, Nash."

He eyed her skeptically. "You're certain you didn't imagine the homicide?"

"Yes, I am. A person went over the side, and they didn't go on their own."

"Again, what did you see? Tell me everything, and don't omit a single detail."

"Two individuals argued. One pushed the other. The other went over, hit the stairs, then the boat ramp, and tumbled into the bay. They haven't resurfaced."

"You can't identify either party, correct?"

She shook her head.

"I noticed Drew outside close to the time you say the homicide took place."

"I don't believe Drew is so violent or callous."

Nash's sympathetic face transformed into suspicious. "You sure? You're not covering for him, are you?"

Teddie went speechless. "Of course not," she finally responded. "Why would I?"

"Guilt, perhaps?"

"I don't do guilt, Nash."

"Don't you? You've been away a long time, but your and Drew's story is well known and still discussed among the locals." A shrewd smile formed across his lips. "Your many successes equated to Drew's. His achievements are feeble by comparison. You don't bear a smidgeon of remorse?"

Teddie hugged her waist and turned toward the water. Waves pitched in the moonlight. She expected Drew and their past to be mentioned. She wasn't surprised their careers were matched, given the circumstances, but she anticipated making it through her first night without the subject being broached.

Except she was wrong.

She reverted to Nash. "Drew and I chose different paths and lead very different lives. We're responsible for our own choices. His regrets are on him."

Nash finished his smoke and tossed the stogie above the guardrail into the rolling seas. "Glad you don't carry torches. He's not the man you once knew."

"Neither of us are the same."

"His feelings for you are still strong."

Teddie stilled, fighting to stay neutral. She didn't need to know this, even if the declaration pleased her. A hard swallow followed a deep inhale. "Of course, I'm special to Drew. I was his first love, and he's mine. It'd be stranger if we didn't care about each other."

Nash narrowed his eyes and leaned forward. "You do seem lucid."

A hand flew to her chest, shocked by his observation. "I keep telling everyone I'm rational, but no one pays attention."

Nash offered a decisive nod. "I'm happy you're improving." He stopped, and his features clouded. "Evie and Drew are experiencing a rough patch in their marriage. Most in Jacob's Cove are familiar with their troubles. You don't want to put yourself in a risky situation by renewing a close friendship with Drew. Especially since your public profile's huge."

"I was lucky enough to sample the Millards' troubles, first hand. Not an enjoyable experience. And I'd never place my family or my professional status in a dicey position. I have too much to lose."

"But you will speak to him, won't you?" He tossed a knowing look her way. "He's a part of the ancient history you're here to resolve."

"There are several issues I came to confront."

"Drew's one of them."

"I won't disrupt his life, Nash. I returned to get answers concerning my parents' deaths. I left soon after they died. When I'm finished, I plan to move on. My sisters intend to list our home and sell it. It's been a constant fight. Me against them. After tonight, I'm starting to believe their way of thinking is the wisest."

"I must agree. Breaking ties with that house and your dreadful memories is a smart decision. The landscape is lovely, but the home contains an obscure stench. Although"—he sifted inside his jacket, withdrew a business card holder and handed her one— "Celia and I are discussing downsizing. Contact me if you decide to sell. We might consider purchasing the property."

She accepted his card, relieved the topic shifted away from Drew Millard. "Downsizing? Isn't our house larger than yours? Or did you move?"

"We're still on Austin Circle. And yes, your house is bigger than ours. We'd buy for the exquisite scenery. I'm sure Celia would insist we tear down the old home and rebuild. She'd never consent to residing in a rustic abode. Particularly one retaining such a dour reputation. We value our privacy."

Given the history, the idea of her family home demolished bothered her, and now she second-guessed her decision to agree with her sisters. Yet, any potential buyer would entertain similar thoughts, if informed of her parents' tragic ending.

"Hey, Nash." Sheriff Breena Dover approached. "We need to chat." She stared at Teddie and nodded. "Sorry, I couldn't come right away, but I had another emergency to tend to. One of my men already spoke to you, right?"

"Yes, I gave him my report."

"I'll study his notes later tonight, and you and I will meet tomorrow. I'd like a more formal setting when we talk."

Nash gave Teddie a final glimpse. "Call if you decide you want me to write you a prescription. My private cell number is on my card."

Teddie was set to accept her reprieve and ready to flee this chaos. She spun to the deputy, who propped against the rail, out of listening range.

Breena returned to address Nash. "Describe Drew's demeanor when you initially spotted him out here. I realize you were indoors, but how would you judge his conduct, body language, and so on?"

Teddie halted. Breena wouldn't permit anybody to eavesdrop on her interrogations, but Teddie didn't want to miss the opportunity to find out any news.

"Angry. Skin flushed, shoulders tense. He stomped around like he was riled over something."

"He was the only person on the pavilion?"

"He had to be if he assisted another over the rail without anyone detecting him." Nash deviated away from Breena as he gazed beyond the pier and concentrated on the darkened waters. "Has there been any validation a crime occurred?"

Breena disregarded Nash's question and continued her probe. "You didn't see which way Drew went? I want to talk to him, tonight." She hesitated. "And we can't seem to find him."

A light touch tapped Teddie's elbow. "Are you ready, Ms. Donavan?"

No, but she consented to let him escort her away before Nash responded to Breena. She scouted the area as they moved. Where had Drew gone? Outdoor lighting was ineffective and didn't provide enough brightness to get a decent look at any one person, but she strained and searched the mass, anyway.

Teddie did spy Evie's buddies still hovered in their rigid circle, their location unchanged, except Evie was missing, too. Her and Drew's absences were very odd.

Teddie entered the ballroom, her guard by her side. Most of the tables were cleared. Only a few stragglers remained as cops quizzed staff members. Musicians had stored their instruments and attacked the near full buffet table.

No sign of Drew or her ex-friend. She was directed to a rear door located next to the entrance and down a short, unlit tunnel.

"Evie Millard headed this shindig?" Teddie inquired casually.

The officer jerked a pair of heavy doors, holding one side ajar. A dim radiance filtered inside. "She's in charge of all Davis Medical Center functions and solicits donations for the hospital. The town's rich and fabulous are always invited to these events. I'm sure you'll receive an invitation, or they may ask you to perform. You'd be a huge draw."

Teddie smiled. "I'm on a sabbatical."

"Hope you'll still sing a song or two."

"My plans are to only sing in the shower. No audience."

"Yes, ma'am." The young man seemed dejected. "This way leads to the beach, which will take you to Main Street. Do you want me to walk you to your car?

Media's restricted to a central location, and Breena ordered them to leave after they get their story. They shouldn't bother you, but you can never tell."

"I think I'm okay by myself, thanks." Teddie patted his arm. "Have a good evening."

She treaded into the open, set to stroll along the cool shores.

"Ms. Donavan?"

Teddie spun to him.

He removed a pen and pad from his pocket. "Would you mind?"

Chapter 5

Glad to escape the commotion, Teddie wandered along the shoreline, content to journey the long way to her rental.

Angry waves rammed the surf across her path, soaking her boot soles with a foamy overflow. Tonight wasn't ideal to stroll the beach, but the ocean's elements presented her a marvelous welcome home. Something she had yet to encounter.

Granted, she didn't expect a sense of ease right away, but again, she didn't predict her comeback to become public her first night in town. While people did seem excited about her homecoming, their enthusiasm didn't encourage her much.

Witnessing a murder and Evie's accusations circled in her head.

Dragging a toe in the sand, she sluggishly came to a halt and stared at the rolling seas as if the water would provide her clarity.

Perhaps Evie was right. She had ignored her hometown and those who resided in the city. In her defense, she didn't intend to put off a visit indefinitely, nor did she plan to skip acknowledging those who supported her and her career during early periods.

Her life took an abrupt turn seventeen years ago, and the arc compelled her to make drastic adjustments. Teddie's flight from Jacob's Cove was essential to her mental and emotional welfare. Devastating events happened while she lived here, and each episode cut her deep. Her pain was profound, so unfathomable those cerebral scrapes still occasionally bled.

In the end, it became easier not to return.

She had tried to tuck those awful memories in a safe place and bury them. Unfortunately, those deep-rooted memories had unearthed themselves and haunted her day and night.

And then there was Drew Millard.

Teddie tugged at her jacket, bringing the edges together as she resumed her walk.

He looked amazing. Mouthwatering. Tall and rock solid. Dark hair and darker eyes filled with spirit and passion. Drew is what bothered her. Not the town or its residents. She'd donate a substantial amount to a local charity or present a concert and allot the proceeds toward a charitable trust. Most townsfolk would exonerate her.

Drew squeezed her heart.

Yet, she must remember what he did to her. No matter how cordially he behaved this evening, he dumped her due to spite, and to twist the proverbial knife in further, he married her sworn enemy.

He may've reconciled his attitude relating to their past, but those old wounds would soon reopen. By the time she headed to Nashville, he may truly despise her.

Teddie's cell buzzed. She reached around to her rear pocket and snatched her phone.

"Hey, Aubrey," she answered, bypassing the caller ID.

"Hi, Teddie. Raven's on the line too."

Great. Dueling sisters. Just what the clichéd doctor

ordered.

"Are you home?"

"Not yet, Rav."

"You're still eating?" Teddie bit her tongue so not to respond to Aubrey's demanding tone. "Your meal should've been over hours ago."

"Uh oh." Raven released a weak laugh. "Your stopover's been discovered. How many people are aware you're in town?"

Teddie would rather not respond. Her life stayed constantly in the limelight, and her older siblings were protective of her privacy. If she revealed what happened, they'd insist they come stay with her or she drive to them. Neither option appealed to her.

But…because of her fame, keeping the night's outcome a secret bordered on impossible. If she didn't reveal what happened, they'd learn the details later through media outlets. Even if Sheriff Dover kept reporters sectioned off, one or more good citizens of Jacob's Cove would speak to them, either innocently or striving to attain their own fifteen minutes off her fame.

She cleared her throat. "I just went to find food." Teddie relayed the last few hours as Aubrey and Raven listened in stone silence.

"Is that all?" Aubrey shrieked, once she was done.

"Isn't that enough?" Raven put in.

"Your physician advised you to rest, and you're not. We're already worried. Your health's a concern, and you're by yourself in the old house. Now we must contend with you witnessing a murder. Then you and Evie Millard spar, *and* you spoke to Drew for a lengthy period. What will you do if paparazzi discovers your link to him? I'll tell you what they'll do, they'll smear you to hell and back."

"I didn't mean to run into him, Aubrey, and no one saw us except Evie."

"You should've walked away when he showed up."

"It didn't cross my mind. The night turned crazy, and everything fell apart."

"Anything involving you and Drew Millard falls apart."

Teddie jerked the phone away and made a face. Aubrey always had to have the final word. She returned the cell to her ear.

"Maybe Raven and I should come to Jacob's Cove. We can ensure you aren't hounded by reporters or fans. After tonight's disaster, you're going to require extra protection."

"You are great guardians"—Teddie treaded carefully—"and I'm grateful to you both, but I'm good alone."

"You're not good," Aubrey insisted. "What you told us isn't good, at all. Your seeing a homicide will generate more rumors. The negative kind."

"No such thing as bad press, remember?" They didn't react to Teddie's attempt at humor. "Interest will subside once another celebrity's implicated in a scandal. Public's fickle. Their attention will deviate."

Raven chuckled. "I doubt if your connection to a homicide will make your situation that much worse, but Aubrey's right. Proactivity is crucial. You'll need to project an upbeat attitude and act like you feel well, too. Call your manager while Aubrey and I work on controlling the fallout."

Teddie did a mental check. "Tabloids need reeled

in before anything else. I'll phone Cliff first thing tomorrow."

"Phone him now. The incident may've already gone viral. If it hasn't, count on it happening soon."

Teddie's chin lowered to focus on the banking whitecaps as they grazed the tips of her boots. Raven was right, yet... "Cliff's with his wife and kids. I hate to bother him. He spends very little time with his family."

"Which is why you pay him the big bucks."

Teddie hesitated, still not convinced she should follow Raven's advice.

"Send him a text." Aubrey heaved a loud sigh. "It's the way you communicate when you want to avoid speaking to us."

"He'll call the second he reads the message."

"I hope he does. Once he discovers this new hitch, he can help squelch adverse speculations. Message him the minute we disconnect. Then head straight to the house and go to bed."

"You know I can't sleep."

"You will if you take your prescriptions." Aubrey halted briefly. "Your whole evening was a disaster. Please reconsider your decision to remain in Jacob's Cove. You won't rest if you're there. Forget the idea and let's go home. Come stay with us tonight, and we'll leave in the morning."

"I won't ever heal until I handle the issues haunting me."

"Anything you uncover might create additional questions instead of answers. You'll search forever and won't be satisfied, nor will you ever recover if you let this consume your life. You'll lose it all. You love your

54

work. Concentrate on recuperating as an alternative to hunting ghosts."

Teddie disconnected the same time she wound up her hike along the shore. Tides were rolling in. A stout breeze whipped her long tresses across her face as the blusters pushed a light spray above her head.

She left the beach and closed in on her vehicle, key fob withdrawn. Climbing inside her parked car, she spared a moment to message her manager. After, she just sat, listening to the distant waves.

Drained and agitated, she felt sure her eyes wouldn't shut once she went to bed.

Aubrey's words echoed. "Take the drugs."

She stretched to reach underneath the seat and grabbed her purse. Her medications were stuffed inside a pouch, still in the sack they were delivered in. Tugging at the staples, she unfastened the top and dipped a hand into the bag for the pill containers.

She twisted the overhead light switch and read the instructions.

May take up to two hours before effective.

Popping the lid, she shook out the correct dosage and deposited the tablets into her mouth. The half-filled water bottle laid on the passenger seat next to her. She unscrewed the cap, placed the edge to her lips, and gulped the meds down.

****

Drew stood in the parking lot, his eyes centered on the circus milling. The sheriff and her brigade appeared to make the rounds and interrogated every attending guest. Breena would want to grill him, too, but his mood didn't suit to be interviewed. He doubted he'd answer any question clearly.

His mind whirled. Marital disputes, a suspicious death…Teddie's surprise appearance.

Seeing her again confused his emotions. While her health dilemmas were common knowledge, viewing her in person verified she wrestled with a lot of struggles. She'd lost a fair amount of weight, which made her frame too thin for her height. Exhaustion had darkened her eyes, and tiny lines strained the corners of her mouth.

Then she saw a murder.

Or did she? Had she developed an addiction as media insinuated and hallucinated the crime amid moonlight and shadows?

He hated to not have faith in her stability, yet her story was hard to buy. Jacob's Cove was a quiet, little city. A fishing town. Numerous townspeople were descendants of founding fathers. No one killed anyone. Ever.

He glimpsed at the turmoil surrounding the Phoenix, then checked his watch.

"Are you waiting to meet your batty girlfriend?" A harsh laugh followed. "Think she's out chasing her presumed murderer?"

Drew swiveled around.

Evie emerged out of the dimness into the moon's glow. She stopped next to Drew. Her body braced as if prepared to go into battle. "I'm surprised you're still here."

"You got more crap of no consequence you want to fight about?"

"No consequences." A slow, crafty grin crawled over her face. "Your name for your willowy blast from the past?"

"Is this necessary?" He allowed his annoyance to seep into his tone. "Can't we keep topics on what's important?"

"Ending our marriage is important? I bet it's super important now Teddie Donavan's in town. Her arrival will impact your impending single life, won't it?"

Of course, she went there. Resolved to endure most of the responsibility concerning their impending breakup, Drew wouldn't permit Evie to insinuate their troubles stemmed because of his involvement with another woman.

"Yes, Evie. You know I'm ready to divorce. I have been for a long time." He flicked a glare her way. "Teddie's not part of our discussion. She's not the reason for our split."

She shrugged. "If you say so."

His teeth clamped down on his tongue. Preferring this exchange not end in the predictable screaming match, he waited until his anger subsided before he spoke again.

"Move on, Evie."

"Fine. What's left to discuss? You already made your decision. You're eager to leave me, even though I'd rather you didn't."

"Sorry, Evie." He stuck around longer than most men, but he was to the point where he couldn't pretend anymore. He was ready to restart his life.

"I suppose I ought to give you credit. You had the balls to tell me you planned to ditch me to my face." She smirked. "I should be indebted to your virtuous character, eh?"

"I don't know how virtuous I am, but I'm not so cold that I'd leave without telling you." He paused.

"You agreed to sign the papers."

She remained silent. Drew's spine stiffened, anticipating her standard outburst. He also feared she'd find another way to stall the proceedings since she'd managed to delay the dealings two years.

"Fine, Drew." She sounded calm. "I'll sign them once I'm home."

Weary of her deferments, he relaxed. Perhaps she'd stop making the process difficult.

"Deal's the same, right? I keep everything." She stopped and examined the sky as if to calculate. "The house, furniture, cars, and bank accounts. You'll take away your ratty, old truck and those ridiculous guitars."

"And my business. The rest is yours."

"I guess all that's left is to add my signature and forward the paperwork to my attorney."

"You made the promise before," he expressed cautiously, almost reluctant to complete what he intended to convey. "This is your last chance. If you don't, you'll leave me no choice but to ask a judge to declare us divorced without your consent. Abel recommended I move forward the last time you reneged."

"What can I say? I'm not ready to let you go."

"We both know I'm not the motivation for us to stay together."

"The past, Drew. I've changed my mind. I see no reason to prolong the inevitable. Although, it wouldn't kill you to stay until we're both ready."

Drew scanned the rows of vehicles scattered throughout the parking lot. He shot a skeptical side glance in his wife's direction. "Sorry, Evie. We've been putting each other through hell long enough."

"Fine Drew. I'll sign."

Drew inhaled, frustrated, after rehashing this same conversation. The initial plan of terminating their nuptials occurred twenty-four months ago. Neither were happy and never had been. While he believed in eternity once a couple said I do, the *for better or worse* mantra lingered on the latter since day one. It was past time to stop pumping oxygen into lungs that never breathed life. Many may call him selfish, but he was ready to live his life, his way. He'd wasted too much time faking it.

"How many times have you made the promise? You've yet to sign a gum wrapper, much less anything legal. I'm fed up sleeping in the basement, and I want a place of my own. I'm also sick of the pretentiousness."

"I'm tired of living a lie too, Drew. I'll sign this time, I promise." Evie released a massive sigh. "I suppose this is our finale. The next time we speak will be through lawyers. I presume this is goodbye."

"Yeah. I appreciate you agreeing to settle reasonably." He remained guarded, hoping not to touch on any subject that may cause a verbal explosion.

"You're certain I can't persuade you to give us one more try?"

Drew rechecked his watch. "Um, Evie, I gotta go. My show starts in thirty minutes, and I still gotta set up." He took a step.

"Oh, right. Your show," she huffed. "Um, but before you hurry off, here's a bit of information you may want to bear in mind."

Drew skidded to a standstill. A huge band tightened around his chest and threatened to explode.

"If Teddie did see a murder"—she held up a

palm—"and I do entertain reservations, but Breena and company are taking her allegations serious until proven otherwise."

"The point, Evie."

"Oh, yes, well. They're requesting to speak to anyone spotted on the pavilion around the time of the *alleged* occurrence."

"Seems the best place to start."

"It does." Her lips expanded across her face. "Funny you mentioned a starting place. You were spied outside the Phoenix around the timeline." Her smile widened. "You may want to make sure your counsel handles a variety of cases."

Drew's features exposed his disbelief. The saying went, hell hath no fury, and he had a feeling this was just the intro of her wrath.

She wiggled her fingers to wave as she spun and ambled toward the Phoenix. "I'll let Breena know where you are."

Chapter 6

Teddie unlocked the entrance to her childhood home and ambled indoors. Keychain dumped atop a tiny table, she switched on a lamp, mounted the stairs, and headed to her bedroom.

The meds worked quicker than she anticipated, or perhaps she was tired due to her long excursion, combined with the jaunt into town, and the uproar that occurred afterward. Whatever the cause, her eyelids became heavy near the drive's conclusion, and she felt relieved she made it home devoid of further incidents.

Exhausted, she plowed into her suitcase to find her pajamas.

Once undressed, she slipped into her pj's and plunged into the bed's softness, glad she remembered to replace the sheets prior to embarking on her disastrous venture. Snuggling into the pillow, she hoped to sleep the whole night.

Almost immediately, her brain emptied, and she drifted into a contented, dreamless doze. But her comfort didn't last long. Foreboding whispers invaded her slumber. Her breathing shallowed as she tried to halt the commanding force. But she was too late. Evil had entered her dreams.

A familiar off-key tune launched and tinkled, cycloning her back in time. She viewed her younger self standing outside her parents' bedroom door, once again eavesdropping on their argument. Her father yelled, but her mother spoke in a quieter tone, and her tenor seemed unusual.

All noises suddenly quieted.

Teddie tensed, aware of what came next.

Gunshots exploded and echoed as if inside a cave.

The bedroom door automatically opened. She floated inside. The room was covered with blood as scents of gunpowder and death lingered. Her mother lay sprawled on the bedspread, her shocked expression still evident on her lifeless face.

"Daddy, how could you?" she sobbed at her father, who lay on the floor with a pistol intertwined within his fingers.

He rose to sit. Blood spewed from the bullet hole lodged into his temple. He bypassed her adolescent version to glare directly at Teddie in the present.

"I didn't kill anyone." The hand that grasped the gun raised and aimed at her frolicking heart. "Beware." A thumb tugged the hammer backward as his forefinger squeezed the trigger.

Teddie's eyes flew open. She sat, tangled amid the covers, her body soaked in sweat. Her heartbeat drummed in her ears. She threw off her blankets. A cool draft surged out of nowhere and swept across her. The cold chills mingled with perspiration made her tremble.

Her brain felt dense and hazy. A dull twinge started to pulse on her brow. She brushed away hot tears and forced her muscles to relax as she emotionally paced through the horrendous nightmare.

"Just a dream." She settled into her pillows and drew the blankets to her chin. "A horrible, horrible dream."

She inhaled deeply and froze. Seizing another breath, she slowly reared up in bed.

Odors of cigar filled the aged house.

Her father's brand. The same as Nash's. Teddie frowned and stared at the hallway, unable to recall if she locked the front door. Nash acted concerned when they spoke. Had an old, family friend stopped by to check on her? Did he roam the bottom floor, searching for her?

Wrapping herself in the sheet, she placed her bare feet on the old hardwood and edged off the mattress. The ancient boards creaked beneath her weight as she crept toward the doorway. She peered down the darkened hall. A muted glow beamed from the first level.

Right, she left on the foyer light.

"Nash?"

She inhaled again, but the smell had vanished.

Scaling the staircase, Teddie lifted her nose and sniffed until she reached the foot of the stairs. Nothing. Maybe the tobacco aromas were an addition to her bad dream.

She remounted the stairway and returned to her room but avoided going back to bed. Now wide awake, she wandered to the window, trying not to replay her recurring nightmare or think about the murder she witnessed.

She gazed through the glass and into the darkness.

Despite her previous insistence, she desired to get out of this house. She craved normalcy. To be carefree. Like her post childhood days. Music soothed her. One of the biggest joys she rarely had time to do nowadays was listen to bands.

She loved the enthusiasm, eagerness, and their rawness. That'd help more than any overpriced pill.

Without checking the time, she redressed and descended the flight of steps. Keys in hand, she dashed through the door and to her rental. Revving the engine, she pointed the car into an obscure direction, blasting the radio. Tomorrow and its worries would arrive soon enough. Tonight, she intended to forget everything else and enjoy the moment.

****

Drew remained in his spot until Evie disappeared, and then started his hike to his pickup, parked a ways off. The evening's affair turned into a weird one. Running into Teddie after so long certainly stunned him, but his interactions with his wife caused him the most worry.

Drew hoped their preceding conversation was his and Evie's last one, except she didn't like to admit to wrongdoing nor did she want her family and friends aware of her offenses. She was prepared to attack anyone who stood in her way, and Drew was a major roadblock.

Drew didn't care what she did. Truthfully, he never loved Evie and married her for the wrong reasons. He craved to end their union the moment they walked down the aisle as husband and wife. Yes, that made him a jerk, but he hated being a source of embarrassment for his wife; therefore, he stayed.

Evie's glittery outlook also faded quickly after she realized Drew wasn't the man she imagined. Most couples would've separated by the second year, but they didn't concede and call it quits, because neither wanted to be divorced.

Circumstances worsened as the days passed. Time moved forward; tensions increased.

By their fifteenth anniversary, the tiny thread binding them snapped and gave way into nothingness. Drew announced he was leaving. Evie begged him not to go, but he refused to relent.

He did his time. Presented his best, contrary to the lack of emotional attachment. If something as common as a breakup mangled Evie's reputation, then she could deal with the fallouts. He was finished.

Drew's lawyer filed the required paperwork to end the marriage. The results were met with constant resistance. Evie's legal team dissected and analyzed every minor detail. Any excuse to prolong the proceedings.

His council informed him, he was stuck unless they took a drastic measure. And his personal attorney provided the tools. Pay extra, and request a judge grant a divorce without Evie's approval.

Drew preferred not to move forward minus Evie's blessing, but his soon to be ex-wife didn't give him much choice. His lawyer messaged her legal associates their intentions, but Drew decided to extend Evie one final opportunity to comply. If he didn't retain the signed paperwork by the weekend's conclusion, he'd proceed with the contested divorce. Once the marriage was terminated, he'd have the freedom to live his life how he always intended, probably the first time ever.

Approaching his vehicle, he fished into his pocket to retrieve his keys and stretched a hand to the door handle.

"Got a minute, Drew?"

He dropped his palm, hitting his thigh, emitting a

loud smack. Expelling a long sigh, he pivoted in slow motion. "Hey, Breena."

"I've been waiting for you." Sheriff Breena Dover leaned on a nearby county car, legs crossed at the ankles, arms folded across her chest.

He played dumb. "Really? Why?"

"You know." Her mouth flattened. She uncrossed her appendages and produced a pen and pad. "Let's chat."

"Sure. But I'm headin' to the Blue Moon. I go on in about forty-five minutes. Can we do this after?"

"Sorry, no. This is too important to let slide, even a few hours." Breena paused. "You're aware Teddie saw someone killed earlier."

Drew gave a noncommittal nod. Even though Teddie would always occupy a special place in his heart, it was hard to ignore the press's insinuations she had mental problems. Like others, he maintained misgivings she witnessed a killing.

"Someone spotted you close to where the alleged homicide happened." Breena strolled nearer and eyeballed him suspiciously. "Timeframe fits, too."

Drew tensed, his fingers dug into his palms and curled into a fist. "You believe I shoved a person into the water and left them to die? Why would I do that?"

"I've known you and your family since your move to New England from East Texas. So no, it's not my inclination to suspect you've done anything wrong. I can't find a reason you'd do something so despicable.

But I'm the law in this community. I'm obliged to follow up on every lead. A bystander says they noticed you on the pier the time another eyewitness says a deadly altercation occurred. I want answers, Drew.

Now." She gave him a stern look. "What's your story?"

"No story. I don't understand what you want me to tell you. I swear, I don't know anything."

"Fine. I'll run the show. I'll ask you questions, and you'll answer them."

"Let's get this over with so I can get to my gig."

"We'll start with the hardest. Were you on the pavilion tonight?"

"Yes. As was the whole damn town."

"Not what I'm asking, and you know it. Were you on the Phoenix's deck, alone?"

"Yes."

"Better." She glimpsed at him in between making notations. "What time?"

"I made three trips." He scratched his head. "First was seven-thirty, maybe a little after. Again, half an hour later, and fifteen minutes afterward."

"Why so many visits?"

"Evie and I were supposed to meet." Drew's gut squeezed. "She kept putting me off."

"Did you see anyone your first time out?"

He shook his head. "Just the third."

Breena arched an eyebrow. "Evie?"

"Teddie Donavan. Evie joined us a few minutes after."

"Bet that was interesting."

"You don't want to know."

"No one else? Just Teddie and your wife."

"Only two people I encountered. And Teddie told us about the murder."

"Okay, I guess we're done." She spun toward her car. "Don't leave town. I'll probably require more information and want to speak to you again."

"Where would I go?"

She glanced over her shoulder and shrugged. "No idea. Just hang around till I tell you otherwise."

Drew extended an arm toward the truck's handle. He stopped within an inch of opening the door and twisted back to Breena. "Do you believe somebody died?"

Sheriff Breena halted. "I confess, I entertain serious doubts, but Teddie reported it. My job is to investigate, regardless." She rotated away. "Stay in town."

Inside his truck, Drew slammed the door the same time his tires squealed, leaving the parking lot. He turned onto the bumpy, graveled road, sparing a peek at the digital clock on the dash.

Damn. He better hurry, or he'd be late.

He pumped the pedal to the floor and headed toward the watering hole situated in the boondocks, fifteen miles away. Ignoring the speedometer, he raced around the winding one-lane rocky road. The vehicle hugged the stony cliffs as his headlights reflected rising clouds of dust.

Teddie appeared into his thoughts. As always, she overshadowed everything.

He never knew how to deal with the flash of emotions that barraged him when she entered his mind. He strained to manage his desires, walling them in a secret, but guarded, section of his heart. Her surprise appearance forced his fantasies front and center, and now they encompassed him.

He'd kept track of her over the years. Why wouldn't he? They sang and wrote songs together. His cock nudged his jeans. Often, the singing, writing, and performing ended with the two of them wrapped around each other naked.

Control, Drew, get yourself under control.

He didn't function well sporting a hard on. Since Evie shut down their sex life not long after their nuptials, he had to find sexual satisfaction on his own. Reminiscences of Teddie and his right hand kept him fulfilled during the dark hours.

Now Teddie was back in town. And he couldn't touch her.

Did he even want to, especially since her health seemed to spiral downward? Stupid question, of course he wanted her. He always yearned for her, but only stupidity would make him act on those desires.

Her recent episodes were a concern. After her wild declarations, could he blindly accept her difficulties were related to exhaustion? Or were the news reports accurate?

With just his gut to listen to—he couldn't fathom. Even his intuition was confused.

He drove into the Blue Moon's parking lot, threw the gear into park, and switched off the motor. The bar, an eroded, crenelated, metal building, was located on a muddy cove's uneven banks.

Neon beams flickered above the admission booth. The steady beat vibrated from inside, loud enough to hear even though the windows were shut. Several patrons surrounded the outer building, tossing down longnecks. They laughed as they drank and socialized.

This is the where his musical aspirations began. For him and Teddie. Their and the band's first gigs. They played and crooned melodies they penned, the place they fell in love.

He surveyed the building a long while, fighting the wonderful memories.

A lengthy groan escaped as he tugged the handle. No use trying to live in the past. Teddie made her choice. Drew rolled out of the cab and marched to the rear to retrieve his guitar case.

And he accepted her decision a long time ago. She didn't choose him.

Chapter 7

"Your first party ended with a dud." Nash stood next to Evie as the final guests filed from the building. "I hope you were able to solicit some pledges before this disaster imploded or your superiors won't be pleased."

"Like I want to hear this," Evie snapped.

Her inaugural position as Davis Medical Center's fundraising operations manager was a major bust, but Evie could do without a reminder of the dismal outcome.

A new trauma unit wouldn't happen with the proceeds they netted tonight. Not only would her bosses knock down her door on Monday, she'd be forced to contend with the town's scrutiny. While responsibility fell on her, Evie blamed the appearance of her husband's former girlfriend as the real cause of the party's catastrophe.

"Drew's pushing me to sign the papers."

Nash's inspection of the dwindling crowd didn't waver. A hand slid inside his jacket, extracting a package of slim, dark cigars. "Is he now?"

"Yes. He informed me earlier. I agree to his terms now or suffer consequences later."

"You've been successful delaying him, thus far. Continue doing what you're doing."

"This   time   is   different.   Drew's   lawyer

71

recommended he request a judge to dissolve the marriage, *minus* my approval. My legal team tells me His Honor will most likely grant the appeal because we've prolonged the proceedings." She twisted toward Nash. "By the way, you can't light up in here."

Nash twirled his cigar between his fingers. "They can do that?"

"The procedure is doable if the divorcer is willing to pay an extra charge. Another option is, the judge requires me to sign divorce papers or holds me in contempt, which results in jail time. Either way, I'm screwed."

"Drew's reasons to leave are valid." Nash's lips flattened into a thin line. Disregarding her warning, he positioned the smoke in his mouth and produced a cigarette lighter, waving the flame underneath. He drew in the tobacco, then puffed out a foggy cloud.

"Excuse me? He thinks he's the only one who lived in hell, well, he's wrong. I had to deal with him, too. Him and his constant sulking and his foul moods."

"No doubt many would applaud your stamina, but you're smarter if you instruct your law firm to keep digging to find something illicit on him and blackmail him into staying until you're ready. He'll never know."

"He may not know, but his good ol' boy lawyer does. I assumed holding Drew off and delaying a divorce would be a slam dunk after he hired the guy, but I was wrong. Abel Fontaine doesn't miss a word."

Nash looked grim. "I suppose Teddie's homecoming assisted in his pressuring your split."

"Of course, his precious Teddie is an influence. I'll make sure the whole world knows they've reconnected, too."

His brows knitted as he inhaled another drag. "Did I catch a trace of jealousy in your tone?"

"No. I just despise her taking anything that's mine." She stomped to the bar and snatched an untouched glass of champagne, then spun to view the messy room.

Nash followed her lead and retrieved a full flute. He took a tiny sip, licked the moist remnants off his lips, then placed his smoke into his mouth. He looped his fingers around Evie's arm and led her past an opened beveled door onto the unoccupied pavilion.

He removed his cigar and took a second drink of champagne. "Let's be real, here. You and Drew never meshed. He was a teenage crush who jilted you to date your best friend, and he rebounded back to you after she left town."

Evie brushed an errant wisp of hair off her cheek. "Be cruel, why don't you? I'm aware he didn't love me. Not in the way he loved her. I appreciate you're a Donavan family friend, but I hate her. Always have."

"True, I consider the Donavans family members, yet I sympathize with your animosity. Teddie is a driven woman, committed to getting whatever she wishes. And yes, she stepped on many toes along the way, including yours."

"I met Drew first. We'd gone on two dates when I introduced them. She saw how much I liked him, but she set her sights on him, regardless. She stole Drew away from me."

"I'm afraid Drew left you without the help of outside influences, and that time was long ago. Sad. You're still bitter over a war you ultimately won, and you no longer care about him. You've talked of leaving for over a year. I can't grasp your hostility."

"Losing my closest friend and a boyfriend," she hesitated and shook her head, "not a pain you easily overcome."

"Stay angry. Your choice." He tossed the ashy butt into the rolling waves below and steered her back inside. The cleanup crew had jumped on the vacant space and were scouring the room. "You forget, Teddie's experienced her share of agony."

"She has not. She's famous. Even if she never sang another note, she'll maintain her fame, and everything that accompanies it. The so-called cottage where she lives is a mansion and sits on a thousand acres of land. The property includes a recording studio, a spa, and an animal habitat, plus a dog rescue. The estate has every amenity you can imagine, and her bank accounts continue to overflow."

"There's more to living than loads of money or a lifestyle. She's experienced a lot of heartbreak too. Her parents died in a tragic way. Drew married you. Tabloids report she and her longtime companion separated, recently. Her fame puts her life out there for everyone to see." He dipped a hand into his pocket and brought out his cell, giving the screen a glance. "She's had health problems, too."

Evie grinned. "Her cheese slipped further off her cracker tonight, didn't it? I mean, seriously, do you believe she witnessed a murder?"

"She seemed fine when we spoke, but in all honesty, no, I can't imagine a person was pushed off the pier." He paused. "I wish she'd let me help her. She's bewildered and despondent. I extended an invitation, but she thinks she's okay."

"I don't get you guys. Does she cast a mystical spell over men? Every one of you scramble to throw yourselves before her thousand-dollar cowboy boots and let her walk all over you. You should've seen Drew." Evie drained her wineglass, set it aside, and seized another. "He hasn't looked at me that way—ever."

"Why are you worried? Let him go and save your heart." A twinkle entered his eyes. "Your little dalliances on the side should help tremendously."

"A *single* liaison."

"More than one, Evie. Our facility is small. We're a tight community, and employees whisper. Numerous doctors or orderlies tended to your desires over the years." He motioned to stop her objection. "No reason to protest. Most moved away, and I've seen to it the board isn't interested what you do in your private life as long as you keep your affairs concealed. You're smart enough to choose side dishes who stood to lose a great deal if word was leaked. Other than what I uncovered, no one is aware. You're extremely lucky."

"No. I'm careful." She sighed. "Drew didn't provide me any alternatives. He's always too busy writing his music and playing in his band. Or he's designing a new project. He stays occupied to avoid me. I have needs, and he never meets them."

"Not necessary to defend your actions to me."

"I would hope not."

Nash chuckled. "Although I think you sleep around because you can get away with cheating as opposed to satisfying your fragile desires. Drew's a healthy specimen. I can't imagine him not delivering, if you made the suggestion."

Debra Jupe

Evie inserted a sharp glare. "Speaking of sleeping around, where's Celia? I noticed her absence. Why didn't she accompany you to the gala?"

"My wife had a conference scheduled." His voice turned dry. "Her antique shop is oh so demanding, and she felt obligated to attend her symposium, instead."

"Have you spoken to her about ending your marriage?"

Nash heaved a long sigh. "I'm deciding how to broach the subject."

"You've said that for months."

"Separations take time. Until now, you and I were on equal ground pertaining to our dissatisfied nuptials. We had time to map out a strategy. Drew's altered that. He's moved along quicker than we anticipated. You can't expect me to go home and do likewise, then the two of us become a public item almost immediately after. People will talk."

"They'll figure us out, anyway. We're colleagues. We work in the same clinic. Our paths cross. A lot. We can say we're comforting each other during a difficult time." She shrugged. "Circumstances progressed, and we became a couple."

"Terminating Celia's and my union isn't as simple as me aspiring to leave, Evie. My wife is a devout Catholic. Her religion doesn't advocate divorce and unlike you, I have children."

"They're grown, Nash."

"Teenagers, Evie. They'll experience the effects, and those results will devastate them. I mean to make this as painless as possible for their sake. I must work on Celia and slowly convince her we'll be better apart. Remember, an instant estrangement would cost me a fortune."

"You mean, cost you *her* money. She's funded your whole career, right? The hospital is financially subsidized by her relatives. She was a Davis before she married you."

"She's helped me by using her personal resources, yes. Another reason I can't suddenly tell her I yearn to leave. She'll make sure I'm bankrupt once we're done."

"You ought've planted the seeds a long time ago," Evie almost shouted.

Nash held up a palm. "Voice down, please. Guests went home, but the staff is still here. They talk too."

"Most don't speak English."

"They understand it."

Evie slanted closer and spoke in a loud undertone. "You said when we began seeing each other, you intended to leave your wife. Later, we'd move in together, and then marry. I never would've gotten involved if I hadn't believed your intentions were real."

She should've seen this coming, but for the first time in a long while her feelings blinded her. "Why is my intuition nagging, saying your attitude has shifted since Drew and I are close to an end?"

"I'm not changing my mind. Celia and I will talk, but I will not end our marriage on the exact night yours collapsed. There are details to discuss, and Celia's emotional state comes first."

"Right." Evie's vocal cords trembled. "I get a boot in the gut instead."

"Regretful, but yes, you're forced to endure the pain until other arrangements are made. I can't just hurt my wife so easily."

A strained silence emerged and continued a long

minute.

"I could, though," Evie suddenly spouted, then she smirked. "Hurt her."

Nash's jaw dropped. "You'd tell her about us?"

"Somebody should."

He exhaled, blowing a stream of air. "You can be hard and mean, Evie. Fine. I'll talk to her. Soon."

"How soon?"

"Give me two or three months."

"What do I do while I wait?"

Nash cleared his throat. "Continue your fight. Direct your lawyer to do the same. What's Drew's timeline?"

"Till the end of the weekend."

"Hmmm, not much time. Perhaps you can shame him into waiting. Use whatever means you have. Discredit him."

"People will support him. I can't believe I'm saying this, but he's got a lot of fans who enjoy his music."

"They're blue collar." Nash's eyes rolled. "Who gives a damn?"

"Their employers are people in our circles, and they do communicate, as in gossip. Most of my connections verify rumors by questioning their staff. Some even solicit. As far as Drew is concerned, you and I may detest his music, but scores of mutual friends love it. Numerous people suggested I use him and his band to entertain at our benefits."

"If you host a honkytonk hoedown, then his group would be appropriate."

"Taste is subjective."

Nash raised a reluctant shoulder. "I'm not a fan of

his musical selections, but you're correct. Enthusiasts are enamored by your husband's talent."

"Many claim Teddie made a huge error bypassing Drew when she headed to Nashville. How would I ruin him?"

"You can't please a whole city. Drew has his supporters. You might use Teddie's return as a catapult to tarnish his reputation. Hint they've resumed their affair."

"Should be easy, since that'll happen."

"Of course, he adores her."

"Thanks."

"You can benefit, leverage the complication to persuade him to delay, which will give me more time to groom Celia. Rumors won't pertain to just Jacob's Cove. Teddie Donavan is famous and coincidently on a downward spiral. The whole world's watching."

Evie's eyes brightened. "You're brilliant, Nash."

"My mind's analytical. After it's all over, you and I will present ourselves as a legitimate couple. Our friends will accept us sans scrutiny or blotches against us."

"What we must do to preserve our social statuses," Evie stated airily. "How will you rise above the stench of initiating a divorce? Celia is well-liked too, and her lineage is traced to the Mayflower era."

"One of the complicated tasks you laid before me, Evie. I haven't a clue. But since you're forcing me, I must bow to whatever ultimatum you administer."

"I hate to be so harsh." She rotated, blinking away pretend tears. "You and Drew are the only men I ever loved. Neither of you care."

He moved behind her and placed a palm on each of

her shoulders. "I do care." He kissed her temple, turned her to him, and sandwiched her hand between his. "Employees are gone. Offices are unlocked and available. Let's borrow a room so I can show you how much."

"While our discreet liaisons are fun, I'm no longer content having you an hour here and an hour there. Especially if Drew and I break up faster than we planned, and you're still married to Celia." She squirmed to escape his grip. "I may decide to explore other options once I'm unattached."

"Ah, Evie. Such a drama queen." His mouth twitched into a smile. "Why don't I give you the rest of the evening?"

"How will you make that happen? Celia's home waiting."

"Actually, she isn't. She booked a bed and breakfast for overnight. We can get a hotel room. I'm familiar with one located on the far side of town. Not a five star, but the beds are comfortable." He smiled again. "What do you say?"

"Hmm, sounds promising."

"Can you escape Drew for one evening?"

"He's set up an apartment in the basement. He doesn't know if I'm home or not." Evie redirected her glare. "I won't play this game long, Nash. Either you talk to Celia or I will."

"I've submitted to your conditions. Are we on?"

"Lucky you're dynamite in the sack, and I'm hungry for some serious physical release. Room charges are on you, baby doll." Evie sat her empty goblet down. "And I demand a fresh bottle of champagne. Most expensive in the Cove."

"You're in charge." He opened the door leading outdoors. "Finest bubbly in the land coming up."

Chapter 8

Teddie tugged her cowboy hat lower to conceal her identity while she waited in line to pay the cover outside a local dive's entrance. Sun-bleached neon letters spelling Blue Moon Saloon hummed above her as forceful wind gusts swayed the flickering logo back and forth.

She quickly progressed to a barred window, slid a twenty underneath a small arch to a bored attendant, and waited to receive her change. Teddie peeked at the woman from beneath her hat and swore this was the same lady who took money when she sang at the club years before.

After obtaining a stamp, she entered the building, stopping to bare her freshly inked hand to a bulky, tattooed guy guarding the doorway.

Inside, the club's interior was smoky and loud. Familiar stenches hovered within the atmosphere, the identical smells she remembered from years before. Maneuvering amid the crammed house, Teddie slipped into a rear corner booth without anyone noticing her. Not that recognition was a problem. Most spectators were too engrossed with the current performer to detect a troubled superstar had crashed their sanctum.

She arrived moments before Drew was slated to go on. The marquee outside listing him on tonight's schedule had surprised her. Even with their obvious discord, Teddie assumed he stayed at the gala to support his wife.

The group onstage completed their set as she settled in her seat. A waiter magically appeared at her side. "Diet soda," she yelled above the commotion.

Roadies quickly hopped onto the stage to exchange equipment. The restless audience circulated to purchase food, alcohol or use the restroom. Within minutes, lights faded as patrons rushed to their stools. The tavern's noise level decreased. Seconds stretched into forever before spotlights swept across the stage.

Teddie's stomach quivered as butterflies flapped. Although she didn't plan to attend Drew's show, a big part of her was excited to watch him perform.

Cheers erupted to a deafening roar. Drew stood onstage with his bandmates, Eight Times Country, ready to entertain. He extended a hand holding a pick and displayed a dimpled grin. He didn't speak, but he didn't need to. All he had to do was pluck a cord, and the onlookers went wild. He sang a few covers, but mostly he crooned songs written by him and his bandmates.

His performance put most megastars to shame. She wanted to lean her head back, shut her eyes, and just listen to him serenade, but she was unable to tear her gaze away because damn, he looked fine. He hadn't changed. His tight t-shirt clung to his torso, the short sleeves strained across his muscled arms, low-slung jeans hugged his hips perfectly, just like the old days.

The old days.

Most of their crew would stumble upon a party or two after a concert such as this. Not her and Drew. They'd find a nearby private retreat, strip each other naked, and rock the nails out of their hideout. Usually their sex-capades occurred in a too-snug janitor closet, located in the back of the building. They used other small havens, too, transforming vertical sex into an art.

Stimulated, her thighs clenched as she craved to run onstage and drag him back to that old storeroom to create new and improved memories. She wiggled in her seat and wondered, had their stolen moments also remained etched in his mind? Or was she pathetic? Were her emotions real? Was Drew the proverbial one who got away? Her soulmate? Or did the illusion only exist in fantasyland?

Her hectic lifestyle kept her too busy to dissect their past, yet his memory constantly lurked in her thoughts. One reason she came to Jacob's Cove was to put her and Drew's past to rest and move on to find a real partnership. Only she still longed for Drew.

How could she survive, knowing she couldn't have him? She focused on the man she'd loved since she was a teenager. Multi-colored beams shimmered across as he delved into a tune he penned years ago.

A song he wrote for her.

She shook her head, reverting to the present. The realization of what the future held for her and Drew hit her like a splash of cold water. She had to forget him.

The forty-five-minute set ended. Earsplitting ovations and shouts for more erupted, only the Blue Moon didn't allow encores. Drew waved as he and his band exited the stage.

Suddenly tired, Teddie finished what she wanted of her soda, tossed some bills onto the Formica, and scooted across the faux leather seat, swinging her legs around.

"Aren't you supposed to be resting?"

A dark, knowing gaze speared down at her. Drew clutched the bench's edge while he rested his other hand on the tabletop, boxing her in. He bent close enough that his warm breath caressed her face. He didn't wait for her to reply. Nudging her knee with his, he urged her farther back into the booth, sank down and scooched in behind her.

A full mug of beer was put in front of him the instant he sat.

His eyes locked into hers as he expectantly waited for her to say something. Except she couldn't find the words. Her fists tightened, gripping her almost filled cup.

He frowned into his beer as he idly rotated his glass. "Why are you here?"

"I needed a night out," she responded in a tight voice.

"And this is where you came?"

She lifted her head meeting his gaze. "I'm shocked the place is still open."

"Name's been switched a few times, but it always goes back to the Blue Moon." He glanced about the bar, releasing a strained chuckled. "The people? Same kind of crowd."

"They're younger."

"More like we're older. Lots of memories were made inside this bar." He fought to restrain a wicked grin. "Lots."

She bit her bottom lip, briefly glimpsing up to view his racy smile. He was too close. Since she became famous, she intentionally minimized her vulnerability as a form of protection, but his nearness uncovered every raw nerve.

"Your band's awesome," she uttered, after a lengthy silence. "Your new songs are great. Maybe I can put in a word to my agent—"

He threw her a sharp glare as his jovialness morphed into resentment. "Don't even."

She shrunk against the vinyl and looked down. Perhaps she deserved his scorn, but the added cruelty in his tone was uncalled for.

"Are you uncomfortable? Do you want me to leave?"

Her head shot up. "Why would you ask me such a thing?"

"You're uneasy. Am I the reason?"

"You're fine sitting by me?"

"Why wouldn't I be? My conscience is clear."

"Drew, I…you know, people make mistakes. Really, do we need to go there?"

"Gotcha." His eyes wandered the room before returning to her. "We can postpone whatever this is indefinitely. Fuck, I've existed this long stifling my feelings."

"Drew, I don't consider what happened my fault."

"Not your fault. Don't mean the whole thing didn't hurt."

"I'm sorry, okay?"

"Yeah, sure. Okay."

Both were quiet again as they sat through another round of unsettled silence.

Drew cleared his throat and adjusted his position, posing them face to face. "You've yet to say what made you decide to come back to Jacob's Cove?"

"Yes, I did. I require a peaceful spot to recover."

"Right. You're exhausted." His tenor held a trace of cynicism. "I'm not surprised you're tired. You're practically a household name. Hit records, sell out concerts in monster-size venues. Hell, I read you're into producing, now. Didn't I hear talk of a TV series?"

"In the works." Her lips slightly elevated. "You kept up with my career?"

"Kinda hard not to. You're everywhere." A large hand swiped over his glass, wiping away the condensation. "You never married."

She snatched her drink and gulped half the cup down. "Nope," she managed after an awkward swallow.

"You were in a relationship. With Jarod Keene. He's a big gun in the industry."

"One of the best."

"You have kids."

"Yes, three. A daughter and two sons. Boys are twins."

"So, why didn't you? Marry."

"I don't know, we discussed it but…" Once more, her words wedged inside her throat. "Mama and Daddy's train wreck soured my impression of happily ever after. My sisters, too. Granted, Raven tied the knot five years ago. I suppose she and Emmitt are happy."

"I see."

"Do you?"

His head snapped around; his expression revealed his irritation. "Yes, Teddie, I lived it too, remember?" Another round of nothingness arose until he ended the stretch of silence. "What happened between you two?"

"Huh?"

He observed her skeptically. Her gut nosedived. While he behaved civilly, the fire in his darkening irises told her he was less than pleased by her unexpected arrival. "You and Keene. Why'd you break up?"

"We drifted in opposite directions. No biggie. We parted amicably. We're still friends, and we continue to work together."

Their conversations treaded on fragile ice since they reconnected, and their talks should deviate to a more frivolous subject.

Instead, she dove in deeper. "And you and Evie? Not my business, but you two don't act like you enjoy each other's company."

"You're perceptive."

"Lose the sarcasm."

He sighed reluctantly. "Like you and your significant other, we didn't work. Never did. I got hurt when you left." He stared straight at her. The darkness in his pupils penetrated her soul. "I proposed and subsequently wedded to overcome my pain. Been miserable ever since."

Teddie licked her sudden dry lips, confused as to her next move. "I'm sorry. Again. For everything."

"Stop apologizing. We each chose our paths." He calmly watched her, laying a hand on the flat surface next to her taut fist. His fingertips tapped the Formica. "Your children, a daughter and twin boys?"

Teddie's insides were paralyzed. She flashed a nervous smile. "Yes. Savannah is a wonderful girl. A joy since day one. Her father's producing a new band in Europe, and she joined him. The boys just celebrated their eleventh birthday. They're at their grandparents in Kentucky while I recuperate."

"Your girl's what? Sixteen, seventeen?"

"Sixteen."

"You hooked up with Keene quick after you and I..."

"You're not the only one whose heart was broken, Drew." Instantly, she regretted her outburst, yet she went on. "You dumped me, remember? I also rebounded." She paused and silently counted to compose herself. "You don't have children?"

He laughed harshly. "Evie's not the maternal type; no, we weren't blessed."

"You two can still, if you chose."

"Don't think that's likely." Another sardonic chuckle erupted. "You and Keene did a fantastic job protecting Savannah and your boys from the limelight."

"Jarod and I live under public scrutiny. We know what that life entails. This business is crazy and unforgiving. We try to shield them as much as possible."

"Guess that makes sense." He stopped, seemingly listening to the music in the background. "Your kids sing, too?"

She smiled. "The twins do, but they prefer video games."

"And Savannah?"

Her smile broadened. "Like an angel."

"Any aspirations? She envisioned following in Mom's or Dad's footsteps?"

"She's interested." Teddie relaxed. "But not in music. She'd rather be an actress."

Drew laughed, but the corners of his upturned lips didn't quite reach his penetrating eyes. "The paparazzi posted some pictures at the last country music awards program. Got closeups of all three. Tabloids published them."

Teddie's lungs congested as if they'd been trapped in a vice.

"Keene's blond like you. He's blue-eyed too, right?"

"Yes," she replied in a hoarse whisper.

"Magazines in the grocery store checkout say his eyes are dreamy." He gave another cynical laugh, then frowned. "The boys. Spitting images of you."

"I've been told."

"But Savannah. She doesn't have your or Keene's coloring. Doesn't resemble either of you." His scowl intensified. "Weird, isn't it?"

Teddie sipped her beverage, wishing she could've ordered something stronger. "Genetics are strange. Darker complexions may run deep in one of our family lines."

"What's her eye color?"

Teddie cleared away the lump in her throat. "Brown."

Drew eased against the wooden back, plucked a napkin, and began to rip it into tiny shreds. "You're right. Genetics are funny."

Teddie shifted farther away. "Blue-eyed people can produce a brown-eyed child."

"Sure they can."

"And she has some of my features."

"A couple, but none of Keene's that I see. She really doesn't resemble him."

He wadded the tattered napkin into a ball and tossed it across the table. A warm palm caught her arm and squeezed. Her skin sizzled where he touched her, but the caress wasn't meant as intimate.

"Maybe that's because Keene isn't her father?"

Teddie's gut twisted. Circumstances had just become no win.

Drew leaned closer and held her gaze. "Tell me what I suspect isn't true." His tone dropped to a dangerous level. "Tell me Savannah Keene isn't my daughter. Teddie, tell me the reason you came back isn't to let me know I'm the father of a sixteen-year-old child."

Chapter 9

Suspicions concerning Savannah's parentage nagged Drew throughout the years. The timeline of her birthday was too much of a coincidence, but the absence of proof and lack of funds to investigate required him to suppress his hunches.

Teddie shielded her children from the public eye, therefore he couldn't even compare Savannah's childhood pictures to his own photographs as an infant to see if a resemblance existed.

Until a month ago. Drew's initial sight of Savannah occurred during an award show on television. His certainty of her parentage avalanched after getting a better look while waiting in a checkout line, and he observed a full-blown glossy family photo, donning the cover of a popular country music magazine.

The girl was a spitting image of him.

Deep in his heart, he'd like to believe Teddie wouldn't bear his child and then fail to alert him. Especially not after this long, but that's exactly what she did.

He glared across the table. Her chin dropped to avoid his prying eyes. He didn't need to press her further. Her body language spoke volumes.

He had a sixteen-year-old daughter he'd never met.

"Explain, Teddie. Make me understand."

Her head raised. Her lower lip quivered as tears

lined her eyes. She heaved an enormous sigh and gulped. "Two months after I moved, I discovered my pregnancy. I wanted to tell you, I should've… I ought to…" Teddie's head shook side to side. "So much you don't know."

"Enlighten me."

"I can't."

Hunkering slightly, he leveled so their gazes matched. "Can't or won't?" Although he didn't require verification, he wanted her to admit what he knew to be true. "Will you at least confirm Savannah's mine?"

"She's your biological child."

Rage erupted inside him, overpowering his shock, and his newly formed anger was directed at Teddie. He suffered disappointment during his life. Occasionally, he even bore resentment that she went on to fulfill their dreams and left him stuck in Jacob's Cove. But once he untangled his emotions, he faced the truth. His feelings for Teddie never changed.

He loved her.

Due to his behavior, she chose career instead of him. His practical side identified with her choices. He couldn't say he wouldn't have picked the same option if the situation were reversed. Their hunger to hit the big time was fierce, and both would've traded their souls to achieve their ambitions.

But to give birth to their child, without his knowledge, and allow another man to rear her as his own was too much to bear.

Unforgivable.

"Why am I just finding out about her tonight?"

Salvaging what was left of her control, she scanned the crowded bar, then slanted closer and lowered her voice. "I realize you have thousands of questions. I'll be happy to answer every one of them, but not here. Reporters like to blend in and pretend they're a part of the audience, but they lurk and eavesdrop on celebrities. I'd rather Savannah not learn you and I spoke through headlines."

Drew slid out of the booth and stood aside. Teddie followed. Together, they walked outside. Neither said a word. Drew halted in a makeshift gravel roadway sandwiched between idle vehicles and the Blue Moon.

"Where to?"

"We can meet, just name a place."

He scouted the sea of automobiles and then squinted at the building. The outer structure appeared dilapidated in the daylight, but the twinkly, neon bulbs lighting the place created an appealing sight during the night. He shook his head to clear it, skeptical as to why such an inane thought entered his mind. Truly, he didn't give a rat's ass about the dump's décor.

"No one's here."

She removed her oversized cowboy hat. "You're fine talking about someone as important as your daughter in a bar's parking lot?"

"Why not?" He glanced at the Blue Moon once more. Music still blared inside. The party would carry on another hour. "Show will continue for a while. It's nice and private."

"Anyone who comes outside might hear us."

"I imagine they'll be too inebriated to notice." Drew motioned toward his pickup. "I'm parked at the end of this row."

Remaining in place, she clutched the hat's brim. This wasn't her ideal spot to talk, he got that, but at the moment, he didn't care.

Then his conscious got the better of him. "My guitar and equipment are inside. I'd rather not leave my stuff, and it'll take a while to load."

"Fine," she relented, obviously still objecting to his choice.

Drew walked to his truck and tugged the lever to release the tailgate and eased it down flat. He hoisted up and slid onto the edge.

Teddie approached his vehicle, turned, and scooted backward until securely seated. She noticeably hugged the other side, sitting as far away from him as possible. "I don't know where to begin."

He shot her a side-glance. "How 'bout when you realized you were pregnant? Did you make a conscious decision *not* to contact me, or were you so busy it just slipped your mind?"

"I was young, Drew. And alone. I didn't know what to do."

"So, you did nothing?"

She didn't respond.

"Fine. Tell me then, why come back now? Why did you choose this as the time to inform me I'm a dad? After Savannah's practically grown?"

"I didn't make any premeditated conclusions. I wasn't sure if you'd agree to see me, much less talk to me."

"Is Savannah aware I'm her natural father?"

"I told her when she was small, and she's understood Jarod isn't her actual dad. She's satisfied concerning her parental circumstances, but lately she's longed to find out more about you. I've tried to answer her questions honestly."

Debra Jupe

"What did you tell her?

"That we met in high school. We wrote songs and sang together. Our friendship evolved."

"Whoa, wait a minute. That kind of thing crops up between band members every day. Nothing but flings. We went way beyond just a hook up. You specified we were more than casual, didn't you?"

"I did." She stretched across the truck bed and placed a warm palm on his forearm. "She's aware we dated before I became pregnant."

Drew froze. The heated contact was too difficult to process alongside the other news he was forced to confront. He shook her grasp away, she recoiled as if he slapped her. He should feel guilty, but he didn't.

"Is she curious why we ended?"

"Very."

"Did you come clean?"

She inhaled through her nose. "I explained it all, although it's a glazed version."

"Sugarcoated the story." He let go a sarcastic chuckle. "She interested why you didn't contact me after you found out about her? Or why you and I haven't communicated?"

"She's hinted." Teddie gazed at her clasped fists lying in her lap. "I've dodged the subject."

"Hmmm. You're good at that."

"What do you mean?"

He eyed her closely. "You've done the same thing to me. I'm still in the dark why you didn't tell me about your pregnancy."

She became still and stared at the starlit sky. "I just explained."

The pair sat for a long period, listening to drums

96

and sporadic laughter echoing from the club's direction.

Drew finally spoke. "Amazing thing about time. Occasionally, you meet someone and you click. You possess this—this bond. It's strong, like your souls are linked. Doesn't matter how long you're apart or the last time you spoke, the connection won't break. So, when one of you isn't straight with the other, you know. You know when they're feeding you a line of bullshit. What else happened, Teddie? How come you didn't tell me about my daughter?"

"I tried to," she whispered. "When I learned I was carrying your baby, I came back. I returned to Jacob's Cove to see you."

"Sure, you did. You came here to talk to me, yet you didn't? Or I don't remember? Pretty certain I'd recall my ex-girlfriend flying in from Tennessee to let me know she's having my baby."

"I swear. You'd just left town." Another silence lapsed. "To go on your honeymoon."

Drew's heart twisted. Air locked inside his chest, and a speck of his annoyance diminished. A palm scrubbed over his jaw as his teeth sank into his bottom lip.

Of all the days to return. No wonder she didn't notify him.

"You arrived the weekend Evie and I got married."

"I didn't see a point pursuing you after I found out you were married. You'd obviously moved on. I'd only complicate your life by telling you, you were about to become a dad." Her head bowed to watch her feet dangle. "So, I went home."

His irritation retreated, understanding her motives at the time. But what occurred over the next fifteen years? Why hadn't she come to him after he and Evie settled?

"Convenient."

"I didn't just come to tell you about Savannah." She spun to face him, staring directly at him the first time since they began this exchange of dialog. "I came to say I loved you. I wanted to try again to talk you into coming to Tennessee. I'd already gotten a bit of experience in the industry and was becoming familiar on how the system worked. I was convinced if you moved with me, you'd make it. On your own. You didn't need my help." Her attention swayed off him and focused on the dirt below her swinging feet. "Except you were married. I didn't want to upset your happiness."

Remorse sliced through him like a double-edged blade. He wished she was spouting nothing but excuses, only every fiber in his core said she spoke the truth.

While he did marry Evie on the rebound and perhaps for spite, Teddie had no reason not to believe he was anything other than a happily, married man. Who knows if he wouldn't have made the identical decision in her place?

Still, his doubts lingered. "How'd Jarod Keene get involved?"

"We just signed on to our label as new artists and recorded at the same studio. Newbies tend to stick together, and we became friends. One day, he caught me crying. He took me to dinner and insisted I explain why I was upset. I craved support, so I told him. He offered to help, and the rest, as they say, is history."

"A huge compromise. To accept and raise another man's child."

"Honestly, it wasn't our plan to get romantically involved or for him to take on the father role. It just sort of happened." She shrugged. "Jarod's a decent guy."

"I guess I owe him, seeing he's the father I didn't get to be." He shuffled off his truck's tail and dusted off the seat of his jeans. "Any more surprises to spring on me?"

"No." She manipulated off the tailgate and onto her feet. "I suppose we're finished, unless there's something else you want to know."

"Nope." He rotated so his back faced her. "We're done, Teddie."

"Savannah wants to meet you."

Apprehension engulfed his jagged state of mind. The idea his daughter wanted an introduction terrified him. He was an average guy, and his mundane way of living compared to her mother and stepfather's glittery lifestyle could only lead to disillusionment.

"I'm not sure if I'm ready, Teddie. I gotta let this whole daddy thing sink in. I'm too stunned to think clearly." Circling the front of his truck, he popped the locks, reaching to grab the door handle. "You can find your way to your car."

"Drew."

He ignored her plea, eager to not participate in more debates concerning his child. Odd crunches rustled nearby. A loud drawn-out moan emitted from Teddie's side, followed by a loud thump. Drew whipped around. Teddie's shadowed form had vanished.

"Shit."

Panic welled in his chest as he willed his feet to move, hurrying to his pickup's rear end. Teddie lay in a heap on the ground, folded in half. He rushed to kneel by her and checked her pulse. Her heartrate battered, yet her skin felt cold and clammy. She required medical care, at once. Drew gathered her into his arms and carried her to the vehicle's opened door, carefully placing her inside.

He slipped his cell phone out of his pocket.

"Don't," she murmured, stretching out a limp arm that didn't quite touch him. As if laded with steel, the hand plummeted and drooped at her side. "Don't call."

Edging nearer, he tilted across to reinspect her condition. Pale skin, fluttery eyelids, possibly coherent, although also extremely woozy.

"I'm okay. Just tired. Want to go home. Please, take me home."

"You ought to see a doctor."

"No. No doctors. Media outlets will…field day."

Drew sighed. Her words faded just like her consciousness, but he got the gist of what she meant. Any trip to the hospital would add fuel to the already smoldering fires and bring further damage to her professional reputation. And to protect her name, he may sacrifice his.

"Fucking hell." He inched her farther into the passenger seat, buckled her in, then hurried to the other side. He looked at her dozing against the bucket seat as he turned over the engine. "Mother of my kid, I guess, I owe you."

Chapter 10

"I'm not finished yet." Evie let go a frustrated groan as Nash dragged his body away.

"No, you aren't." He whipped her around, snatched her hands, and held them behind her, bending her over the bathroom counter.

She inhaled noisily as he jammed himself into her and pumped. His other palm snaked across her stomach, his fingertips skimmed until settling between her thighs. Helpless, her head fell backward and rested on his shoulder.

They gyrated in rhythm.

A buzz whirred in the bedroom.

Nash stopped. His attentiveness diverted to where his phone rested. "Fuck, I'm almost done."

"Me too," Evie panted. "Ignore it."

He tightened his grip and drove into her again, shoving in and out at a careless rapidity. Each shouted amid moans until they collapsed onto the countertop, drenched from the exertion. They remained motionless several minutes.

Evie unfolded her upper body. She brushed the dots of moisture off her brow and stared into the mirror at her contented image. When it came to sex, the man played her like a symphony, every note synchronized in perfect harmony.

"Hmmm, Nash. You always manage to touch me in

all the right places. You're so creative." Her smile widened. "An artist."

He lifted his head, his face reddened and damp. "I'm pleased you appreciate my originality."

He moved off her, seized a towel hanging over the toilet, and patted the perspiration off his cheeks. Then he unrolled the filled condom from his limp penis.

"My wife never enjoys venturing outside the realms of propriety, even in the privacy of our bedroom." He tossed the used rubber into the commode and flushed. "Celia's such a prude. Her strict upbringing makes her uptight between the sheets. I begged her to try more adventurous escapades, but she always ignored my pleas. She only consents to missionary position, and the room must stay in total darkness."

Evie propelled off the edge of the counter, spun to him, and glared. Unadulterated resentment blinded her. Arms folded, she concealed her bare breasts as once again the ugly insinuation arose. Nash lied to her. He and his wife were still a couple, and she was nothing more than his side dish.

She refused to allow him to use her. "You told me you and Celia haven't been intimate in years. Now you're insinuating different. Which is the truth?"

"I've always been honest as to where Celia and I stand. She refuses to modernize her outdated religious beliefs. Intimacy ended after our last child was born, fourteen years ago, which was the last time we shared a bed."

He pitched the towel aside, tilted toward her, and pinched her nipple. Evie whimpered as her head released and angled backward.

"As I explained a thousand times, I moved into the study during that time." His tone softened. A hand careened across her torso and slipped downward to caress the center of her legs. "I could never resume those old, dull sexual antics after the stimulating adventures you provide."

"You'd get it every day if we were together. Like you promised," she breathed.

"Patience, Evie. We'll be paired, soon." Slanting closer, he nipped at her earlobe. "I can't wait. I'll quit the hospital or retire and be at your disposal sunup till sundown."

"Ummm. My disposal. I like the sound of that."

"Me too. My fantasy is to be a subordinate to my partner's Master. Would you consider becoming a dominatrix? You're a natural, you know."

"I do enjoy being in control."

"Perhaps we can try a smidgen of my vision during out next round of fun?"

"We've done it all night, but I'm game." She moaned as he continued to stroke her. "You're amazing. You're ready to go so soon."

He chuckled. "I'm not. But who's to say I can't whisk you away on a sensual quest while I recharge."

"I bet I can revitalize you."

"How, my sweet?"

"As your Master, I'll need your belt. You deserve a good spanking."

"Love when you talk dirty."

Nash's phone chirped again.

"Shit," he grumbled and pulled away. "I should check my messages."

"Not fair to leave me in such an overheated state,"

she teased. "I demand immediate gratification."

"Hold the thought." He strolled into the main room, retrieved his cell, and moved a thumb over the screen. "I'll return to complete my obligation once I'm done here."

Evie followed him, ambling to a curtain covered window, and yanked the tie off a hook. She held the bind at each end, raised the material overhead, and snapped it.

"I'm coming up with a ton of exciting ideas."

"Interesting. Look inside my briefcase. There's one condom left."

She walked to a nearby shaker desk and deposited the fabric strip on the top. Searching the opened case, she located the protection and displayed the square packet in Nash's direction.

"Last one. You better have a finale planned."

"We'll savor this time." His lips elevated higher. "Remember, you're in charge. I do whatever you say."

She relocated in front of him and sank to her knees. "Let's find out how well you obey."

"What do you plan to do?"

She licked the tip of his penis.

He discharged an amorous hiss. "You're a naughty girl."

She giggled, circling the end with her tongue, then she drew away. "My first act as your Master? I'm going to make you so hot—and then I won't let you have me."

"Bitch." He laughed as he put the phone to his ear to listen to his voicemail.

She stifled a snicker, grabbed his jutting shaft, and squeezed. Burying the head between her lips, she gave him a hard suck.

Eyelids shut, he relaxed his neck. "Feels good, baby." He hitched a growl. "So good."

His relaxed frame suddenly tensed. Eyes open, his head jolted upward. He smacked her forehead, using the heel of his palm to knock her away.

Her teeth scraped against his tender foreskin, but he didn't flinch.

Evie cried and then scowled. "What's the matter with you?"

Nash's complexion had swiftly paled to a whitish hue. He flung the phone onto the tussled bed and paced.

Evie sat on her heals and wiped her lips with the backside of her hand as she curiously watched him.

He dashed to his phone, dug it out of the mass of tangled sheets, and pressed in a number. "Come on, come on." He waited. "Breena, its Nash." A moment's pause ensued. "Yes. Certainly." More silence. "I'm on my way." He disconnected and scanned the room. "Damn. Breena's requested I come in."

"Now?" Evie glanced at a digital clock. "What time is it?"

"Around nine a.m., I think."

"I didn't realize it was so late."

"Evie, the time isn't important. Breena has called me into her office. Where are my pants?"

"Why does she want to talk to you?"

"To go over last night's incident, again."

Forgetting his boxers, he nabbed his trousers draped on a chair rail and shucked them over his legs. His eyes flickered across the space as he zipped his fly. "Where did you throw my shirt?"

Evie pointed to a miniature wet bar. "It's—I think, umm, maybe, over there?"

He hurried to search for his button down and discovered it underneath a cabinet. He swiftly grabbed it and tugged an arm through a sleeve.

"Will you tell me what's wrong? How come you're so jittery?"

He adjusted his shirt and jammed the buttons into their matching holes. "I'm jittery because I'm rushed. She expects me as soon as possible."

"No, you're more than rushed. You're nervous. I mean, seriously, did you change your mind? Do you believe they found a body?"

"You never know. Why else would she insist we meet so quick?"

"She's evaluating the interviews. I'm sure she's gotten many conflicting stories, and she's trying to narrow down the specifics."

"I see no point her making efforts to meet unless she's found a clue. I assume there's been a development, or they discovered crucial evidence. She wouldn't summon me to her office to discuss the weather."

"What exactly did she say?"

"You heard the conversation. Short and not so sweet." He turned to her, his expression worried. "She said we should chat more about the details I provided last evening."

"This is ridiculous. If any other Cove resident claimed to see a murder that didn't happen, this would've been wrapped up already." Evie rose to her feet, scooped her panties off the carpet and slid them up her legs. "Today, the whole town would be at the coffee shop, chuckling how so and so drank too much bubbly and hallucinated. But the great Teddie Donavan says she witnessed an imaginative homicide and every public official can't wait to prove a killing occurred."

"We can't be one hundred percent positive a crime didn't happen."

"You're kidding me. Last night you didn't believe her." She pouted. "Why the change of attitude? Does this new faith in Teddie have anything to do with you once having a serious relationship with Aubrey Donavon?"

Nash swung toward her. Crimson spread across his face. "My former romantic involvements aren't any of your business."

"Why so defensive? Everyone knows how torn you were after she dumped you."

"Again, off limits." His intonation dropped an octave. "Unless you'd like me to remind you of your past. Your romantic history stems from either pining for or chasing Drew Millard."

Evie swallowed past a newly formed lump. "Why not just rip out my jigglier?"

Their slandering words resulted in moments of uneasy silence as the room thickened with a growing rage.

Nash let go a long exhale. "I apologize. I was way too harsh. This talk has catapulted me over the edge."

Evie lowered and submerged into the mattress. "Forgiven." Her vocal cords stiffed as the sting of his hurtful words still lingered. "I'm not getting the reason you're so uneasy about visiting Breena, but you need to chill or you're going to blow an artery."

Nash dropped to his hands and knees to drag his shoes from beneath the bed. He crawled to his feet and glided them into his loafers without bothering to locate his socks. Walking to the dresser, he peered in the mirror to straighten his hair. "I hope you're right and nobody's missing. I'd hate to find out one of our own met their untimely demise or one of our fine citizens took the life of another."

"No one's gone. Do a head count. You'll find every person present." Evie wandered into the closet and removed her dress. "Except your wife."

His reflection froze. "Why would you make such a vile statement? Celia's alive and well."

"My, you're jumpy. Just calm down. My inference was because Celia's out of town. She's at a conference, remember?"

Nash appeared appeased, but Evie didn't miss the instant specks of secretion spouting over his temples. Whatever he hid would evidently cause him a load of trouble, and she aimed to learn his secret.

He fastened the lid on his briefcase, then rotated toward her. "I'm ready," he announced in a doubting tone.

"Wait. Let me finish dressing, and I'll go with you. You're so tense, you'll need moral support."

His head shook. "No. You can't accompany me. Breena asked to see me alone. I prefer not to activate suspicions concerning you and me. We can't let anyone speculate we're more than friends."

"No one will. Our friendship formed years ago and enhanced because we're employed at the same facility."

"You'll probably find yourself amid a nasty divorce soon. You're accompanying me wearing the same outfit you wore last night will start tongues wagging. You're also disheveled. Your hair's a mess, and you fucked off your make-up." Evie's hand shot up and grazed her fingers over her naked cheek. "Breena's a trained law officer. Her skills are sharp. She'll recognize we're having an affair the second we enter the building."

"I suppose," she agreed, though she felt dejected. Her eyebrows slashed in confusion. "What about your appearance, Doctor? Your normal wardrobe is usually impeccable, but you're scruffy, too."

"I'm a physician. I can say I stayed with a patient."

An eerie sensation scuttled up Evie's spine. "Convenient. What happens if you're required to verify your account? Which of your patients will lie for you?"

He paused to contemplate. "You. We can say you became ill after your fundraiser spurned into such a debacle. I remained by your side most of the night. We can even use the same excuse to vouch for each other if an alibi is necessary. We can say you weren't feeling well prior to the festivities, and I took you into the rear office for an examination."

"Sounds plausible." Evie gave a slow nod as she mulled over his explanation. "One question, though. Why do you need an excuse if nothing happened on the pier?" Crisscrossing her arms, she leaned closer to him as her eyes tapered. "Spill. What aren't you telling me, Doctor?"

Chapter 11

Drew rested on the porch, watching the sun slowly peek above the mountaintops. In his right hand, a steaming mug filled with coffee. A spiral notebook he found on a table inside lay across his legs. He ignored both and relished the sight in front of him. The wilderness views never ceased to amaze him, despite the years he resided in this area.

Teddie's family quarters sat secluded, near the edge of town. Granite cliffs towered beyond the three-story rooftop. A span of summer jade swept around the dwelling. Pine tree forests and sapphire waters located mere feet past the initial acreage sandwiched the log home. The beauty should inspire him but too many anxieties circled his head.

The main issue. The confirmation he had a daughter.

Savannah was his child. Now that her true parentage had been established, their lost years created havoc. How could he salvage so many missed events? Countless firsts were gone forever, moments he'd never enjoy, since her mother chose to cut him out of her life.

Could he forgive Teddie for stealing their time?

It wasn't just history he fretted about, he also worried over their future. His almost grown child desired to meet him. Did he feel the same? Of course, he did, but would he be satisfied after an introduction or would he yearn for a relationship to develop?

They were strangers, and his opportunity to step in and be her father was no longer available. Jarod Keene had held that title since she was born, and Drew had no illusions he wouldn't continue to act as her actual dad.

Drew was grateful for the other man's sacrifice, yet he'd stay an outsider because of it. But if they did try to forge a bond, would Savannah accept him? A man who didn't function as a wealthy, heavy weight in the music industry, but instead a part-time guitar player and singer, and a full-time carpenter and renovator who earned just a sufficient income? Was he strong enough to deal with the disappointment if everything fell apart?

"You're here?"

Drew twisted to glance as Teddie emerged outdoors, still wearing pajamas. Her surprise to find him on the wrap-around veranda was evident by the look on her face. Truthfully, he sensed shock at his decision to hang around. He didn't respond immediately, instead, he resettled into his rocker, his gaze returning to the ridged peaks.

She yawned big, shaking off fatigue as she lowered into a rocking chair by his.

He placed his half-filled cup on the ground near his seat. "Coffee's fresh. Found an unopened can and an old coffeemaker in a cabinet. I set it up next to a butt load of vitamin bottles scattered across the counter."

"In a minute," she mumbled, dabbing her fists into her heavy eyelids. "What happened last night?"

He stared in disbelief. Did she not recall their discussion or that she collapsed? He should've followed his instincts and driven her to the emergency room, but her garbled pleas had him abandon his common sense and do as she requested.

"You had an incident."

Her eyelids rapidly blinked, like she tried to remember, but couldn't quite catch the memory.

"You passed out in the Blue Moon's parking lot."

Her face went blank. "The evening's vague. Clearest I recall is changing into my pajama's."

"I suggested we drive to the hospital. You vetoed my advice."

"Not necessary to bother doctors. Just the effects of my exhaustion. I blackout when I'm overly stressed. I also swallowed a sleeping pill at my sister's instance. I'm sure it didn't help."

"You ought to visit a doctor to make sure. Better yet, let me take you to emergency now and get you checked."

She shook her head. "Reporters will swarm the medical center if I show up. A lot of unnecessary hindrances will arise and get in the way of people who truly require medical attention. Plus, the media insinuated I suffered a breakdown due to Jarod's and my separation, which is the pretext of my supposed narcotics addiction. The Phoenix scenes will create more negative headlines. I prefer to forgo any more exposure."

The cause of her sudden unconsciousness bothered him all night. First, a fall off stage and now this. Drew would rather not rely on the gossip, but after the questionable episodes, he was wary of her stability.

He sipped his cooled coffee. "So, did you?"

"Did I what?"

He tucked a finger underneath her chin, gently prodding her to face him. Instantly, he became absorbed in her sleepy eyes.

Despite his anger or worry, the woman stirred him in a way no other had or would. Those feelings spanned his motivation to remain by her side today, regardless of her betrayal.

He forced his mind to focus. "Did you have a meltdown because of your and Keene's split?"

"No, Drew. Our parting was mutual. There's no bitterness between us."

"That's unusual." He released her and readjusted so he sat farther away.

"We outgrew each other. Our personal lives branched in opposite directions, and we didn't spend much time together. We acted more like friends than a couple. We decided to go our separate ways. We're still friends."

"You told me, and it's best for your kids."

"Drew, I told you about Savannah, didn't I?"

"In a roundabout way."

"You're mad at me. Still, this is your daughter."

His fists tightened into firm balls. "Not discussing her."

"You can't just sweep her away and pretend like she doesn't exist."

He refused to talk about his girl, even with her mother. The only emotion he radiated was outrage, and he had to maintain his cool.

A change of subject was in order.

"Those pills. Do you take them often?"

She spun toward him, her irises flashed. "How dare you ask me such a thing."

"I dare, because I expect an answer."

Turing away, she concentrated on the lake

bordering the property and sat in obstinate silence.

"Teddie? I don't judge. I'm just curious."

"Yesterday was the first. Aubrey insisted I take one, and I regret listening to her."

Although he wasn't sure he trusted her, he chose not to press her further, since he felt she was done providing him information.

She motioned at the spiral lying in his lap. "Does that belong to me?"

He raised the notebook to sift the pages. "You left it on top of the table in the entryway. I couldn't sleep. I had to wind down after I brought you home and was hunting for something to do when I found it. They're good. Your songs."

"I wrote these years ago. My time is limited nowadays. I hardly ever sit down and write." A tiny smile teased her lips. "I thought I might use this sabbatical to try and pen a few tunes."

"You pack your guitar?"

"Yes, but I rarely touch it either, but creating melodies wasn't my strength." Her mouth boosted higher. "That was your specialty."

"Yeah, but your lyrics danced rings around mine. Still, I practice and a few expert friends say I've improved."

"You were blessed with the talent to do both. I love your words and music."

He tossed the notepad onto her knees. "I can put some notes to those, if you'd like."

"You would?" Enthusiasm gleamed in her eyes. "That sounds wonderful. I'll pay you for whatever I use."

"No way." A chill penetrated his voice. "I refuse to

take a penny."

"Ditch the ego, okay? Payment is standard due to legalities. I can't use artists work unless they're compensated. You're an artist, and you'll receive a paycheck like my other contract employees. Deal with it."

His mouth gapped to argue, but he rethought exerting his efforts to oppose. Pride wouldn't take precedence. She was a superstar. Her attorneys would insist on a written agreement and an imbursement plan in place if she utilized other's material.

"Understood, but I'll only consent to scale."

"Scale, whatever." She huffed and rolled her eyes. "Nice to see your stubbornness has remained intact."

Drew shuffled to readjust and studied her. "When's the last time you've eaten?"

"What?"

"Food. Have you eaten a decent meal or even enjoyed some French fries within the past twenty-four hours? Lunch? Dinner? Either or?"

"I nibbled some bread at the café before the excitement occurred at the Phoenix."

"Perhaps you fainted because you're hungry."

"I'm not. I'm too frazzled to eat. I'd get sick if I tried to swallow a bite. My stomach can't handle me even thinking about sustenance."

"Well, I'm starved." He clutched the rocker's rails and pushed to his feet. "And your pantry is sad."

"I only got here yesterday. Grocery store is on today's list, but you'll need to drive me to my car so I can go."

"Later. I gotta make a run into town and speak to Abel Fontaine."

Her brows raced up her forehead. "Isn't he an attorney?"

Drew faltered, uncertain if he should reveal more. His and Evie's turbulent nuptials weren't a secret. The whole town was aware they didn't get along, but he preferred not to expose too much of his personal life.

Except this was Teddie.

"I've spent the past two years trying to end my marriage. Evie and her high-powered legal team keep installing tactics to postpone the proceedings, but I'm done. Abel recommends we press forward and ask a judge to grant the divorce without Evie's approval.

I gave her one last chance, until the end of today to sign the papers. She constantly says she will, and then she always reneges, so I have my doubts. I gotta firm the details with Abel, and we can prepare to move forward if she doesn't agree again."

"Wow, Drew, I'm at a loss. I mean it's obvious you and Evie aren't happy, but I'm surprised it's gotten to this point. I assume she has her reasons to oppose you?"

"Won't delve into particulars, but it's a status thing."

"Gotcha. I recall Abel's a competent lawyer. I'm glad you hired him to represent you."

"He's the best."

"Today is Sunday. Is his office open?"

"We're fishing buddies. He's always open when I call." Drew plowed a hand into his pocket to search and find his keys. "I know of a place off the square on my way. They sell homemade breakfast tacos, and they're delicious. I'll stop and grab us a sack full."

Her nose wrinkled. "Grease, Drew."

"Good grease, Teddie."

She laughed. Seeing her smile was wonderful, but her expression sobered right away. "You might drop by the police station, too. Breena intends to speak to you at some point. Pertaining to what I witnessed on the pier. Might ought to find her first."

"An actual crime's been determined?"

"I don't know, but Nash Sewell arrived after you left." Nervous fingers raked through her blowing tresses. "He claimed to've seen you on the deck near the same time the homicide transpired. He loosely deemed you as a suspect."

"To what? I was on the pavilion. I needed fresh air." He hesitated. "I saw absolutely nothing. I can't be held accountable to an offense without evidence to reinforce it."

"You don't believe I witnessed a murder, do you?"

"I'm certain you saw something, but it was dark, and darkness distorts. Plus, you're exhausted. Your tired mind might've played tricks on your eyes."

"The night was murky, but the moon was full. Granted, I only distinguished shadows, but I'm sure what I saw."

"I can't agree or disagree since I wasn't around. As far as me speaking to Breena, Edie pointed her in my direction. Breena and I spoke last night."

"You're in the clear?"

"Unless they discover proof."

"I hate how I'm being placated." Teddie scowled. "I saw someone killed, Drew, I swear."

Drew sidestepped the topic. "Go upstairs and rest until I get back." He clumped down the steps toward his pickup. "I'll grab us some scrumptious tacos. We'll eat, and we can talk more, then."

Chapter 12

Teddie chafed her arms as she watched Drew's truck disappear into a veil of dust. The man exasperated her to the brink of annoyance. Perhaps she deserved his suspicions, but she couldn't endure his doubts much longer.

He didn't believe she witnessed a murder. The odds weren't in her favor to change his mind since they hadn't located a body. Tie that in with last night's episode, which she now recalled, plus recent less than unflattering headlines, and he'd assume she was ready for a straitjacket fitting.

Except they went way back, and he should know better.

Why his opinion bothered her was another mystery. She didn't owe him anything, other than what she accomplished the night before. She set Savannah's parentage question straight, thus her and Drew's future conversations should pertain to their daughter.

The remainder of her retreat could go as planned, minus Drew Millard.

The problem? Drew's re-entrance into her life and the explosive bomb he delivered, that he intended to divorce Evie, shattered Teddie's vow to curb her emotions. Or did it? Should she allow herself the luxury of wishing they had a future together once he was single? Her sensible side said to move on and forget him, while her heart soared, urging her to seize the opportunity and experience true love.

Her pajama pocket buzzed, drawing her away from her dilemma. She slid a hand inside, withdrew the phone, and glanced at the readout. Grimacing, she swept her index finger across the *accept* icon, and cautiously answered.

"Hey, Aubrey."

"Checked online this morning?"

Teddie braced, prepared to listen to the latest outrageous updates. "Internet reception's iffy, so no. I assume details concerning last night are viral, and reports aren't spinning pleasant overtones."

"Not even. Every media outlet has exposed your murder mystery. Implications are you've suffered a mental breakdown."

"I can't figure out how these rumors got started. A fall off stage and a breakup shouldn't spawn such nonsense."

"Seeing a murder without evidence doesn't help. I wish you would've postponed disclosing that until the dive team made a recovery."

"I can't help what I saw, and I couldn't wait. I had to report the crime. It's the law."

"You spoke to Cliff, right?"

Teddie sighed. "I texted him, but he didn't respond. I'm surprised, if allegations are as damaging as you claim."

"Bet he's busy extinguishing the fires."

"I'll try to call once we're done talking."

"Let me. You're expected to take it easy, and so far, you've done everything but."

"No time. I must make a trip into town and buy

food. I also plan to hire a cleaning service."

"I'd put any excursions off until the hoopla dies down. Lay low. Your location's been outed, too. Lots of Jacob's Cove residents are speaking to reporters, recounting your antics at the Phoenix, *and* their talking about your past."

A wave of nausea quivered through her. "How much of Drew's and my story did they reveal?"

"They've only skimmed over specifics, but that could change. Make sure you stay away from him if you want to keep your secrets hidden. You don't need a romance involving a married man added to your rumor list. Your manager already has tons of holes to plug." Aubrey paused. "One more thing. Many Cove citizens knew our parents and remember how they died."

"Oh, please tell me the press hasn't gotten a hold of that report."

"Not yet. But the fine folks of Jacob's Cove are primed to spread gossip and are talking to the paparazzi. Everything is at risk of exposure. I'm relieved you waited to tell Drew about Savannah."

Teddie groaned.

"Oh great. Don't tell me, Drew knows, doesn't he?"

She longed to avoid confessing, but Aubrey was a pro at catching silent gaps, even if miles separated them.

"You're just sinking deeper and deeper," Aubrey told her after she finished her account.

Teddie didn't reply as she'd chose to skip additional harsh reproaches by omitting her fainting spell or how Drew spent the rest of the evening by her side.

"I'm serious, Teddie. Pack your clothes, drive to Cerulean Beach, then let's fuel up the plane, and fly home. You've worked too hard to let the good citizens of our former hometown destroy your career over events that happened almost twenty years ago."

"I won't allow anyone to take me down."

"You can't stop them. If you could, you would've. The longer you stay, the worse the gossip will spread, and the world will discover your connection to Drew and hurt Savannah. Seriously, no good can come from you being near Drew Millard."

"Drew knows Savannah's his daughter. Our paths are tied, forever."

"Whose fault is that?"

Teddie ignored the implication because she couldn't argue. "Savannah asked to meet her dad. Drew deserves to know his child."

"Since day one, but you made the decision to conceal their true association, which is on you. Accept the consequences and go forward." Aubrey paused a moment. "Let's be real. You informed him he has a kid. You achieved your goal. Your purpose to revisit Jacob's Cove ceases to exist. Time to head home. You and Drew can communicate long distance."

"Drew's and my business is complete, but he's not the only reason I came home."

"That again." Aubrey's tone patronized. "If Mama and Daddy are still haunting you, then you shouldn't be in the house by yourself. You should contact a shrink. You're not even there twenty-four hours, and you're dreaming, plus you smelled Dad's cigar. Creepy, if you ask me."

"The odor was weird, but not weird enough to

leave."

"Teddie, your mind's lethargic due to fatigue. Added trauma may trigger an emotional collapse and a long hospital stay. I'm not referring to a regular hospital, either. I'm talking about the kind which requires lots of meds and padded walls."

"So glad I can count on you."

"I'm here, and I'm trying to prevent you from making a career ending mistake."

"I'm not leaving. But after today, I promise to take it easy during the remainder of my stay."

Her sister huffed. "Not what you should do, but whatever. Call if you decide you need us."

Teddie stuffed the phone into her pocket and rose out of the rocker. She swept up her notebook and wandered indoors, placing the spiral on an entryway table. Curving to the left, she halted at an archway leading into the main living quarters.

A staleness hung in the air. Sooty sheets covered the furniture. Wallpaper patterns had faded, and the worn floors were submerged in grime, yet a familiarity lingered. As did a chilling sensation.

Placing a hand on the doorframe, she scanned the space, resisting the urge to shiver. Thus far, she'd struggled with the idea of touring the house, but if she desired to resolve her nagging acuities, she'd have to explore the home top to bottom.

She stepped down a lone stair and strolled to the fireplace. Rows of photos were perched on the mantel. She retrieved the print nearest the edge and used her shirttail to wipe the filth off the glass. The picture displayed her smiling, happy family. Memories tucked away and forgotten, reappeared, and flowed. Some joyful, but most were bittersweet.

Blinking away a rush of tears, she replaced the photo and drifted to a bay window to peer at a sea of indigo. But she didn't see the water. Captured in the past, those moments she realized what her father did to her mother and himself appeared before her eyes as if she experienced night terrors while wide awake.

A faint hum startled her into the present. Needles spiked over the backside of her neck. A warbled tune— the same music from that day that haunted her dreams, chimed upstairs.

Teddie left the window and stood at the bottom of the staircase, staring up at the second floor. A shaky foot boosted to mount the steps. The melody grew louder as she climbed higher. Reaching the upper level, she paced down the hallway as the peals persisted to amplify.

She slowed by her parents' bedroom.

The strain weakened and then died. Another series of chills peppered her skin. Her chest tightened as blood inside her head drained. Perfume. Mom's favored scent. She threw out a palm and used the wall to avoid a collapse to the floor. The bouquet was light, almost not there, but she clearly sensed the featherlike tang.

Her dizziness subsided, and her fingers slipped away, landing on the knob. Did she dare? She had to discover the cause of these peculiarities, and the secret was inside.

She stared at the closed door. What did the interiors look like? Last time she viewed the space, there was a tremendous amount of blood splattered, and a reeking stench. A crew had been hired to come in and scrub the place clean, but could they scour away every speck of carnage? And did a company produce a strong disinfectant to cleanse the memory from her head?

Gradually, she twisted the doorknob.

"Don't."

She winced and quickly spun around, bouncing into Drew. Warm hands seized her shoulders and gripped to hold her upright.

She cleared her throat to rid an abrupt lump that formed. She wondered why he was here, but she was too surprised to inquire.

"I didn't make it very far." Drew breathed in and blew out a stream of air. "First time I've been up here since…"

"Me too," Teddie whispered in a trembling voice. "When I'm somewhere else, their deaths are just my bad dream, but now that I've returned, everything's so real and final."

Powerful arms encircled her, and he tugged her closer, strengthening his grasp into a protective embrace. Her arms slipped around his neck to bury her face into his chest as his familiar scent attacked her nostrils.

Instinctively, his body aligned with hers. A tingly sensation erupted in her stomach and warmed her insides as her mind drifted to other things that once happened in this house. When her parents weren't home.

Overwhelmed by the sudden memory, she wiggled out of his clutch and stepped away, unable to manage the current eeriness and tender moments between them.

Drew's skin flushed to a deep red, his expression a mixture of infuriation and embarrassment.

He shoved his balled fists into his front pockets and

paced the floor. "I listened to a call-in radio show while I was out. They discussed your Jacob's Cove visit, which means your hideout has aired around the country. You're lucky. No reporters can get near your property entrance because Breena's posted a couple of deputies."

"Thank goodness for that, but my whereabouts aren't the only thing disclosed. My twilight viewing last night also went public." Teddie shrugged. "Not much I can do."

Drew gestured at the doorway. "Hunting ghosts won't help your image."

"I came home for answers. I need to find them."

He glanced at her parents' closed off bedroom. "Today?"

Teddie licked her lips. "Did you notice anything odd when you came in?"

"No why?"

Discreetly, she sniffed the air to make certain the perfume odor hadn't returned.

"What's going on, Teddie?" Drew's brows dipped low. "Tell me what's bothering you."

"I dreamed about my parents."

"When? I stayed awake well after midnight. I peeked in on you numerous times. You seemed a little restless, but not agitated."

"It happened before I went to the Blue Moon. The tablet I ingested earlier made me drowsy." She faltered. "Or maybe the effects of the long journey or the Phoenix episode. I went to bed immediately after I came home. Then it began, always the same."

"Always the same? You've had the dream before?"

"Since that day."

"I'm sorry." He shuffled his feet, dropping his chin

to center on his shoes. "I didn't realize what you've gone through all these years."

Teddie didn't respond.

"Wait." His head raised. "You asked me if I noticed anything odd when I came in. Did something happen?"

She turned away.

"Teddie?" His palms encased her shoulders and tenderly reversed her to face him. "Tell me."

"My mom's music box."

"It was playing," he broke off to swallow, "that day."

"I always hear it in my dream, but this time the melody played while I was awake. I followed it and was led to this room."

"Is that all?"

She clamped her mouth shut, refusing to reveal more. He wouldn't believe her, and she was tired of everyone's skepticisms.

"What else, Teddie?"

She expelled a breath. "Mama's perfume. I caught a hint of her favorite fragrance when I first arrived. Did you smell a lilac scent when you came upstairs?"

His nose tipped upward and breathed in. "Air's musty, but that's all I smell." He gripped her forearm and tugged her down the hallway, putting a distance between them and the bedroom. "Leave this alone, Teddie. It's too much pressure on you."

She wrangled free of his grasp. "I have to do this, Drew. Don't you understand? If I don't confront my demons, these visions will plague me the rest of my life."

"Not this way. You found your mother and father

dead—the tragedy will never leave you. The whole thing still disturbs me, and they weren't my parents."

"I'm grateful you stayed with me that day, despite our personal circumstances."

"I'm glad I was here for you, but that was a long time ago. It's over, Teddie. They're gone. Let it go."

"I can't."

Their gazes connected. The morning sun blared past a window, situated near the end of the hall. Darkness in Drew's eyes intensified. Time stopped. Passion from long ago vaulted between them. Regardless of his lack of faith, Teddie craved for his mouth to touch hers. The gleam in Drew's eyes expressed identical yearnings.

But instead of reacting, he retreated. "I never understood why you and your sisters didn't sell this place."

Searching to find her composure, Teddie hurried back to the room, reeling in disappointment.

Their moment had passed.

As it should have.

"This house has been in our family for generations." Teddie's speech went hoarse. "My ancestors built it and enlarged the home as their families multiplied. My heart's not ready to let strangers live here. Besides, a murder and suicide aren't great selling points, no matter how long ago it happened."

He moved nearer. "You ever find out if your mom really had an affair?"

"As far as I know, it was a lot of speculation. Daddy may've killed them for no reason." She found the nerve to look at him. "You settled in town after I left. No whispers?"

"People guessed. Names were mentioned as possibilities, but no one owned up, then it dropped." Drew glimpsed at the bedroom's access. "I suppose if you insist on doing this, we should get it over with. Are you ready to go inside?"

Teddie turned to the threshold and nodded. He tilted forward and rotated the handle. The door squeaked ajar.

"After you."

Chapter 13

Teddie nervously drifted into the moldy smelling bedroom. Drew followed her inside, his boots echoed eerily against the hardwood. He strolled past her to one of two windows flanking a king size bed. Leaning on the sill, he shoved a sheer curtain aside to peer out, allowing her a private moment.

She stopped in the center of the room, combing to find traces a tragedy occurred seventeen years prior. Like the rest of the house, dusty sheets concealed the furniture, and an inch of grime littered the floor. The walls were painted teal green, which shouldn't be significant, except it was.

A slight smile formed across her lips as she recalled how Mama chose the color, and the way they giggled over her daddy's predicted conniption about the color. He did blow up. For a minute. Then as always, he yielded and claimed he found the hue attractive.

Whatever made Mom happy.

Until that day…and now, not a remnant from the time existed. Not a shred of evidence her father released a bullet into her mother's temple and then aimed a revolver at his own head, shooting them both dead. The haunting vision which plagued her for years seemed like nothing more than an overactive imagination.

"Are you all right?"

Teddie flinched and snapped into the present. "I'm

fine." Though her declaration sounded weak to her own ears.

Touring the room twice, she chafed her exposed arms, wishing she had grabbed a robe when they trekked by her bathroom. Although donning additional garments wouldn't warm the internal chill clutching to each of her nerve endings.

"The memory of us bursting in and finding them is distinct, but I'm fuzzy on what happened after."

"The sheriff, the coroner, and Nash came over." Drew folded his arms across his chest. "Not sure why Nash showed, maybe Aubrey called him. He took charge after the authorities finished their part."

"I'm missing a clue."

"A clue to what?"

"That's my problem. I don't know. The memory's not clear."

"You're referring to the day they died?"

"Yes, there's something else, but it's vague. I see the image in my dream, but I can't remember after I wake up."

"Teddie, I was here, too. Our view was identical. Other than the bloody mess, nothing else stood out."

Teddie let the subject drop. She had yet to persuade her sisters evidence in their parents' deaths had been disregarded, why would Drew trust her? Especially since he was aware of her deception involving Savannah, plus the dogging media hypes would cause him to entertain reservations about her reliability.

"I often wonder if I had arrived five minutes earlier." She stopped. "I might've prevented him firing the weapon, and they'd still be alive."

"Don't do this." He pushed off the windowsill and

rushed to her. Placing his hands on her shoulders, he gripped tight and gazed into her eyes. "I think about that, too. Maybe we could've altered the outcome, but I hold serious doubts. Your dad was irrational and had already made up his mind. If we went in sooner, we might not be here either."

"Daddy would never harm us."

"But he did, Teddie. He discovered your mother's alleged affair, and he killed her."

A shudder shimmied up her spine. She disengaged, wiggling out of Drew's grasp, and ambled in a circle. She felt her parents' presence. Like they hovered nearby, wanting to relay a message, but they couldn't cross the realm into the living world to deliver it.

Halting by the bed, she eyed the floor. She swiped a foot over the hardwood, brushing away the dirt. A deeper shade of brown blemished the wooden planks. Unnoticeable unless standing over it. Her stomach capsized. The last place she saw her mother was here, where her bloodied, lifeless body lay.

A movement in her peripheral brought her back to reality.

Her chin raised to encounter a pair of worried eyes. She blinked away a sudden threat of tears. She lost so much in Jacob's Cove. Exhaustion abruptly overwhelmed her, yet she couldn't walk away. She was determined to find what she overlooked, end her nightmare, and advance toward an untainted future.

Unable to remain in the spot, she hastily strayed to the dresser. The drape across hung cockeyed and wasn't as dirty as the others. Like someone recently moved it.

On impulse, she snatched the ends and tugged it away. A music box sat in the center. Mom's music box.

Teddie's trembling hand stretched to the ornament and elevated the lid.

A trilled tune began to hum. She froze as if drawn into a trance.

"Teddie?" Drew spun her to face him, grasped her palms, and squeezed. "You're drained." He directed her to the doorway. "We should leave." Drew released her to sweep past her and slapped the top shut. "I don't want to ever hear that again." He gave her a side glance. "You're ready to leave, right?"

She hugged her waist and nodded. "I'll come back, later."

Drew gave her a gentle nudge and guided her toward the exit.

"I'm glad you went inside with me."

"You shouldn't singlehandedly try to relive such a traumatic event."

Using the top of her hand, she grazed her cheek, and was astonished to find her skin damp from crying. "I assumed it'd be easier after so much time's gone by."

"Can't understand how a first visit to such a tragic event would turn out easy."

They walked across the hall in silence. Drew led the way downstairs and into the living room.

"Are you planning to stay, or are you going to try and run your errands, again?"

"I should go"—he shot an anxious glimpse her way—"but you're still pale, which concerns me after last night. I'll stick around until I'm sure you're okay."

Weary, Teddie motioned at the couch indicating for him to sit, then she hurried to her father's favorite chair, sitting to the side.

She tossed the cover to the floor, dusted the edges,

and sank into the cushion, craving space. She longed to feel safe. Safe from the past and future. She peeked at Drew, who perched on the sofa. She specifically had to keep her heart safe from getting broken.

"You can take off. I'm fine."

"No, you're not. You're shaking." He shifted anxiously. "Maybe exploring your folk's room this soon wasn't the best idea."

"Possibly. But I can't turn back time. It's done." Teddie chose to switch topics. She needed to process and reflect, before discussing the journey. "Have you considered furthering your music career? Beyond the Blue Moon Saloon?"

He looked stunned. "You mean like you and relocate to Nashville?" His head shook with a careless shrug. "Evie never supported my music."

"But you anticipate becoming single, shortly."

"I'm too old to start over, career wise."

"You're a talented musician." Her lips slightly upturned. "I know talent too. I worked with most of the greats. You're a gifted songwriter. Even if you preferred to not sing, your songs would sell. There's not a singer in Nashville who isn't seeking to find fresh material."

"You're bias."

"Probably, but I'm also right."

"Thanks, but I'll pass. What you're suggesting is a major life transformation."

"You'll undergo a huge adjustment if you end your marriage. You might as well do a complete overhaul."

"Don't take this the wrong way, but I don't think we should live too close to each other. And by close, I mean in the same town. Besides, I could never afford the real estate in your neighborhood."

Teddie's eyes widened, shocked by his remark. She swallowed, straining to control her emotions after his verbal cut oozed.

"I'm the reason you won't give Nashville a try?"

He stared into her eyes. "What do you want me to say, Teddie? My head's spinning. I just found out about my daughter, who you kept a secret for seventeen years."

"I'm sorry, Drew, whether you believe me or not, I do regret my decision. Keeping her away from you has caused a lot of grief on both sides."

"It doesn't change what happened. You left. You had our child. You went on to live our dream. All without me."

"I know. You deserve the success I've enjoyed. I just hate to see someone with your capabilities waste their talent."

"I don't consider what I do a waste." He forced a grin. "My band has a recording set up, and we've cut a few demos. Our Blue Moon gig gets us plenty of downloads."

"But you could have so much more. Nashville is a big city. You could live anywhere in town, and I can indirectly put you in touch with the right industry people."

"You don't owe me, professionally. I didn't mean to mention it. You tried to sway me to join you. I'm the one who refused. I was mad, childish, and stubborn. I have regrets, too, mainly because of my pig-headedness."

"We were young and strong-willed."

"True. But I won't lie. Your fame bothered me.

Still does, sometimes, but I'm happy playing with the guys. Not exactly what I envisioned, but I'm putting music out, and I get to do something I like."

"But you're the one who convinced me we could expand further than Jacob's Cove and chase our crazy dreams." She hesitated. "Don't you still want that?"

"Yes, but I'm a realist. I missed my chance when I turned you down."

"If your minds made up."

"It is." He stirred in his seat and propped his feet onto a coffee table's surface, appearing calm and relaxed, yet Teddie suspected he was anything but.

"Since we're being open and honest, I want to ask a question." He scanned the room, then returned to her. "How did you manage to conceal your mom and dad's death? I don't recall reading any later reports relating to how they passed away, and it was in all the newspapers back then."

"The media didn't possess the abilities to gain as much access to celebrity's privacy as they do now. Then, my first album took a year to finish, and another three or four years went by until I became well known enough, and people became curious about my background.

Mom and Dad had been gone a while. When questions arose concerning my family, I explained my folks were killed in a terrible accident. Which was true, sort of." She heaved up a shoulder. "Reporters accepted my version at the time and no one's probed since."

"People are nosy."

"And it'll get worse if my spotlight stays the way it is now. I'm not sure how much longer I can keep it quiet or if the public would care. My visit home has sparked attention, but honestly, everyone's more absorbed with Jarod's and my break-up, and speculations why I fell offstage."

Teddie hoped they were done with their exchange, but she sensed Drew had more inquiries he wanted her to answer. And she would, however anguishing, reply truthfully.

"Your and Keene's quickie coupling, plus a pregnancy never generated interest, either."

"By the time Jarod and I were noticed, Savannah was four. We'd been together a while."

"He's a good father?"

"Huh?"

"Keene? He's a good dad to Savannah."

"He's an awesome father. They love each other very much." Drew's expression twisted into resentment. "Drew, you did ask."

"Teddie, I get it. You were young and given a chance of a lifetime. Your dad and mom died in the most horrible way possible. I dumped you and made the stupidest decision in my life by rebounding and marrying your ex-best friend. What I can't wrap my head around, is after the dust settled, you elected to not find me and tell me. It wasn't necessary you make the call. One of your assistants could've contacted me."

"Drew, I wrestled this issue every day. There were days guilt consumed me because I decided to keep the two of you apart. I knew you'd be a great father, but her life is a circus due to Jarod's and my profession. At the time, it seemed simpler to leave things alone. I put her, first. Not fair to you, but she's my daughter, too, and I had to consider what was best for her." She studied his demeanor, which gave away nothing. "Can you forgive me?"

His mouth opened to respond. Teddie braced, prepared to hear the worst. A buzzing noise drew his attention downward. He fished into his pocket and removed his cell phone. Glancing at the screen, he frowned as he leaped off the couch.

Teddie watched him as he wandered to the entryway, out of listening distance. Evie. He didn't go home last night, and she may be trying to locate him.

Drew should stay away from her and this property. If Evie found out he spent the evening at Teddie's home, she'd punish him, even though their night was innocent.

His face transformed, to first confused, surprised, then concerned as he walked toward her. "I'll drive over and get her. We'll see you soon." Appearing troubled, he slipped the cell back into his jeans. "You need to get dressed. Breena's requested a meeting."

"With both of us?"

"She tried to call you, but your phone went straight to voicemail."

"I silenced it after a way too long conversation with Aubrey." She wearily regarded him. "What does Breena want to discuss with us? Did they find a body?"

"Not sure. She said she wants to review the Phoenix story once more. And me? I get to be interrogated. She says we need to chat about my time on the pier." A hand raked through his hair. "Damn Nash. Not only is he screwing my wife, he's gonna screw me too. Right into jail."

Chapter 14

Evie stood in the hospital corridor, arms across her middle as she peered into an ICU window. Orderlies had flattened the automatic bed so the woman rested in a supine position.

Nash stood by her side. His expression was saddened and drained. He tilted across her, her blanch, limp hand clasped between his.

A crisp, white sheet was tightened around her chest, her arms uncovered. Machines surrounded her, tubes spidered from every orifice. Eyes closed, she appeared comatose as the power-driven devices maintained what little existence she possessed. Family members sat on the far edge, their vertebras facing her. Hunched shoulders and bowed heads displayed their evident grief.

Evie's attention refocused on Nash. As if by telepathy, his head elevated. His sorrowful façade morphed into instant annoyance. He leaned across the mattress speaking to the relatives in an inaudible tone. His lips thinned as he disengaged, deserting his near-death patient, he marched to the glass and swiped the curtain shut.

Evie sighed and pivoted, prepared to return to her office. She wouldn't learn the details concerning his and Breena's conversation or why he behaved unusual after he received the summons, but she meant to get an explanation later.

The ICU door opened emitting a soft click. Evie heard the snap and spun toward the noise. Nash exited, quietly sealing the doorway behind him.

"Why are you here?"

His head orbited one side to the other as he rushed to where she waited. He grabbed her upper arm and guided her away from the scene. Their shoes scrapped noisily against the tiles as they moved, but they didn't utter a sound until they relocated farther down the hallway.

"You shouldn't be seen near my patient's room," he scolded, keeping his vocal cords low. "People could start wondering, and speculations can lead to unflattering rumors."

Evie screeched to a halt, her high heels shrieked on the scrubbed floors, sounding comparable to fingernails screeching over a blackboard. Her anger soared, having enough of her rank of importance lingering at the lower end of his personal totem pole.

Tired of him placing his entire world in front of her, she wiggled out of his grip and whirled to face him. "You forget I work here, too, Nash." Her hands lodged onto her waist, her ridged fingers jabbed into the fabric of her dress. "Despite our shared intimacy, I am also interested in the welfare of the patients who require treatment at this facility. My job hinges on understanding theirs and personnel's essentials. My superiors would deem me inept if I didn't daily assess the center's occupants."

Nash skimmed his palm across his cheek. "I'm sorry, Evie. Of course, you're right. Situations like the one in the trauma unit distress me. My brain is unable to center on logics."

He tapped her lower spine and pointed her to an empty vestibule within eyeshot of his patient's room. They halted near a row of seats, next to a garden window, though neither chose to sit.

Nash mindlessly analyzed the manicured foliage beyond the glass rim. "I'm always in such turmoil whenever I'm close to losing one. I'm confused as what to feel."

She patted his forearm. "I understand, you're upset."

"I'm juggling a multitude of issues."

"You mean, your interview at the sheriff's office? What did you and Brenna discuss?"

"Not much. I retold my version of what transpired at the Phoenix. She thought perhaps I recalled additional particulars once I had a good night's sleep."

Evie chuckled. "You would've had to've slept."

Nash didn't share her humor. He pressed his forefinger and thumb into his eye sockets and stifled a yawn.

"We stayed awake most of the evening. You ought to head home and rest for a short time."

"I'd like to, but…"

"Celia's on her way home?"

"She hasn't responded to my text or phone calls."

"Does she make a habit of not recharging her battery? Maybe her phone died."

"She's not speaking to me. We had a tiff prior to her departure. If I go home and she's there, the whole incident will be rehashed, and then she'll force me to redeem myself. I loathe the idea of devoting a perfect afternoon to an argument." He yawned again, only he didn't attempt to contain it. "I don't foresee a nap in my future."

Evie almost informed Nash, he made the choice not to unwind, but she bit her tongue. She preferred not to allow herself to become too affected over Nash and his wife's relationship. Conversations involving Celia merely reminded her how his wife's status overshadowed hers, and the realization angered her.

"Back to your talk with Breena. Did she drop any hints, like they've confirmed a crime occurred?"

"None other than she's taking Teddie's claim seriously. She's called in an elite forensic team. They're upstate and driving in today. She expects them to arrive this afternoon. They plan to examine the pier, board by board, and they intend to dredge the waterways encompassing the Phoenix."

Evie shifted to glance past the window. "I'm betting they'll come up empty. I don't believe a murder happened."

"Regardless, Breena's forging a full investigation as if one did."

"If that's true, the supposed proof was compromised by her CSI wannabe's. The pavilion was flooded with people attending the party. After Teddie made her crazy announcement, stragglers and news people showed up, tainting the hypothetical evidence even more. Breena's hot shot crew won't find a spec of untainted blood."

"You're right. But Breena must investigate, just in case. She's serious, Evie. Our sheriff will not abandon this task until she's assured a homicide didn't transpire." His head dropped backward, and he used his first two fingers to massage his temples. "I reiterated she needed to question your husband since I witnessed him outside alone during the approximate timeline."

"I don't understand his relevance other than his appearance outdoors. Drew's a decent guy. Many view him as a model citizen."

"Even the best can be pushed to their limits."

While no fan of Drew Millard's, she couldn't imagine her husband deliberately injured another human and not take responsibility for his actions. His conscious bothered him too much. "Except if Drew overreacted and harmed another person, he'd own up. He's disgustingly honest."

"Did he ever mention he desired another woman throughout your marriage?"

"He never confessed his preference for Teddie, although he did tell me our marrying was a mistake. Or more appropriate, his mistake."

"Model citizen? I think not. I'm surprised you aren't elated he's a possible suspect. If a misdeed did take place, and he's guilty, you can leave him without the scorn of your family and friends."

"He's divorcing me, remember?"

"Yes, well…I should check on my patient." Nash glimpsed at the ski-blue doorway situated ahead of them. "I want to speak to her family. Her children are getting ready to leave and review the options I gave them earlier. If you're staying, I'll swing by your office later." He touched her elbow and flashed a sly smile. "For coffee?"

Her eyes brightened. "I'm tallying the gala's donations, so yes, I'm scheduled to hang around for the next several hours."

"Excellent." Nash strutted to the entrance and

stroked the knob. He paused and looked at her over his shoulder. "A little advice? Rethink your loyalty toward Drew. A man who marries a woman he doesn't feel affection for isn't authentic. He's a user and users simply want to please themselves. Keep that in mind, Evie."

****

"Evie and Nash," Teddie cried. "You're sure? Did you catch them?"

Drew clamped his tongue between his teeth. He shouldn't blurt and expose his wife's transgressions. Abel hired a private investigator, and he collected enough facts to nail the pair, but his attorney advised him not to disclose the knowledge, lest the word spread before they were ready.

"You can't tell, Teddie."

"I won't. Do you have verification?"

"Pictures, video, phone records. We've acquired what's needed to take her down." He hesitated. "But my intentions aren't to broadcast, because I'd rather not hurt Nash's wife and kids. I want to walk away without complications."

"My visit to the Cove won't help. Especially since you stayed at my house last night."

"Evie will try to make a big deal about your homecoming and attempt to stall the proceedings, but I have proof to support my allegations. She's got nothing on me."

"Can I ask again why Evie's fighting a separation? I don't get how come she wants to remain married when she's dating Nash, and you want out?"

Drew squirmed as the heat inside the room escalated. Propping an ankle across a knee, he cleared

143

his throat and peeked at Teddie. "Evie and I never jelled as a couple. We headed down the aisle too quickly for the wrong reasons."

"Evie cared deeply for you before we got together, Drew. She terminated our friendship as you and I grew closer."

He frowned, surveying the boot perched on his thigh. "Her feelings for me were strong at one time," he admitted in a quiet voice. "I took advantage of her affection after you left because I craved comfort."

"Using somebody isn't a sympathetic trait."

"No, and I hate I did that to her." He realigned his position to stare into her wide-eyed gaze. "You broke me, Teddie. Once you took off to Nashville, I quit caring. I abandoned my music. I went to work every day, but my heart wasn't into my job either.

If anyone other than my daddy employed me, they would've fired me, and it didn't bother me. I lost interest in life." A cynical chuckle escaped. "Evie rescued me. She made sure things got done. I owed her. So, I stayed."

"I'm sorry, Drew."

"Enough apologizes. I don't deserve pity. It's on me."

"You're implying my exit was the catalyst to your downward spiral."

He studied her. "Who's to say I wouldn't have done the same as you, if we reversed roles? I created my own chaos. I'm struggling to repeal my errors and convert into a respectable man. But I can't change myself into reputable when I'm married to a woman I never loved. It isn't fair to either of us."

"You made mistakes, but you're a moral guy."

"I act more honorable than I am. I just confessed to not ever loving my wife, and I exploited her to dull my pain. Evie's conduct now is the result of my past attitude toward her."

"You're saying Evie's cheating is your fault? Wrong. Like you, she's accountable for what she does. I watched you interact. She isn't very nice to you."

"She can be a bitch."

"And she's intimately involved with another man. A married one."

A tired smile strained his lips. "My inability to care drove her to seek male attention elsewhere. She boosts her self-esteem by sleeping with other men."

"Men?"

"She's had numerous affairs."

Teddie's features remained impassive as she let his remarks process. "Yet, you're still with her."

"Guilt makes you do crazy stuff."

Her brows rose. "Guilt makes you willing to take the verbal abuse she doles?"

"I tune her out." Drew caught Teddie's eye to challenge her. "Honorable, huh?"

"What changed your mind?"

"I'm tired of her fucking around, and I'm ready to be free." Drew relaxed into the sofa cushions. "No matter how bad our marriage is, it's still humiliating when you're cheated on, although I'm almost grateful she did. It assures me, I'll get my belongings and freely walk away. Her indiscretions and prolonged proceedings should persuade a judge sign off on the papers, immediately."

"I hope you're not experiencing remorse having to end it this way."

"No. I tried to finish us the right way, but she refused. She's all about pretense, and she wants to make me the bad guy so she can divorce me. I won't let her, so she stalls."

"You may've had your flaws, but it sounds like you've done your best to do right by her."

"I'm not so wonderful. I mean, I wasn't unfaithful to her. Not in a physical sense, but that doesn't mean I didn't cheat in my heart." His chin sank to his chest. "And Evie knew. She always knew."

"She knew?"

He raised his chin and stared into her eyes. "That I'm in love with someone else."

Chapter 15

Drew's confession hung in the air and circled like low clouds in a brooding thunderstorm. Teddie's heart smashed into her ribcage as she averted her eyes away, refusing to confront Drew's hopeful gaze.

The man she loved since she was a teenager felt the same as she did. This news should bring her happiness and complete her, but it didn't. Instead, his acknowledgement thrust her into added despair.

Countless obstacles blocked their road to happiness. Not only his existing marital glitches, and the barrage of unsubstantiated, publicity that harassed her, she continued to reel over last night's unconfirmed homicide he didn't believe she witnessed.

She also had her reoccurring nightmare, and the first-time visit to the final spot her mother and father congregated moments before their death to emotionally contend with. Lastly, he hadn't forgiven her for keeping their daughter a secret.

Drew nervously shifted. "I oughta keep my feelings to myself."

Teddie struggled to find her voice. "Yes, you should."

"Only it's too late to take it back."

Regrettably, this was true. No matter what else life presented, neither would forget his disclosure, and his words would dangle between them, long after she departed for home.

As Savannah's parents, they may correspond and presently those communication lines were clogged with lost years, passions, and other complications. They had to find a way to backtrack and put his admission behind them or their relationship and their daughter would suffer.

"We'll just pretend you didn't say anything and ignore the awkwardness."

A split second of agony flashed across his face, before his features reverted into an unreadable expression. "You can do that?"

"I have to and so do you. Think of Savannah. Our words and actions affect her."

Drew nodded, after a moment of reflection. "Forgive me. I'm not used to fatherhood or putting someone else's needs ahead of my own."

Teddie chose to let the topic drop and rose to her feet. "Breena is waiting. I'll hurry and dress so we can head into town." She maneuvered past him, careful to keep out of his reach, not trusting he'd just let her go by without physical contact. Traipsing to the stairway, she mounted the first step, then hesitated. "Drew?"

He glanced over his shoulder, raising his brows.

"Phone Abel. Tell him to join us at the sheriff's office."

A frown creased across his brow as he twisted around to fully see her. "Why? I haven't done anything wrong."

"You need to expose Evie's affair. Abel's your proof."

"Um, no. What's happening in my marriage is no one's business. I only intend to use the information if

Evie decides to go for the jugular during the divorce proceedings. Up until now, she doesn't know I'm aware of her flings. I want to keep my secret until I need to use it."

"Nash indicated you were on the deck the same time I saw the victim forced into the water. His sleeping with your wife may motivate him to implicate you. Abel can bring the file and insert doubts."

Her observation registered across Drew's face. "But no one's verified anyone's been killed."

"Even if nothing's substantiated yet, I did witness a person pushed off the pier. The dive team will find a body, and an official investigation will follow. Your name tops the list of suspects because of Nash."

Exiting the stairwell, she ambled to the sofa and tilted across the back, relaxing her forearms over the summit. "I get it, Drew. You're not convinced I saw someone die, but Breena isn't entirely sure or she wouldn't want to speak to you again."

He faced frontward and sank into the cushions. "She's just doing her job, Teddie."

"And when she finds out I'm right? You'll wish you'd taken my advice and brought Abel in." Teddie orbited the couch and lowered next to him. "I guarantee somebody will come up missing."

His scowl relaxed, but he contemplated, fixated on the dirty fireplace. His head vaguely shook. "I can't win this. I guess I'll call Abel. Not only to protect myself from a possible murder charge, but to defend yours and my reputation against Evie."

"I'm not following."

"Just occurred to me. If I divorce her, Evie will shout to the world I left to resume yours and my relationship. And by shout to the world, I mean, she'll use every media source available. It'll be easy too, since reporters are in town trying to get your story.

She'll make herself appear the wronged ex-wife, me a cad, and you the other woman." He paused to wipe his brow. "She'll ruin you, if she can. If she messes with us, she messes with Savannah. We're fucked, Teddie."

Teddie sat, staring straight forward, realizing the consequences which could be thrust upon them. "Is she that clever?"

"Unfortunately. She's dropped some strong hints about us since you've returned." A hand lay on his thigh moved, and his fingertips grazed across her arm. The gentle stroke was meant to reassure, but instead, the touch provoked a sharp current between them. Teddie winced as Drew jerked away, shoving the culpable palm back onto his leg. "Don't worry," he went on as if nothing happened. "I'll fix this. I'll stop Evie's revenge."

"How will you stop her?"

"I'm bringing in Abel and those documents, and I'll request he postpone our divorce."

"Drew, you've waited so long to move on with your life."

"I'll just have to wait longer." He stood. "I'll go outside and phone Abel."

"If you're sure." He didn't respond and Teddie didn't press. "I'd like to take a shower before we leave. Your conversation should give me the time to grab a quick one."

****

Drew rang off his lawyer, glad he made the call.

Abel agreed to meet him and the sheriff. Under the circumstances, Nash Sewell's affair with his wife would initiate an alternative facet in a police probe, if a body was recovered, but he'd also use it as a buffer in case Evie decided to play dirty.

Once Drew disconnected, he phoned Breena and explained he and Teddie were delayed but planned to arrive soon. Abel would also attend and bring documents, which may assist if the enquiry unfolded. Breena was tentative but grudgingly allowed the postponement, synchronizing a firm time to gather later.

His stomach interrupted his exchange by rumbling noisily. He was starved. By Teddie's too thin frame, she'd benefit eating a breakfast taco or two. He checked his watch.

Breena arranged the appointment early afternoon. Plenty of time to drive into town and purchase food. Drew texted his attorney the timetable as he trod back indoors.

He peeked upstairs. Rushes of water strained the plumbing, inciting the old house to whistle as the heavy streams churned amid the rusted pipes. He hustled into the kitchen and searched cubbies and cabinets.

After ten minutes of rummaging, he found a scarcely, sharpened pencil and aged paper. He scribbled a swift message to Teddie, then scrambled up the staircase, scampered down the hallway and to the bathroom, halting by the doorway.

Teddie was in the shower. Naked. The interiors of his mouth moistened. Every inch of her body stayed embedded solid in his memory. The thought of her so near, in an undressed state enraptured his pulse into a frenzy.

He blinked rapidly to erase the image. Now was not the right time. He'd already messed up enough by revealing his feelings. Not that he experienced any embarrassment or regret over sharing his sentiments. Teddie may feel the same, in fact, he was almost sure she did, but she had been brutally honest as to why they couldn't be together.

He had to be realistic too. If they somehow managed to cut through all the intricacies and reunite, what could he offer her? She was a big star. If her light burned out this second, she was still fixed financially and had access to any materialistic item she desired. Employees assisted in whatever whim that hit her. He'd be no use to her.

She may dabble with him a while, but Teddie wouldn't want him for the long haul, even if he was the father of one of her children. She advised they act like he hadn't let anything slip. For Savannah's sake. Who was she kidding? They were never meant to be.

Hurriedly, he tucked the paper into the crack where the door met the frame and turned away.

"Get the woman out of your head, Millard," he said aloud. "She's made it clear. You're not in her league anymore."

****

"Teddie?" Drew hollered as he walked into the house. He moved past the ingress, depositing their food bag on the catchall table and scanned the living room. No Teddie. He hiked to the foot of the stairs.

"Teddie?"

Once more, silence replied. Sounds of water streaming above ceased, she'd finished her rinse.

Gradually, he climbed the flight of stairs. Reaching the highest level, he strolled across the hall, pausing at her parents' room, relieved to find it still sealed. He trekked by the bathroom. The door was left ajar, his folded note had dropped to the floor, unread. No noise came from within, but he peered around the edge, just in case.

Empty.

Next and last place to check was Teddie's bedroom. He treaded across the corridor until he came upon her closed door. A sudden burst of perspiration beaded over his forehead as his fingers touched the knob.

"I'm eighteen again," he muttered.

Slowly, he rotated the handle, easing the entry open. Quietly, he crept inside and stood motionless at the entrance, once more transferred backward seventeen years. Teddie's teenage room was identical as to how he remembered, down to the opened window that allowed a cool, summer breeze to drift inside.

Curtains covered a pair of windows, facing the house's frontage. They slightly waved as the draft fanned them. Teddie lay face up amid the crumpled sheets, of an unmade, four-poster bed, her eyelids shut. Her damp hair was slicked away from her face as a tiny, serine smile teased the corners of her lips.

A regular-size bath towel concealed her torso and lower extremities, leaving her shoulders exposed, and her beautiful, long legs were also uncovered.

His first thought was concern. Was she okay and just overly tired or was there another reason she'd fallen asleep in the middle of the day? Should he get closer and check? He surveyed her again. He couldn't tell this far away.

As if an invisible power propelled him, he wandered farther into her room and to her. Unable to discern if she breathed normally, he leaned across, flattening a hand into the mattresses softness to retain his balance.

Teddie's eyes flew open as she lurched upward to sit. Her cover-up crumbled into her lap. "Drew?"

Stunned, he didn't move. He stared at her bare chest, incapable of tearing his eyes away. Teddie released a loud gasp. Yanking the cover upward, she crisscrossed her arms to conceal her nakedness.

Wide eyed, she glared. "What are you doing in here?"

Drew put his hands up in a surrender pose and backed away. "I, um, you were sleeping and I was worried, and…"

"You need to get out," she shouted.

"You need to get dressed before you lay down," he yelled back.

"It's my house and my bedroom. If I want to walk around naked, I can."

"Did you forget I was here?" He shoved his fingers through his hair and forced his gaze away.

"I checked when I finished my shower. You were gone."

"I left a note saying I'd be back."

"I didn't see…" A slam of the front door came below and interrupted their heated discussion. Teddie snatched the sheet to shield herself over the towel. "Company's downstairs."

He moved close to the bed and uttered low. "I heard, but who?"

Their gazes reunited, both fearing the worst. If

Evie caught them in this circumstantial compromising situation…

"Teddie," yelled a familiar voice beneath them. "Teddie, where are you?"

"Great." Teddie fell back into the headboard. "Aubrey."

Chapter 16

Nash's chair squeaked as he reclined. Scrubbing a palm across his face, he released a defeated sigh and sealed the envelope containing a freshly signed death certificate. A nearby chirp, beeped inside a drawer, located on his right.

Tossing the packet into his *out* box, Nash opened the drawer and retrieved his cell phone. He swiped the pad of his index finger over an icon and scanned his latest message. A smile warmed his features as his gaze flitted across the screen.

"Wifey finally reply?" Evie edged around the corner of his office. Sauntering inside, she halted near his desk, folding her arms over her middle, eyeing him suspiciously.

He placed the phone down and stood. "No word, yet. She's ignored my efforts to communicate the entire weekend." His lips smacked in indignation and glanced at his watch. "I'm sure she's relishing in my groveling."

"Poor you." Evie gestured at the phone. "Who's sending you messages triggering your gigantic grin?"

"No one. A colleague forwarded some information I requested."

"I bet." She circled the desk and plucked the cell off the top.

Nash bent and snatched at Evie who swung her arm behind her, securing the phone in the small of her back.

"Evie, this is ridicules. My patient just died, and I'm in no mood for your overblown drama."

"Sorry, the lady's gone, but her death wasn't exactly a surprise. We were supposed to meet for *coffee*, but you didn't show." She held up his cell and wiggled it. "I came to find out why."

"I told you, the woman in ICU passed away. Each death hits me hard. I needed to compose myself."

"Sure, you do." Evie spun away and scrolled. Doctor Sewell had a reputation of having a roving eye. While he swore he'd stopped wandering, she never was sure.

"You're behaving childish. Return my property at once."

She continued to browse.

He tilted across the desk, and extended an open palm, his face stern. "Evie, do *not* read my private messages."

She tossed a glimpse over her shoulder. "Why not? They're all innocent, right?"

"Yes, but you'll dissect every word and misinterpret their context."

"No doubt."

Nothing caught her attention, but she knew Nash too well and recognized the familiar glint in his eyes. She experienced his game when he was driven to convince her to become his pastime. He was up to something, probably no good, which meant he was nattering with other women.

And another woman entering the picture would not happen. His wife rivaled enough. Besides, she labored to create a future, she refused to consent to his shoving her aside and swap her for a younger model.

"Evie, I'm serious. I insist you give me my phone." Nash swept around his desk, ripping the mobile from her grasp. He stretched an arm above his head, holding the devise out of reach. "Most of my connections are business related and aren't your concern."

"You're right. Your business interactions don't interest me. However, you speaking to a prospective new girlfriend, does. Or are you chatting up an old love? Maybe you're sweet talking your wife to draw her attention away from your indiscretions?" She made a waving motion with her hand. "Red flags are flapping all over the place, Nash, and I want answers."

"Your imagination is extremely active. You see things that don't exist."

"Do I?" Evie's mouth curved up. "How long have you and Aubrey Donavan been hooking up? Did you two renew your friendship before her trip home or after she returned?"

"Aubrey and I go way back. I consider her father a mentor, and he was a dear friend." Nash's sudden anxious expression transformed into a blank. "That's it."

Bingo. Sparks of anger ignited and burned inside Evie's gut. She hadn't identified any names among his list of contacts. Aubrey happened to be a lucky guess. "Too vague and your response doesn't satisfy me. When did you begin communicating with Aubrey Donavan?"

"We've always exchanged a few lines to check on each other. All innocent, I assure you."

"But I'm not assured, not one bit."

"Jealousy isn't a becoming trait, Evie."

"Neither is lying, Nash."

He strolled behind his desk, tucked the phone inside his pocket, and lowered into his chair. "You're overreacting, as usual. Former lovers often turn into friends."

"Or previous lovers may become new lovers again." Evie's eyes narrowed. "I remember how hot and heavy the two of you were. I'm thinking your little exchanges are more than friendly."

"Truthfully, Evie, I lost touch with Aubrey several years ago. Both of us were occupied in our own lives, and we let the friendship dwindle. I only discovered her visit minutes prior to you barging into my office to spout off unfounded accusations."

"Well, pardon me, but I'm watching out for myself. I won't allow you to blindside and dump me because you suddenly prefer antiques."

Nash drew in a deep breath, exhibiting his irritation. "The idea never entered my mind."

"When it comes to women, your mind usually doesn't do the thinking." She paced the floor, stomping her high heels to drive home her point. "The huge smile plastered on your face is a clear sign of what's on your," she paused and cleared her throat, "mind."

"You're exaggerating. Nevertheless, I won't pretend Aubrey isn't important to me. Certain memories tend to bring back pleasant moments, but our time is in the past, and we've moved on."

"Maybe you have, but has she? Last I heard, she's too busy catering to her famous sister to enjoy a love life."

"I'm unsure of her relationship status."

"Bull. Everyone knows she's Teddie's assistant." She kept pounding the ceramic tiles with her angry gait.

"Reporters recently interviewed her. She stated her time is so limited, she rarely socializes, much less has time to connect with a special person. I'm wagering you still light her fire, if you get my drift."

"Your allusive drift is like a piece of wood battering my skull."

Evie walked to one of two chairs set ahead of his desk and dropped into the nearest seat. "The Donavan sisters strike again. They're both into chasing men who belong to others."

"You're relating two different scenarios. Neither are correct. If you're worried about obsessive men, your ex would qualify. Thus far, I've not seen or caught Teddie's attempt to win Drew back, but if she decided she wanted to rekindle their romance, he'd simply follow her lead. As for Aubrey carrying a torch for me? She deserted me like her sister left Drew."

"She may entertain regrets."

"Unlikely." His chin thrusted in defiance. "You may believe whatever you choose, Evie, but Aubrey and I aren't contemplating a reconciliation, secretly or otherwise."

"Did she suggest you meet while she's in town?"

"Yes, for a drink. Mean's nothing. She wants to discuss Teddie's condition. She swears Teddie isn't taking medications, and she is interested in finding alternatives to help her get healthy. She asked for suggestions. If I decide to accept her invitation, I'll inform Celia and may include her in the outing."

"A threesome. Intriguing. What's missing from this little party?" Evie looked at the ceiling and feigned concentration. "Hmmm, oh, wait, I know." Her glare returned to Nash. "That would be me."

"I intended to tell you. After we met."

Evie's face changed to scarlet as her fingers rolled into a tight fist. "How thoughtful of you. And yet, you can't fathom why I don't trust you."

"Evie, no amount of reassurance from me will satisfy your uncertainty. If I told you, Aubrey and I planned to meet, you'd jump to conclusions, incorrect ones, and make an appearance at the tavern. Your presence would alert and raise Celia's suspicions."

"Goodness, no, we can't offend unfortunate, depraved Celia." Her fingers uncurled and flexed. "Will the day ever come when you put me before her?"

"We've rehashed the subject hundreds of times. I will speak to her soon, per your mandate. But until that day, yes, she does come first. After all, we made a commitment to one another, and once again, we must consider our children."

She shot out of the armchair to her feet. "I'm so tired of this. Excuse after excuse, and nothing changes. I don't know why I bother."

"You're not the only one who suffers. I must play the devoted husband to a woman frostier than the North Pole."

"Really? You're expecting me to pity you when it's your choice?"

"Evie, you want to put this on me, but may I remind you, you're not free from marital bliss, either."

"I'm about to be, and you're not."

"Evie." Nash moaned impatiently. "I'm aware of your position, and I understand your annoyance. But you've just given me a time limit to end my marriage, and I haven't even seen Celia to start the process and I must let her down easily. Once done, then we can proceed as a couple."

"Proceed as a couple to what? I need to ask, Nash. After we're no longer married to our current spouses, what's our next step? Where will I stand after we're divorced?"

Nash avoided Evie as his gaze darted around his office.

"Nash?"

"You're asking me to predict the future. I can't do that."

"What you're saying is, we won't marry."

"Us married?"

"Yes. I assumed we'd tie the knot after we're divorced. You suggested it, saying we'd make an awesome power couple. Your words, when you began to pursue me. Or was that just a line to convince me to sleep with you."

He remained quiet.

"Nash? I need to hear the truth. Is marriage in our future?"

"We'll just see how it goes, Evie." He stared past her and centered on a wall. "We'll see how it goes."

Chapter 17

"Teddie, where are you?" Aubrey shouted from the lower level of the home. "Are you all right?"

Teddie heaved in a breath, raised, and slapped a palm into a surprised Drew's chest, giving him a hard shove. His boots smacked the hardwood emitting a soft thump as he stumbled backward. His upper body weaved side to side, while his legs scrambled in the opposite direction.

Teddie feared the worst. Any odd commotion would entice Aubrey to zip up the stairway. She couldn't permit her sister to detect Drew in her room with her undressed.

Drew tipped farther sideways, about to succumb to the power of gravity. Arms flailed, he managed to catch himself before he crashed to the floor.

A nervous smile flickered her way as he re-aligned. "Close one."

She released the air, thankful he averted tumbling to the ground, making a mountain of noise.

"Too close," she agreed, in a whisper. "Now, disappear."

Drew frowned. Teddie glared, shooting daggers his way. "Drew, did you hear me? Vanish. Aubrey will be up in seconds."

His face registered. Shrugging, he spun at the waist, twisting one way, then the other. "Where should

I go?"

"No clue, but we can't let her find you in here. She'll never let me forget it."

"You? What about me? She'll put me six feet under if she sees me in your room with you…"

"Then our concerns are parallel."

Voices echoed below.

Drew's forehead lined. "She brought someone with her?"

"Raven I bet. Checking on me too, no doubt."

"Do you live in a sealed vacuum? Are you allowed air to breathe? You don't get a free moment."

"Success isn't free. I sacrificed a lot of my privacy so my music is recognized all over the world. No, it isn't pleasant or convenient, but I'm fortunate my family protects my little bit of sovereignty."

"Those two never give you any space."

"Sums it up, but this isn't the time to discuss my lack of seclusion. Butts are on the line. Make yourself scarce."

He nodded, rushed to the far side of the room, and grabbed the doorknob to the closet.

Teddie sprang to her knees, clutching her towel nearer. "Not in there. That's the first place they'll look."

"What are they looking for?"

"You."

"Well, if they're looking for me, they'll find me."

She sank onto the mattress and peered at the window. "Hide somewhere else."

Frustration swept across Drew's features as he combed the diminutive area. "I think I'll go with my first choice. I refused to climb out that window you're eyeing and drop two stories." A corner of his mouth lifted. "Sprained my ankle last time. I'm seventeen years older, now. The touchdown would put me in traction."

Footsteps tapped the staircase as the excited chatter grew nearer. The panic attack Teddie struggled to control morphed into an outbreak of anxiety. Moments stood between her sisters finding them.

"Under the bed."

Drew squatted to peek beneath the bedframe then straightened, shaking his head. "No way. Nobody's cleaned under there. Dust bunnies are cohabitating and they've multiplied." He ambled back to the closet. "This small space isn't much more than coffin size, and I'm claustrophobic. I'm iffy about hiding inside, but if it helps avoid Aubrey's brand of crazy, I will." He walked in and pulled the door behind him, then cracked the opening and inched around the edge. "Does this whole thing remind you of prom night, senior year?"

"Get back in there," she hissed, worried they wouldn't pull this off.

He shut himself inside the same instant her bedroom door exploded.

"Teddie, you're..." Aubrey burst in, Raven followed and both halted.

"Aubrey, Raven." Teddie brushed away a strand of damp hair and bowed her head to conceal the heated crimson crawling across her skin. "Why are you here?"

"We're worried." Raven strolled past Aubrey to Teddie. She squeezed Teddie's shoulders and pecked her on the cheek. "Another massive media blast hit the airways a while ago. You'll need our support after this one."

"Are things that bad?"

"This morning's report was just the beginning." Aubrey informed in a terse tone. "You're a short leap from becoming fodder for the late-night talk-show hosts."

Teddie witnessed these frenzies happen to others, but this was a first for her. Friends in the business had encounters of adverse publicity due to fallouts involving personal matters. While a few were warranted, most were exaggerated or worse, fabricated like hers.

Bottom feeder journalists thrived by pouncing on entertainer's tragic events. Careers had been ruined, although the majority weathered the storms and continued forward. Teddie anticipated the latter to occur, but she lived in the real world and realized the other scenario could easily transpire.

She forced a cheerful smile. "Don't knock gratis exposure, even negative. My greatest hits album is scheduled to release at Christmas. This news should make those tunes jump off the shelves."

Aubrey glowered. "This isn't a joke, Teddie."

"I'm not laughing, Aubrey. But I won't let this senselessness make me insane."

"Insinuations indicate it may be too late on that front. As in you smashed through the looking glass and slipped down a rabbit hole."

"I get it. My screws aren't only loose, but they're missing. They can believe whatever they chose. I'm fine." Her lips elevated higher. "They'll see."

"Sure, they will." Aubrey raked a wise glimpse over her. "Or not.

"What do you mean?"

"You're a mess." Aubrey waved a hand in her direction. "Be grateful Breena had enough sense to station twin deputies at the entrance to the property or the tabloids would be breaking down your door. But Breena can only do so much. If a brave reporter scales the cliffs across the way, and has a zoom-in lens…"

A hitch wedged in Teddie's chest. Usually she was careful, but her return to Jacob's Cove gave her an abnormal sense of security. One that didn't exist. Aubrey was right. A climbable overhang sat level and gave a clear view into her bedroom.

If a photographer captured her and Drew on video earlier, she was sunk.

"Then they're out of luck," Teddie denied. "My morning consisted of a shower and sleep, which explains my disheveled appearance. Not very interesting."

Aubrey drifted near Teddie. "Sleep, huh?"

Teddie gathered her towel, scooted across the wrinkled sheets, and touched a toe to the floor. "I followed your advice and took a sedative. My brain's been foggy since. I told you meds weren't the way to go."

"Food might alleviate your blurriness. A bag of breakfast tacos is in the kitchen." Raven gave Teddie a sly gaze. "They smell delicious."

Aubrey indicated toward Teddie's absence of attire. "I hope you didn't go grocery shopping dressed like that."

Teddie rose off the bed. "I didn't leave the house."

Drew had to bring sustenance. She told him not to, because she wasn't hungry.

Aubrey folded her arms across her chest and shot

her a haughty look. "Did your food just appear?"

"Delivery."

"The sack is full." Raven grinned. "You must be starved."

"I ordered a week's worth." She blew out a frustrated breath, uncomfortable fibbing. "Why don't you head downstairs. Find plates and silverware, while I put on my clothes."

Raven rested against the windowsill, wearing a small smile. "You sure you don't want to confess before we go?"

Teddie hurried across the room and rifled through her suitcase. "What would I confess?"

Aubrey shadowed her, swiped up a t-shirt Teddie tossed aside, and thrust it at her. "Come on, fess."

She snatched the shirt and wrangled it over her head. Quickly, she slid into her underwear, dropped her cover-up, and seized a pair of shorts.

Aubrey and Raven divided a glance between them.

"Fine, then." Aubrey shrugged. "Your life, your mistake."

Teddie guided the shorts up her legs. "Please go down and locate some dishes so we can eat."

Aubrey gave her a quick onceover. "You're as ready as we are. You can come with us. Unless there's something—or should I say someone else who'd like to join us?"

Teddie folded her lips under her teeth, unpacking her shoes.

"Teddie. We aren't idiots." Aubrey's mouth flat lined. "Hot food, a hundred-year-old monstrosity parked in the drive. I'd guess you enjoyed one hell of a welcome home party. I'm betting it didn't involve medications or bad dreams. So, tell us. Where'd you stash our old friend, Drew?"

Teddie fumbled her flip flops, dropping them onto the wooden planks with a plop. She was so busted.

"You ought to break your old habits, Ted." Raven sauntered to the closet and turned the knob. "Do you think we'd buy the ancient pickup in the driveway is your rental?" She peeked around the rim, flashing a cagy smile. "Hey, Drew."

Drew treaded out of the gloomy cavity, scowling. "Quit raggin' on my truck, Raven."

"Oh, great." Aubrey rolled her eyes. "Another nightmare. Did you stay here all night?"

"No, I didn't." Drew glimpsed at Teddie. "Well, I did, but it's not what you're thinking."

"Drew." Teddie shook her head frantically. "Not helping."

The elder siblings shared another meaningful look.

"Seriously, nothing happened. We met at the Blue Moon by accident, and discussed Savannah, like I explained earlier. I fainted when we left." Uneasiness fluttered across her spine as she eyed Raven, first and then back to Aubrey. "He wanted to take me to the hospital, but I insisted he bring me here. He stayed to make sure I was okay."

Aubrey's eyes held a perceptive glint. "You're telling us he spent the night in the closet while you slept in the bed? Naked?"

Teddie started to reply, but her defense deflated as did her vindication. What they assumed was incorrect, but how could she convince them when their circumstances appeared guilty?

"We're adults, Teddie. Maybe you're expected to

account for your every move, but I'm not. I don't owe them anything." Drew stomped to the exit, pivoted, and directed a forefinger at Teddie's sisters. "I get you're worried about Teddie, and you should be. But I'm not part of the problem. I just want to help." His hand fell. "This morning was rough. We went into your parents' room."

The duo gasped.

"The trip was traumatic, and she wanted to shower after. I'd left to run errands and returned to check on her. I found her asleep. You barged in as I attempted to wake her. We imagined you'd get the wrong idea, but we didn't do anything. End of story." His eyes darkened, filled with anger. "You're truly concerned? Be alarmed over the stress she experienced after reliving such a horrible day. The visit was so intense, she thought she sniffed your mother's perfume before we entered."

Aubrey's brow creased as she turned to Teddie. "You got a whiff of Daddy's cigar last night."

Drew stared at her. "You never mentioned anything about tobacco."

"Smoke or perfume?" Aubrey grilled. "Which was it?'

Teddie sighed, not wanting to answer. "I smelled both."

Aubrey's faced turned grimmer. "This is too much. Time to go, Teddie. If you refuse, I'll take drastic steps to ensure your wellbeing."

"What kind of steps?'

"The type that will force you to seek the help that's necessary to get you healthy again. Pack your stuff, and tell Drew so long. I'm phoning your pilot and instructing him to prepare your jet. We're going home."

Chapter 18

"Are you able to identify the parties involved in the alleged murder you witnessed?" Breena tore her concentration away from writing to center on Teddie, who sat rigid on the other side of her desk.

"The pavilion, wow, really dark, even the moonlight didn't help. I only saw silhouettes."

"You can't recall particulars? A night's rest sometimes helps process missed details."

"I didn't sleep much. Just short restless naps full of nightmares, so no."

"Not surprised, you being alone in the house the first night since your parents' tragic deaths." Breena wrote another notation on a legal pad. "Could you hear anything?"

"Voices yes. They were strained, like they argued, but I didn't catch any distinct dialog."

Breena's eyes flickered, shooting her a doubtful glimpse.

Teddie fidgeted. "The tide rolled in. Waves were loud and drowned out sounds."

"Gender? Male or female?"

"Not sure"—her brow furrowed—"but I got the impression a man and woman quarreled."

"What makes you think so?"

"Their movements. One was graceful, the other more masculine."

"Which individual hit the rail and fell into the ocean?"

"The lady."

Teddie shifted in her seat again. Her battered nerves distracted her. Too much transpired this morning. Her sister's surprise appearance, followed by a huge argument over Aubrey's insistence she go home. She won a reprieve, thanks to Raven and Drew's support. This appointment helped too, although at the moment, she wasn't sure she counted this interview as a victory.

Her focus transferred past the large window dividing the private space to the main office. Drew sat near a drink machine, his fingers curled around a soft drink can. Officers and personal occupied the scattered work stations, attending to their duties. Those nearest Drew sporadically engaged him in a quick chat.

One discussion triggered a roar of laughter, loud enough to penetrate the glass. Drew's lips upturned and his eyes crinkled with charming creases as his shoulders bounced.

Breena's squeaky chair whined and jerked Teddie back to the interview.

"You also mentioned one individual was taller than the other, so we can presume a man had the height advantage. Although, Jacob's Cove does have its share of taller women, me being one." Breena consulted her notes, then peered at Teddie. "You've been diagnosed with exhaustion and returned home to recover. Ugly rumors are also dogging you."

Teddie's stomach lurched, her reply silenced by uncertainties.

"Understand, I'm not judging you, but I must ask,

did you take any medications before you observed this murder?"

"My doctor prescribed medicines to assist in sleeping and pain. I took a sleeping pill, but after the homicide occurred."

"You're fatigued and experience fainting spells. Extreme tiredness causes hallucinations or bad dreams. You think you're awake when you're not."

An assumption, not a question. Teddie sat quietly, winding her fingers around her chair's wooden arms. How could she disagree without a sliver of proof to validate her? Yet, instincts told her, she was right. She *did* see a person killed.

"I also find it odd," Breena continued punching holes in Teddie's scenario. "Plenty of guests attended the benefit, and the building is closer to the outdoor deck than you were. The whole backside is glass."

"Curtains had been drawn."

"Fair enough. Still, no one noticed or heard any activity. Yet you viewed the entire assault across the street. I'm surprised you're the only witness."

Teddie wondered where the exchange was leading. "Weird, I know, but Breena, I'm telling you the truth."

"We also spoke to Darby, your waitress. She didn't see anything either."

"I gathered, since she ignored my instructions to call the police."

Her attention drifted to Drew. He'd left his seat to toss his soda can into the trash, then he hurried to greet his attorney who just entered. His t-shirt spread across his sturdy torso, his faded jeans tapered perfectly over his hips and thighs, his arms muscled and taut. Well-built men were the norm in her business but were contrived by their record and management companies.

She moistened her suddenly dry lips.

Drew didn't possess an artificial bone in his body. He was the real deal.

"Tell me about Drew."

Teddie flinched, spinning toward Breena. "Drew?"

The sheriff's usual veiled features converted into shrewd. "Nash Sewell says Drew Millard was on the pavilion the same time the apparent dispute went down."

"I spoke with Drew after the argument and subsequent death. I can't corroborate Nash's story. I sat across the street, remember?"

"History has a powerful hold."

"What's that supposed to mean?"

"You're protecting Drew."

Teddie felt her face warm. She inhaled, fighting to reel in her temper, weary of the assumptions she'd go the distance to shield her former flame. "I'm loyal. Under certain circumstances I'd defend to the max to help someone I care for, but not when a life is at stake. Why would I report a homicide, but protect the murderer?"

"Good question." The old chair screeched as Breena pushed against the back. "I contacted a forensic unit upstate. They arrived two hours ago and are conducting a thorough analysis. They plan to drag the water surrounding the Phoenix." Breena gathered a stack of papers and bounced the bottoms on the flat surface in front of her to straighten the pile. "We're done, here. You're free to leave, but until this issue is resolved, I need you to stay in town."

Teddie nodded.

"Send in Drew."

Teddie stood and moved to the door. Her hand clutched the handle, ready to twist. A flit of memory darted through her mind, then disappeared as quick as it emerged.

Breena looked up from her work. "Did you forget something?"

"Not sure." She fought to refocus and grasp the fleeting thought. "Nope, lost it."

Breena's face displayed her disbelief, which was a huge disappointment, but there was little Teddie could do. She carried a lot of clout in the music world and learned long ago she couldn't control what others believed. Breena formed her opinions, and while she may not have faith in Teddie's story, she'd couldn't prove it false, either.

Teddie strolled out of the office. Like a magnet, her gaze gravitated and latched onto Drew. His attention veered away from his lawyer and brightened as his eyes connected with hers.

She threw a thumb over her shoulder. "Your turn."

"How did it go?"

"Great. Except, like everyone else she doesn't believe me."

"Well, Teddie…"

The warm affection he generated instantly vanished. She was tired of the skepticism, especially from Drew.

"You know what? I'm done with this, done with you. I'm so outta here." She turned and headed toward the door.

****

Drew wanted to chase after Teddie, but Abel

blocked him and shook his head. Ignoring Breena's summons wasn't an option. He walked into the office, attempting to forget Teddie's anger, but that wasn't easy to do.

Breena stood behind the desk. Extending a greeting, she then motioned for them to sit opposite her. She eyed them curiously. "Must be some confession if you're bringing council, Drew."

Abel rose to his feet, opened the dossier, and placed it before her. "Read for yourself."

The rolling chair squealed as she lowered onto the cushion. She opened the packet as she simultaneously began to skim. Numerous "hmmms" escaped as she held each photograph eye level.

One she completed the report, she seesawed an inquisitive look from one man to the other. "Evie and Nash have a major fling going on. Not sure why I need to see them in action." She almost grinned at Drew. "But then again, it makes interesting reading."

"We're exposing their affair because the good doctor seems intent on fingering me as a suspect in a possible homicide investigation. He has a reason for wanting me out of the way."

"Your theory, if you're in prison, then he has a straight shot at Evie?"

Drew nodded.

She chose a picture to study. "Looks to me like he has a straight shot, regardless." She tossed the photo back onto the desk.

"Has evidence been uncovered to reveal any crime occurred?" Able asked.

"None's turned up, yet."

Drew's mouth leveled. "Then I'm not a suspect."

"Not so fast." She slapped Evie's affair file shut. "You're not excused. No proof, doesn't mean Teddie's account isn't true. Bodies can take a long time before they wash ashore, or they may never emerge. All the citizens in Jacob's Cove must be accounted for, and we haven't even started counting."

"But no one's been reported missing, correct?"

"No, Abel, they haven't. But relatives and friends don't always come forward right away, for a variety of reasons." Breena looked at Drew. "Which side of the pier were you on last night?"

He glanced at Abel, who bobbed his head. "East, most of the time."

She studied her notes. "Hmmm. Teddie claims the victim went over the west rail." Breena frowned. "And Nash stated he saw you on that side, too. Was he mistaken?"

"I moved to the western side, later."

"What went on next?"

"I, um, I ran into Teddie."

He peeked past the office window and sighed. Teddie hadn't left, but then again, he was her ride. She was seated, arms across her chest, her features showed her rage. He felt awful, he couldn't offer her support. Unfortunately, after all her strange claims, he was beginning to agree with the rest of the world. Teddie was unstable.

"You and Teddie met last night?" Breena coaxed, dragging him back to the conversation. "But you didn't plan to meet her?"

"No, our meeting was coincidental."

"Then what?"

"Teddie told Evie and me someone was pushed off

the pavilion and showed us where. I rushed down to the boat dock, but it was dark, and couldn't see anything."

"Back to you and Evie." Breena snatched a pen and clicked the top. "Did you argue with her?"

"We had words."

"What kind of words?"

"Snappy, insulting, the normal." Drew raised a shoulder. "What are you insinuating? Evie didn't go over the side. She's still alive."

"Thinking aloud." She surveyed Drew. "Something bothering you?"

He hoisted a leg, propping his left ankle across his right knee. "I hate the idea of a person in our community slaying another."

"Funny." Breena smiled a smile that didn't show humor. "You're saying the possible killer and fatality are Jacob's Cove residents?"

The foot on the floor, bobbed. "I assumed?"

"Know what happens when you assume, Drew?"

His crossed ankle slipped back to the tiles. "Isn't assumptions part of your job?"

"Not really. I'm investigating. Can't have anyone turn up dead without an inquiry in place. But other than Teddie's word, there's nothing to go on. Her mental state should compel me to shut down this whole operation. Save the county a buttload of cash. On the other hand, my palms itch."

The sheriff chuckled at Drew's and Abel's obvious confusion.

"Itch like crazy. Do you know what that means?" She stood, knuckling her desk, and leaned forward. "That's my gut speaking. My intuition tells me, Teddie might not be as irrational as the world believes and a killing did happen." She gestured toward the folder containing Evie and Nash's affair. "Someone isn't giving me all the facts. Maybe you? Or Nash? How about Evie? One or possibly all of you are hiding the truth. Don't worry. I *will* find out." Breena's intense glare speared into Drew, holding his gaze as if she held him hostage. "And watch out when I do. 'Cause somebody's going down."

Chapter 19

Drew and Abel emerged from the sheriff's office, stopping before they reached the main area. They stood nose to nose, speaking in quiet tones, immersed in an intense discussion. Drew's features were tight and drawn, while his attorney's complexion was enflamed and dour.

Apprehensive, Teddie grabbed her purse and rose out of her chair. After a quick goodbye to the surrounding crew, she hurried across the station to the debating men.

She lightly touched Drew's elbow. "What happened in there?"

"You won't believe."

A rigid Abel tapped his other arm. "Breena's bluffing, but be careful what you say. She's trying to trick you into admitting something." He shot a glare toward Teddie. "You're not the one who should confess."

"Nice." Teddie's scowl followed the lawyer as he shoved the door open and stomped away.

She returned to Drew, who scanned the room. Teddie trailed his gaze. Everyone in the room was watching them. Breena remained in her office, also kept her attention focused, observing them through the glass partition.

Deft fingers clutched Teddie's upper arm, tugging

her toward the exit. "Let's find someplace less crowded to talk."

He released her once they left headquarters and hiked past the town square. The hour was late, and it was Sunday, most businesses remained closed, the noiseless streets were empty. Cool, light summertime wafts drifted off the bay, preserving the warm temperature at a bearable degree. Colorful blooms bordered the sidewalks and gracefully danced in the breeze, their scented fragrances saturating the air.

On a normal day, Teddie would deem the tranquil sight, total peace. Restful. The reason she came to Jacob's Cove.

But this day was far from ordinary.

She glanced at Drew. His lips flattened, and his eyes squinted against the bright sun. He seemed unaware of his surroundings and in deep concentration.

"You hungry, yet?"

"Burritos?" She scrunched her face, shaking her head. "No, thanks."

"Tacos, and you missed your chance. Breakfast is over. It's past lunchtime. A burger sounds good."

"Too heavy. A salad, maybe."

"Superstardom trashed your appetite. You used to devour a thick, juicy double meat and cheese."

"No thick, double or otherwise. So not on my diet."

Drew gave her a swift onceover. "Wouldn't hurt you to gain a few pounds."

"Yes, it would. Cameras add ten to fifteen extra, so I watch what I eat." She hesitated. "Now, what went down in Breena's office?"

"I'll tell you as soon as my stomach is filled."

He led her across the street and circled into an

obscured alley. A smaller size hamburger stand sat buried inside a nook, among a slew of structures. Brightly painted tables surrounded by mismatched benches dotted the side street. Napkins and salt and pepper shakers sat on a platform was positioned in a central location. Smoke curled and flowed out of the stall's glassless window. Sizzles of beef on charcoal inundated the crammed space.

Drew directed her to the nearest table and dragged a bench forward, the legs scrapped noisily against jagged concrete. He patted a seat. "Sit."

Teddie obeyed and inhaled, adding a hmmm. The appetizing aroma spurred her empty belly to rumble, even though she'd sworn off junk food years ago.

"Not much foot traffic passes on Sunday, so no one should bother us, but if you packed shades and a hat, I suggest you wear them."

He ambled to the counter and chatted with a beefy man who inclined forward to peer out the opening. The duo peeked at her as they spoke. Concluding their dialog, Drew paced back to her, gripping two extra-large drinks in each hand, and a ticket lodged between his lips.

He deposited one of the beverages next to her, tossed the receipt onto the table, sinking on the stool farthest away. "Ordered the biggest meal on the menu. The works." An eyebrow cocked. "Don't argue, you'll eat every bite."

Teddie stripped the paper off her straw and speared it into her drink. "Now explain why Breena upset you and Abel."

"In a minute. I've got something else to say, first." He scouted the empty alleyway, sipped his soda, then grazed a sleeve across his mouth. "I want you to introduce me to my daughter."

"Oh, Drew, she'll be so excited."

"I hope so. I'm still not happy how I found out about her." He held up a palm to stop her from responding. "Let me finish. I'm working on understanding your reasons. You say you wanted to protect her—but truthfully, wasn't your aim to protect yourself? You're famous. Stating your child was fathered by someone other than your companion wouldn't generate great headlines."

"You're saying I hid Savannah's parentage to safeguard my career? That's not true. I found out I was pregnant with your child, and you married somebody else practically the same time. What I was protecting was my heart." She snapped her mouth shut. Immediately, she wished she could retract her words, but it was too late. They were out there.

"This puts us at an impasse."

"Forget I said that. I'll tell Savannah you want to meet her and give you her number. You two can arrange to meet in the fall, or if you prefer to see her sooner, you can fly to Europe since she intends to continue her travels with her da—um, Jarod."

"I'm just getting use to the idea of being a father, so I'll wait till she comes back."

"Maybe you can communicate through social media or speak on the phone before you actually meet in person."

"Sounds easier. I'm apprehensive and nervous about the whole thing."

"You'll do fine."

The guy leaned out of the stand and hollered at

Drew, telling him their food was ready. He left her to collect oversized baskets of burgers and fries, sitting one in front of her when he returned. "Every bite."

"Your talk with Breena?"

He unwrapped his sandwich and took a big bite. "Can't really say," he answered after he swallowed. "Abel gave her the file on Evie and Nash. She didn't say much or if it helped me. She asked me a couple of questions, I replied. Pretty much it."

She dragged a fry across a pile of catsup, bit the potato in half, then shifted nervously. "Why were you and Abel upset when you left her office?"

He released a cheerless chuckle. "I made a comment how I hated the idea a Cove resident killed another. She pounced on me, like I knew something I wasn't telling her. I tried to clarify, explain I just speculated, but she wasn't interested."

"Doesn't sound positive."

"Was your interview positive?"

"You're already aware it wasn't."

"Right. She went as far to say she should shut everything down and save the county's money."

Her heart faltered. If they didn't carry on with their investigation, they may never find the victim. "So, why doesn't she stop?"

"Her palms itch."

Teddie's brow wrinkled.

"Baffles me too, but she claims itchiness is her intuition telling her something's up."

A smile crawled across her face. "She has a gut feeling?"

"Must be a woman thing."

"I'm so happy. She's taking me seriously."

Drew paused in mid-bite. "Teddie, nothing's substantiated." He laid his burger on the wrapper, snatched a napkin, and wiped his fingers. "Breena's operating on instincts. Feelings can be wrong, especially if you didn't include all the information. How honest were you?"

"I answered every question."

"Did you reveal your recurring nightmare? Or hearing your mom's music box? What about the smells?"

"My bad dreams came up..." No longer hungry, Teddie pushed her lunch away. "No, I didn't say anything about the other stuff."

Remorse spread across Drew's face. "Let's be real. Not a shred of evidence has been found that suggests somebody's dead."

"Yet."

"Think, Teddie. Consider where you are. Maybe you're working through something, I don't know, but you're not in your right mind, and you haven't been since you've arrived."

Teddie's eyes narrowed. "When did you become a shrink?"

"I'm not a shrink. I'm trying to be here for you."

She leaped to her feet, flattening her palms onto the table, and tilted toward a guilty-faced Drew. "I don't *need* your kind of help. You don't believe me, my sisters pacify me, because I pay them well." She whipped around, extended her arms wide, and shouted, "The whole damn town, no wait, the entire planet sees me as a nutcase, and I'm sick of it."

"Teddie. Calm down." Drew patted the air as he moved toward her. "Relax."

"Appreciate your advice, Doctor Do Nothing." She turned to face him. "I'm stuck in this nightmare, and I don't know how to escape. What's your opinion, Doctor? How do I make a graceful exit?"

Drew stole a peek at his shoes, lifted his head, and sighed. "Take Aubrey's advice. Leave Jacob's Cove, go home. See a therapist. Then your problems will be solved."

Chapter 20

"We'll see how it goes?" Evie bolted out of her seat. She leveled her palms across the surface of Nash's desk and tilted closer as sparks of anger flashed in her eyes. "Hold on, mister. I put my reputation in jeopardy because you convinced me you were the man for me, and now I'm holding you to your word, the best I get is, we'll see how it goes?"

"I didn't force you to sacrifice anything, Evie. There were no expectations when we began. You chose to start seeing me, and you also made a decision to risk it all when we became involved."

"I'm calling BS. I let a whole year pass before I gave in and slept with you. I came to you as a trusted friend to discuss Drew and our problems. You used my vulnerability and took advantage of my circumstances."

"I didn't promise you an immediate future. Our matrimonial states were parallel and made us kindred spirits. The common bond instigated our friendship to grow into something more. As far as my quest for you, our attraction was mutual, and we *both* acted."

Evie rounded the chair, then plopped back into the seat, her legs rubbery after receiving a cold punch of reality. "You and I retain extremely different viewpoints on how we got together or where we are now. Your pursuit of me was relentless, you showed up at every function I attended, phoned me every day, sent loads of text messages, and bought me gifts, which rarely happens since we became a *couple*."

"I assure you, we'll be what we were and more, but that day is a long way off. Nevertheless, until we're official, planning a future is useless." He glimpsed at her. "Meaning, we're still married to others, and this discussion's pointless."

Evie opened her mouth to reply, but a soft tap outside Nash's office curbed their conversation. The door cracked as Sheriff Breena peeked around. "Got a minute?"

Nash's complexion whitened, but he tried to sound friendly. "Sure, come in."

Breena strolled inside, halting beside Evie's chair. She didn't speak right away, but a sly gaze jumped first on Evie, then Nash.

"Glad you're both here. I need to address a situation concerning you two. Actually." She deposited a folder in Nash's viewing range but positioned it so Evie could see. "It's better just to show you." Opening the file, she spread an array of photos across the desk. "These were delivered to me." A wry chuckle slipped. "Not much discussion's warranted. These pretty much tell the whole story."

"Drew, the bastard. He's known all along." Evie raised her head, wide-eyed. She glared at Nash. "Or is it Celia?" She turned to Breena. "Who gave them to you?"

"Can't say."

Nash's complexion went paler. He opened a desk drawer for a handkerchief and dabbed his sudden sweaty temples.

Evie waved a hand above the pictures. "What does

Debra Jupe

this mean? Why are you showing us these? To tell us something we already know?"

"Be quiet, Evie," Nash demanded. "Admit nothing."

"No need to confess, Nash." Breena gathered the snapshots into a stack. "Pretty obvious you are in what I can only describe as"—she waggled the prints—"a torrid affair."

"We're guilty of cheating. Last time I checked, fooling around's not a crime. I'm still unsure how you fit in or…do you intend on holding these photos over our heads?"

"Evie, stop."

"She has us, Nash. We're buck naked doing what we do. In color and black and white."

"They're available on video, too." Breena replaced the images into the folder. "You've been outed. Doesn't matter who exposed you or why, it won't be long until the entire town is aware." She returned to Evie. "You asked if an affair was illegal? While some do, our state never passed an adultery law, so no, Evie, it isn't against the law to sleep with another woman's husband."

"Like Evie, I'm confused by your motives." Nash rubbed the hankie across his face again. "Why did you bring those here? Do you intend to expose us or tell our partners?"

"No, I do not. Isn't my business. I showed you these because you should be aware of what's about to come down. People will find out. They always do."

Evie exchanged a worried glance with Nash. "No one's knows yet, right?"

"I do. The photographer and…" Her phone buzzed.

She extended a finger and spun away.

Evie tamped down her irritation and moved closer to Nash. "How'd we get caught? We were so careful."

"I believed we were. Whoever was hired to follow us is a crackerjack tail. I didn't notice anyone following us, much less snapping—those." Nash inhaled his first smooth breath since Breena's arrival. "I'm acquainted with people who can handle this. They'll claim the pictures are doctored. They'll even invent a source, and they'll testify in court, if we need them too. We'll emerge virtually unscathed."

"You're sure they can make this go away?"

"All it takes is cash." He looked at the ceiling, adding a defeated sigh. "Lots and lots of cash. Until then we should steer clear of each other. I'd rather not throw more suspicions our way."

"Well, of course not," Evie spouted, louder. "As long as your sweet ass is covered."

Nash motioned for her to drop her intonation. "This isn't the time or place to air our—"

"Okay, folks." Breena disconnected and tucked her cell into her pocket. "I'm needed elsewhere."

Nash's skin lost pigmentation again, but his features looked relieved.

"Another flock of reporters rode into town. Like the others, they're wanting a story about Teddie and creating a ruckus trying to find the Donavan house. I'm obligated to meet them and explain how to act when visiting another city." She held up the binder. "As far as your fling. You probably think it's none of my concern, what you do in private, and you're right, it isn't. I'm just here to give you a friendly warning. Clock's ticking. Once your sideline is out, it'll unfold faster than a wildfire burning during a blue norther."

"Which one of our spouses do you think found out?" Evie asked after Breena left.

Nash appeared anxious. "I can't fathom why either would give Breena the information. But if I had to choose, I'd pick Drew. He's more suspicious. Celia's the type to bury her head and behave as if everything is perfect."

"You sure? Maybe that's why she's not taking your calls. Drew would've attacked head on and confronted me. Celia may be more passive aggressive and contact Breena on the sly."

"Whichever spouse turned us in is moot. We have to make this go away." He opened the center drawer on his left and shuffled, withdrawing a worn spiral. He thumbed through the pages.

"I'm glad you're connected."

"This'll only solve half our problem." He looked up. "I'm serious, Evie. Keep your guard up. We can't be seen together until this blows over."

"You're certain this is the game you want to play?" She rose to her feet, resting her fists on her hips. "Because I don't think so. You lured me with your sweet talk and gestures, made sure I fell in love with you, and I insist you stand by your word."

"Evie, this isn't the time to engage in your silliness."

"Silliness?"

He slapped the notebook shut and stood. "I'm going to try and find my wife. I don't enjoy her silent treatments. I need to know if she's on to us and smooth things over if she is." He marched out the door. "Lock up when you leave."

Chapter 21

"I'm not seeking psychological help, Drew, nor do I intend to return to Tennessee until I find out why this dream keeps haunting me. If you're thinking all I need is a shrink, there's nothing left to talk about."

"What do you expect, Teddie?" Drew almost shouted. "You're irrational. There's no evidence to validate your story. Maybe you were misdiagnosed, and you're ill rather than exhausted. Regardless, you need help."

"I'll concede to the music and smells may've been part of my dreams, but I didn't imagine the murder."

"No body's been found, and no one's been reported missing."

"So you've said." She wandered to their table, snatched her soda, and sucked angrily on the straw. "We go way back, Drew, yet benefit of the doubt some how's gotten lost on you."

His hard mouth flattened into a line. Her allegations were outrageous. So outrageous, he couldn't even pretend he believed her.

He stole a glance her way. She remained in place, her long, golden tresses lifted in the breeze, giving her an air of innocence. Her expression was sad, and she appeared at war with her emotions.

Guilt tugged at his heart. This was the mother of his child, and he'd loved her since he was a teenager.

Teddie needed him to back her, and he owed her.

"You're right. I wasn't there, so I can't dispute your claim. I'll keep quiet until Breena issues the results of her investigation."

She didn't instantly answer. Instead, she stationed her cup on the tabletop and clutched it tight with both hands. "You're pacifying me, and I don't appreciate it."

"Give me a break. You've laid a lot on me since we reunited, and in a short amount of time."

"Not on purpose."

A sympathetic smile touched his lips as he pitched his trash in a nearby trashcan. "I'm aware, but from now on, I'm behind you one hundred percent."

Teddie's eyes flickered, demonstrating suspicion. "Why the change in attitude?"

"I failed you too many times when you needed me. You were always the strong one, and now it's my turn to be strong for you."

"I just said I don't want pity, Drew." She bowed her head and stared at her feet. Finally, she lifted her gaze. "I think we're finished here." To reiterate her point, she spun away and stormed toward the alleyway's outlet.

A knot instantly materialized and weaved through his chest. While he encouraged her to go back to Nashville and get help, he also just found her again. A big part of him didn't want to lose her.

"Wait. Teddie, don't do this."

She slowed until coming to a standstill, but she stubbornly refused to turn around and look at him.

"It's not pity, I swear..." His voice faded as he held his arms out to his sides.

She shook her head. "Seriously, I'm done."

****

Teddie adjusted the radio, unable to find music that satisfied her mood. Singing along to happy songs soothed her, and she hadn't sung in weeks.

Everything sounded like noise and grated on her nerves. Finally, she relented and muted the radio, so the only sound was gravel crackling beneath the tires.

After miles of quiet, her house appeared. To her dismay, her sister's rental was parked in the drive, and both relaxed on the porch in the old-fashioned rockers. Preferring to be alone, Teddie glided the gear into neutral, cut the engine, and slowly exited.

Aubrey straightened as she approached. "New car?"

"Yeah, the other's still at the Blue Moon so I ordered a new rental."

"How was the meeting?"

"Uneventful." Teddie moved to the veranda, stooping to perch on the top step. "Breena's guys haven't found evidence to show a homicide occurred, so now she's bringing in a forensic team from upstate."

Raven cocked her head to the left. "Sort of an uplifting negative?"

"She's covering her butt in case a body does emerge. But if one doesn't, my sanity—" Teddie shrugged. "You know."

"We'll always stand by you, but the rest of the world? Not so much." Aubrey elevated her phone to display the current newsfeed. "Did you and Drew argue earlier today?"

Teddie groaned. "Argument's way too gentle of description."

"Whatever happened is blaring across cyberspace.

Video's had thousands of hits. The fallout's bad. Very bad."

Teddie buried her face into her palms. "I was so upset. I didn't consider reporters may be around." Her head popped up. "Wonder where they hid? We ate at an outdoor site located in a back ally. There was just one access."

Raven's brow puckered. "Surrounding building windows?"

"Today's Sunday. Everything's locked up."

"Rooftop, perhaps?"

"I suppose." Teddie paused. "Wait." She looked at her sisters. "The guy who grilled burgers. He watched the whole time. I bet he recorded us."

"Too late to worry about the who's, what's, when's, and where's. Damage is done." Aubrey's face twisted. "And it'll will only get worse. People are speculating about your and Drew's connections. Only a matter of time, and they'll find out he's an old boyfriend. Who's married. And father of your firstborn, whose parentage you've lied about."

"My child's father isn't the world's business."

"Your followers won't agree," Aubrey warned. "You'd be smart to keep away from Drew Millard."

Teddie inspected the tower of cliffs situated beyond the property line. "Not a problem."

Aubrey hoisted her brows. "You and Drew didn't forgive and forget after your performance went live?"

"No. Essentially, I did what I came to do. He and Savannah are aware of each other. If they chose to go further with their relationship, it's on them. I'm out."

Raven placed a toe on the wood to sway the chair forward and back. "What did he do to make you so mad?"

Aubrey handed her phone to Raven. "You can watch the uncut version in its entirety." She refocused on Teddie. "I'm glad you put Drew Millard and your history to rest. I never thought he was good for you."

The hole in Teddie's heart expanded. Many dreams died today. While she realized roadblocks to any future between her and Drew was set years ago, she hadn't foreseen their conclusion to be so harsh or final.

"I don't feel like talking about him. Can we end this conversation?"

"Understood," Aubrey consented. "How are you? Physically? Psychologically?"

"I'm beat."

"I can imagine." Raven shifted. "How awful was the trip into Mom and Dad's room."

"About what you'd expect."

"You're braver than me. I had trouble walking past the door."

Aubrey released a cheerless laugh. "I won't even go upstairs. You sure you're handling this okay, Teddie?"

"I guess. Maybe. I don't know."

"No resolutions to end your nightmares?"

Teddie shook her head. "Nope. Nothing."

"Then you've tapped all your points in Jacob's Cove," Aubrey announced. "I'm sorry you didn't find the solutions you hoped, but it is time to pack and head home to Nashville."

Uneasiness swept amid Teddie. Aubrey was right. She did what she came to do, sans an outcome. Yet... "I agree. We should leave, soon. But I mean to stay till the end of the week."

"Why are you so determined to destroy the years of respect you've earned from your colleagues and fans, not to mention a long-term career." Aubrey thrust her cell screen to give Teddie a clear view of the train wreck. "You can't take too many more of these media poundings. We won't recover."

"A few days. Besides, Breena insisted I stay in town."

"A decent attorney can solve that problem." Aubrey looked toward Raven. "Can't you?"

Teddie rolled her eyes. "No, she can't."

"I don't get you."

"This fuzzy memory won't go away. I want to give it a few more days."

Aubrey grimaced as her hand fell into her lap. "You're hopeless."

Teddie leaped to her feet and grazed her clammy palms across her shorts. "Your support's a bit underwhelming, dear sister."

"I am trying to get you going in the right direction, but you refuse to move."

"I hear what you're saying and more importantly, I hear what you aren't saying. You see me as someone who can't distinguish truth from fiction. Ingesting *one* pill made me a little loopy, and undoubtedly instigated my nightmare, but I've had it for years, and I want to know why."

"Keep doing what you're doing, Teddie." Raven tossed a glimpse Aubrey's way, then returned to Teddie. "This is your journey. We can't make demands or expectations until you're at peace. Finish."

Aubrey's features showed her disapproval, but she begrudgingly nodded. "Do what you need to, and we'll pick up the pieces after it falls apart."

Not exactly positive encouragement, but she and Aubrey quibbled often. She flashed Raven a quick grin and mouthed a "thanks."

Tired, she climbed the stairs to go to bed soon after they departed, and long before the sun dipped below the mountain peaks. She fell asleep the moment her head touched the pillow, but restfulness didn't linger.

A recognizable out of tune jingle faintly chinked. Once more, a youthful Teddie waited beyond her parents' bedroom door as she eavesdropped. Her father screamed, and her mother spoke barely above a whisper.

Their argument abruptly silenced.

Teddie's frame stiffened.

Pop. Pop.

She sprang to a sitting position. The faint music box trill echoed throughout the house. She flung the covers off her shaking body and dashed down the darken hallway. Splatters of moonlight shimmered from her parents' bedroom. She froze and stared. The door stood ajar, which was not how she left it.

Her pulse vibrated as chills scattered across her skin, like the devil himself snuck up behind her and breathed down her neck.

The melody escalated, sounding sharper as she scampered down the hallway. Suddenly, it stopped. She lithered to a halt and peered past the doorway. Rounding the corner, she entered the room. Scents of cordite emerged like someone had fired a weapon.

Teddie strained to focus, adjusting her vision to the dimness. Her gaze swept the moonlit filled room. Everything seemed normal, nothing disturbed. She stepped to the bed and stared at layers of grubby blankets. Something seemed off. She leaned closer and squinted.

An object rested in the center.

She inched nearer, gaping at the entity. A scream burned the back of her throat. Backpedaling, she hurried outside, fleeing down the staircase. She sped to the foyer and threw the door open.

An elongated shadow obstructed the doorframe. Teddie shrieked again.

"Teddie, it's me." Drew surfaced out of the shadows. Grasping her arm, he guided her to the sofa and gently eased her to sit. "Hold on, let me turn on a light." He clumped across the hardwoods, his boots ringing in the blackness. A click snapped. A dim glow flooded the room.

Drew strolled to the couch and lowered next to her. He turned to study her, worry etched across his face. "What happened? Another bad dream?"

Her shaky hand swiped at the wetness, moistening her cheeks. "The gun, the one that he—Daddy, used…" Her voice wobbled. "I saw it, just now. Lying on their bed."

Chapter 22

Drew bolted off the sofa, bouncing to his feet. "Stay put," he yelled over his shoulder as he sailed up the flight of stairs.

Teddie tucked her calves beneath her rear and circled her arms to envelope her middle. Images of her father's gun lingered, inciting constant shivers to flutter across her skin.

She leaned backward, shut her eyes, attempting to ease the tenseness. A strong, cordite odor still stung her nostrils. Instead of relaxing, the smell had her heartrate soar at rocket speed and ricocheted a deafening drumbeat inside her ears. Interiors of her mouth had parched and were more arid than a bale of cotton.

Footsteps thumped above had her refocus. She lifted her eyelids and stared at the ceiling. Drew was in her parents' bedroom, stirring between morsels of stillness. After a few minutes of the same pattern, his paces shifted.

A moment later, he stood at the edge of the staircase. "Teddie?" His vocal cords had elevated higher than usual. "Are you well enough to come up?"

No. A blaring headache had begun at the base of her skull and crawled upward, adding to her other discomforts, but she refused to elaborate, fearing she'd worsen the already escalated situation.

"I'm coming."

Slowly, she scooted across the cushion and stooped frontward until she could stand. Her legs were heavy as the ache in her head intensified. She forced herself to move, grabbing onto nearby furniture for balance. Her strides strengthened as she forged ahead, but she fumbled at the bottom of the stairwell in Drew's viewing range.

"Do you need help? You're awfully pale."

"I can do this."

Struggling to lift her foot, Teddie only made the third stair before Drew rushed to meet her. He ignored her scathing glare of protest, clasped her wrist, and tenderly guided her to the second floor. Teddie peered down the hall when they reached the top. A spectral glow gleamed a squatty cone shape and circled the vicinity of their destination.

The light became more ubiquitous as they traveled across the hallway, approaching her parents' bedroom. Frosty air coiled around her as they halted at the threshold.

Drew hiked farther in and stopped next to the bed. His brow furrowed. "You're sure you saw a gun?"

Her eyes drifted to the mattress, centering on the location she'd seen the weapon. A nauseating horror pierced her stomach. Empty. Not even a minor dent in the quilt.

"I don't understand," she whispered, gradually advancing inside. She indicated at the bed's center. "It was right here."

"Did you turn on the lights?"

She shook her head.

"Then how can you be sure? It's a dark night."

"Moonlight gave off plenty of radiance."

"The moon can also distort. Did you hear the music box, again? Or smell any odd odors?"

"I was asleep, but I heard music." Her speech sounded faint, even to her.

Drew glanced at the covered dresser, his mouth stretching into a hard line as he noted the sheet hadn't budged. "What happened, next?"

"Shots. Gunshots," she finished, emotionally preparing to endure his scrutiny.

Drew looked shocked. "You heard actual gunfire?"

She gave a feeble nod as the ache in her head began to skyrocket. "Two. Just like the day Mama and Daddy died. I got a whiff of gunpowder after." She touched her forehead. Perspiration speckled her temple. The room started to revolve, accelerating at each round.

"Are you sure this wasn't another bad dream?"

Her jaw locked. Teddie couldn't part her lips to respond. Heat charged through her veins as the brightness dimmed, shrinking to a pinhole, and then gave way to obscurity.

****

"Teddie? Teddie, wake up."

Teddie attempted to stir, but her limbs were stiff and weighty. A cerebral objection suppressed her cognizance from emerging.

A warm hand clenched her upper arm and gently shook. Teddie tensed, wishing whoever disturbed her would leave her alone.

"Come on, Teddie. Open your eyes."

Time inched and raced by as Teddie laid motionless, her body limp, her breathing slackened. Drowsiness swept her into deep sleep.

A damp, iciness swabbed and compressed onto her

forehead. Teddie's eyes snapped open. The coldness paralyzed everything but her eyelids. She blinked at a vibrant beam piercing her corneas. Semi alert, she focused on a shadow towering over her.

"Who are you?" she demanded, straining to see.

"You don't know?"

Her eyes tapered.

A silhouette standing against the bright light, twisted. "I'm phoning an ambulance."

"An ambulance?" She repeated. "Are you ill?"

The darkened profile froze. "Teddie." The fuzzy form walked out of the sheen of light and lowered next to her. "It's me. Drew. And no, I'm not sick."

"Drew," she panted as her vision began to clear. "What happened?"

"You really don't remember?" Holding a damp washcloth between his palms, he maintained a wary observation. "We went into your mom and dad's bedroom after you thought you'd seen your father's pistol lying on their bed. It wasn't there." He brushed away the moist strands of hair bonded to her cheeks. "You fainted after."

Her chest caved, like an anvil had been dropped in the middle. Glimpsing at her surroundings, a tremor shimmied up her spine. Fragments of memories flitted as she methodically pieced the last few hours' events.

"I'm so tired."

"Glad you're finally getting that."

"Fainting's probably a delayed reaction."

"Except you passed out twice within a twenty-four-hour span. Last evening you behaved lucid when you awakened, but this time you had an attack of amnesia."

"Perhaps it's my way of coping with stress."

"Still not right, Teddie. Your brain is not receiving oxygen and losing consciousness isn't a normal coping mechanism."

She didn't agree but chose not to argue since that's all they'd done today. Which made her wonder why he was here? They had parted in a swell of anger. She was still mad, and sensed he might hold on to various annoyances, too.

"Why are you in my room?"

"I came to—" Drew broke off and sighed. "I'm bothered by the way we left things. We haven't spoken in years." He rose and orbited the space. "We have a child. We can't be hostile toward one another."

"She's almost grown. Why does it matter?"

His eyes narrowed impatiently.

Warmth flooded her face as her heart squeezed painfully. "Seriously. You think I've lost my mind."

"No, don't ever say that. I'll admit, you're going through some odd stuff, and I don't understand. I want to help you, but I'm not sure how."

Teddie lingered, hesitant to go on. "That's nice, but…" She extended an arm to the nightstand and retrieved a bottle of water. After a long swallow, she recapped the drink, and replaced it on the table. "The best way to help me is to stay away."

Drew didn't offer a reply. He strolled to the window, propping on his rear against the sill, and eyed her. "I'm not leaving you by yourself." His voice quietened. "I hate to ask you, but I need to." He paused. "Did you take any meds, earlier tonight?"

"No, I did not."

"You're sure?"

"Yes, Drew, I'm sure. Why?"

A grimness spread across his face as he straightened and sank his fingers into his front pocket. He pulled out an object, walked to her, and extended a flat palm.

A small container lay in his hand.

"This is one of your prescription medications. I found it inside your purse after you collapsed. I couldn't rouse you, so I checked to make certain you didn't ingest anything because I planned to call 911." He positioned the bottle next to the light fixture to display the content, then shook it as if to prove a point.

"Half empty." He repositioned and rattled the tablets in front of her nose. "Explains a lot." He glared at her. "Now, let me ask you again. Did you take these?"

Chapter 23

"Where are you, Drew?"

"In the dungeon." Drew marked a note on the sheet music resting on a black, metal stand in front of him. "You banished me down here, remember?"

Tossing the pencil onto the stand's edge, he twisted to the basement's staircase, regretting his retort. He ought to repress his sarcasm. Smartass comments often put him in a vice. Yet, he couldn't restrain himself. Thoughts formed in his brain and just tumbled out of his mouth.

A glimpse at the stairwell instilled a guarded relief. So far, the upper floor remained noiseless. Maybe he dodged one, the first in a long while. Stifling a yawn, he reviewed his music and plucked a string on the acoustic perched upon his lap, then paused.

Teddie had left him frustrated. She wouldn't admit she ingested the prescription meds, although she couldn't explain what happened to the missing tablets. After hours of arguing and against his better judgment, he left her, coming straight home. He fell into bed, but sleep escaped him, and he lay awake most of the night, tossing, and turning.

He had to help her.

While he'd rather chose a different method, he couldn't think of an alternative, so he sought out her sisters. Knowing she wouldn't divulge the half-filled pill bottles to anyone, Drew thought her family should be aware.

He, Aubrey, and Raven made decisions, verdicts Teddie was furious about, but she could stay mad. An intervention had been called for. Today, he made a side trip after he ended his twelve-hour shift, and the visit had a devastating outcome.

Now here was home. The evening's goal was to create melodies and add them to Teddie's lyrics. Later, he planned to relax with a cold one, tune into a ballgame, and try to forget his part in betraying the mother of his child.

The door above squeaked.

He looked up. Shit. So, close.

The dwindling stitch of anxiety swelled in his chest as high heels echoed inside the stairwell, the sound strengthening as they approached. He swiped up Teddie's songbook, raised his butt, and sat before returning to the ten-bar intro he'd almost completed.

Evie burst into his sanctuary, dressed to kill, same as her expression. She circled his hardback chair, intending for him to get a bird's eye view of her raging fury.

Reluctantly, he ceased playing. Although he preferred to skip her latest drama, he was shit out of luck.

Arms posed across her torso, she faced him ready for a fight. "I don't want a divorce. If you insist on us splitting, then you need to leave my home. Pronto."

Drew ignored her death glare and edged nearer to his tune, electing to take the simplest route and keep quiet. This wasn't the first time they engaged in this debate, and if he tried to reason with her, the argument could go on all night.

Evie's speared daggers into him. "I'm speaking to you."

He maintained the silent treatment.

Evie closed in and yanked the sheet music off the stand. She held the top center as a vengeful grin crawled across her face.

Drew bolted out of his chair, but he was too late. He watched in horror as she ripped the piece in opposite directions. He lowered into his seat and clutched the neck of his guitar.

Halves realigned, she split the doubles into smaller pieces and performed the procedure once more. She opened her palms to let the tiny bits float to the ground.

A satisfied smile appeared as she brushed the remaining scraps from her hands. "I'd appreciate a response."

Drew studied the sown fragments, while he worked to tamp down his anger, unsure how much more of her nastiness he could take. "Do you know how much time I spent on that piece?"

"I don't give a damn about your stupid music," she shouted, twisting her wedding band around her finger. "Your ending our marriage concerns me."

"We've talked the subject to death." Drew rose and set the guitar in its case. Still focused on the shreds scattered across the floor, his lips extended into a thin line. "My decision is final."

Evie snorted. "I'm sure, now that your precious Teddie's back in the picture."

He sat down and leaned against the back of the chair, struggling to keep his attitude impassive, and not allow her to provoke him. "You're one to talk."

"Then it was you."

"What was me?"

"You took the photos to Breena. She hand-delivered them to Nash and me. We were both humiliated."

Drew inhaled deep. She sounded accusatory, like he should be remorseful. What nerve. "You aren't the least bit ashamed, are you? Not a smidgen of embarrassment."

"Are you?" she shot back.

"I'm not cheating."

"You expect me to believe nothing's happened between you and your sweet Teddie?"

"Do you have proof?" Teddie wasn't a part of the equation, and he wouldn't allow Evie to use her as a catalyst in their divorce.

"No." She stomped to him, and bent forward, placing her face inches from his. "Maybe you haven't cheated in a physical sense, but she's always been between us. I never could compete."

Drew cursed under his breath. He should sympathize. He did, but his guilt didn't stem from the right reasons. "I'm sorry I caused you so much pain."

"Save you're regrets," Evie snapped as she straightened. "I don't give a rat's ass what you do."

"I'm aware. Except, you didn't sign the divorce papers like you promised."

"We're not finished discussing our marriage."

"You don't care what I do, but you want to stay married?"

"My family and friends will not understand."

"Too bad. You had the weekend. Weekend's over and no signature. You know what's coming next."

"Not fair, Drew."

"I'm miserable, and you're sleeping with another guy. You've been sleeping around for years."

"Like it matters to you."

"Or to you. It's over, Evie."

"Fine." She glowered, her face transformed, flushing crimson. "I wish you and your psycho girlfriend all the happiness." She spun to the exit. "Just so you know, I've never loved you, either. I married you just to get back at *her*."

"And we're both unhappy. We suck the life out of each other, and yet you want to continue to live in misery."

Evie swung to him and glared, then her tenseness transformed. "What if I behave? I won't cause you any trouble. You can even be with Teddie in secret."

"Can't see how I'd benefit."

"You get your precious Teddie, and I won't reveal your relationship to the press."

"Speaking to reporters wouldn't be in your best interest and in the end, would bite you in the ass." His mouth curved into a knowing smile. "But you already know that, don't you?"

"Do your worst. I'm not scared."

"Neither am I."

Color drained from Evie's face as her mouth fell open. Her nostrils flared as her scowl deepened. Blaring silence crushed the room.

"Pack your stuff and get out. I'll give you until tomorrow," Evie asserted calmly, "or I'll call Breena to evict you."

"I'm hunting for a place, but I can't find anything. Not a lot's vacant this time of year."

A few free rentals were booked the next coming weeks. He couldn't afford to buy a home, and he had no place to go, which she knew, though he doubted she cared.

"You can live inside your truck or in the woods. You can even die, because I never want to see you again." She whipped around and stamped up the staircase. "Tomorrow, Drew," her declaration boomed before the door slammed.

Chapter 24

A chilled Teddie hugged her knees to her chest as she sat huddled, staring at the stagnant, black liquid. Her mind was wedged in bitter, dark confinement. Something had happened. Something undefined, nameless, but sinister nonetheless. She wanted to run, to escape, but the unknown wickedness had her trapped.

Still, she must take a stand and fight whatever—or whoever this was, until her private war ended.

"Teddie?"

A cool hand grasped her shoulder and shook.

Teddie's body braced as her breathing became labored.

"Teddie?"

Her mind reversed, capturing her mental state in a murky vortex until it collided with a blaze of white light. A raze of shock almost brought her accelerated heartbeat to a searing halt.

She sprang upright. Her eyes flew open. She examined her surroundings. She was nowhere near water. Another dream? Possibly. Not as horrendous this time, but just as strange.

So, where was she? She scanned the airy, open space, surrounded by peach tinted walls, stark white floors, and one window. A scent of chamomile mixed with a trace of disinfectant lingered.

She laid in an unfamiliar bed, a crisp sheet and thin

blanket covered her below the waist. Various parts of her body had been bonded to a tube and a hum of equipment droned behind her.

"Are you all right? You moaned like you were having a nightmare."

Teddie glimpsed to her left. Aubrey stood next to her, watching, her face full of concern. She peered past her sister at a clock placed on a nearby nightstand. The digital readout was 8:39. It didn't indicate whether the hour was a.m. or p.m., and since curtains covered the window, she couldn't tell if it was day or night.

"Where am I?"

"In the hospital."

This revelation didn't surprise her, she suspected as much. Still, she wanted to know more. "I don't remember anything. How long have I been here?"

"Almost a week." Aubrey turned and strolled to an oversized, wingback chair situated on the room's far side. Lowering into the seat, she gazed guardedly at Teddie. "You've been kept sedated, which is why your memory is sporadic."

A frown clouded Teddie's features. "Are we in Nashville?"

"Jacob's Cove. Davis Medical Center."

When did she return to Jacob's Cove? Once again, she fought to remember. Pieces flashed inside her head, but like everything else, nothing came in distinct.

She closed her eyes and relaxed. Harsh realities pierced her drug induced thoughts. Recollections flooded and burst through the dam, allowing mental pictures to progress in gradual flow.

That awful night. The gun. The smell. And none of it real, or she was told. An almost empty pill bottle sat

214

perched at the edge of the coffee table. Her sisters, Drew, and Nash Sewell gathered at the house and cornered her.

Fearful, Teddie tried to flee, but they captured her and held her down like a wild animal.

Demands ensued.

See a shrink. Get help.

Angry, she refused. Arguments arose. Her against them. She lost. A sad faced Raven went upstairs to gather her belongings. Aubrey, with Nash's help, forced her into a foreign vehicle.

Hours later, she was admitted into the hospital. Although she protested, her objections went ignored. They strapped her to a gurney and pierced her arm, inserting a drip.

After that, everything was a mystery. She skimmed the area one more time. The outer appearance of her room was attractive, but appearances were deceptive. Her family had committed her. Imprisoned her into her own nightmare.

Drew…she didn't know what happened to Drew. Him, settled on the porch steps as silent tears spilled across his cheeks, zipped through her mind. A final impression or one more dream?

At this point, did it matter?

Furious over his participation in her intercession, his desertion still saddened her.

"It's best he stays away, Teddie." Teddie stared at her sister. "Drew can't help you, even if he's in your corner."

She didn't argue. Instead, she sought to recognize her options. How long would she remain confined? Could she freely depart if she chose?

Teddie eyed Aubrey. "What's the plan?"

"Plan?"

"Can I leave?"

"No, your doctor has to sign off to release you."

"How do I make that happen?"

"You can't make anything happen. You stay until the doctor says you're ready to go."

"And then?"

Aubrey stood and sighed as if she were weary of replying to Teddie's questions. "Once you're discharged, we'll head home to Nashville. You can continue your recovery at a local facility." She smiled. "Don't worry. Teddie Donavan Enterprises is running smooth. Cliff and your team composed carefully worded press packages and added believable spins. The media is under control. Your career will survive and thrive."

Teddie eased into her pillows.

"That's the positive," Aubrey resumed. "Your secrets have been revealed, which is the negative."

"My secrets?"

"Details of Mama and Daddy's death, you audibly witnessed the shootings, and later finding them. Your and Drew's past was also exposed."

An overflow of air inundated Teddie's lungs. "The public knows Drew's Savannah's father?"

Aubrey shook her head. "Fortunately, Savannah's parentage is still safe."

Teddie exhaled. She could deal with everything else, but she couldn't bear the paparazzi exposing and shoving her unsuspecting daughter into the limelight. She needed to leave so she could begin repairing the damage before the final tidbit became common knowledge.

"Why've I been kept under sedation?"

"Staff kept up the anesthetics to give your body time to rest. Since you're conscious, I assume you're improved enough to awaken."

Teddie looked about. "Where's Raven?"

"She's left already. Problems with Emmitt." Aubrey paused to roll her eyes. "I don't know about that husband of hers."

"Not our business, Aubrey."

"True. Anyway, we packed most of your things and shipped them home prior to Raven's leaving." Aubrey gave her a bland smile. "Now, we wait for your doctor's word."

"Who's my doctor?"

Aubrey gave her an odd look.

"I recall Nash's presence at the ambush you staged. Did he continue on as my physician?"

"I'm sorry you felt trapped, but choices were limited. You had extreme hallucinations, and Drew found your medication bottles almost empty. He suggested we stage an intervention and institutionalize you."

Teddie's heart froze. Committing her was Drew's idea? She breathed in so not to expose a flow of tears that suddenly formed.

"We feared for your safety, and we were correct," Aubrey went on. "Phlebotomist did a blood panel. You showed a high dose of amphetamines in your workup. You overdosed, which has invoked your delusions."

Teddie wouldn't discuss the beginnings of this incarceration or what technicians claimed to find in her plasma. She was pissed at Drew, both sisters, and everyone remotely involved, but her main goal was to break out. She intended to play along until she understood how these incidences tied together.

"You didn't answer me. Is Nash Sewell attending to my…"—she swallowed—"illness?"

Aubrey's hands joined, her fingers clutched tight. "I phoned Nash because we required support from a trusted healthcare professional. Nash kindly agreed to come and assist us in the intervention, but he is not a part of your therapeutic unit. Dr. Ramey took over your case."

Teddie sensed relief, since *she* didn't trust Nash. Or anybody. Nor was she comfortable in this facility. Gut instincts whispered her stint at Davis Medical Center wasn't near done, and those associated would placate her until she quit asking.

"Go find this Ramey and notify him I'm ready to leave."

"Teddie, I can't just give orders to your doctor. He'll need to examine you before he discharges you, and that won't occur until he's certain you're healed."

"I'm cured."

Aubrey patted her arm. "Of course, you are."

"I *am* better." Teddie loathed how Aubrey appeased her.

"I'm glad you're recovering. I'll go alert the nurses, and they can inform your doctor." Aubrey spun and hurried away.

As soon as she was gone, Teddie tossed the covers off and climbed out of bed, immediately snatching onto the edge of the mattress. Her legs wobbled and dizziness whirled in her head, nearly toppling her to the ground.

An empty IV was jammed into her skin and hooked to a rack on wheels next to the headboard. She sidled against the bedrail and backtracked to the rear, unhooking the transparent container. Slowly, she trekked to a wardrobe situated by the bathroom, needing several breaks in between steps.

The interiors of the closet had a plastic grocery sack sitting on the lowest shelf. She peeked inside and let go a quiet whoop. She moved as fast as possible to re-hook the IV bag, then gripped the bottom sheet and hoisted up. Short of breath, wooziness prevailed. Her heart banged into her ribs by the time she lay supine.

A clicking noise of the door opening had her briefly freeze. Quickly, Teddie tucked her bag underneath her calves and drew the sheet up before Aubrey sauntered in shadowed by a woman dressed in blue scrubs. They both smiled at her, but neither grin seemed genuine.

Aubrey walked over to stand by her. The nurse halted and studied a chart linked to end of the bedframe.

Once she was finished, she looked past Teddie and spoke to Aubrey. "This is a mistake. The patient is supposed to remain anesthetized."

"No, I'm fine," Teddie claimed. "You're not putting me back into a coma."

"Teddie, your physician makes your medical decisions," Aubrey hissed.

The RN disregarded Teddie, still directing her comments at Aubrey. "I'll fetch a fresh saline solution and another round of medications."

She was gone before Teddie had a chance to protest. Infuriated, she glared at Aubrey. "She ignored me. That women will not touch me."

"Calm down, Teddie."

"No, I won't. I'm done playing Sleeping Beauty."

Within minutes, the rude nurse reentered the room, carrying a translucent plastic bag of fluid in one hand and an IV catheter in the other. She rapidly exchanged the empties and left the room without touching Teddie or speaking a word.

Aubrey's expression altered into irritatingly sympathetic. "Do what's expected tonight, and we'll speak to doctor in the morning."

Teddie's eyes skated over the drawn curtains. "It's nighttime?"

Aubrey checked her watch. "After nine. I should go. Guests must be off the premises by nine-fifteen. Lockdowns at nine-thirty." She kissed Teddie on the cheek and headed toward the door. "Behave and cooperate. I'll see you tomorrow."

Finally, Teddie found herself alone. She inspected the tubes connected to an intravenous drip that pierced into her vain. How would she remove this? She had viewed actors jerk ports out of their arms in movies, but that was make believe. What if she tried and accidently damaged a major artery? Ripped flesh and gushing blood didn't appeal, especially if it belonged to her.

But if she wanted to leave, she must go now, before the replacement medicines took effect or the entrances were locked for the night.

Using her thumbnail, she nudged the tape's border until it loosened, then she gently peeled the strips off her skin. She inspected the hypodermic spear implanted into her flesh. Carefully, she extracted the needle from her skin. Thankfully, the prick didn't bleed much.

Edging off the mattress, she grabbed her sack which held the clothes she wore when she checked from under the top sheet. Still lightheaded, she managed to change and stuff her hair into a ball cap she wore when she entered to hide her identity. On tiptoe, she walked to the door and cracked it ajar.

The hallways appeared empty, even though dark blue bubbles donned the ceiling, indicating security cameras recorded every move. She slithered outside, then strolled down the hall, not knowing where the corridors led, but tried to appear natural, like a guest who knew the way, and was departing after a visit.

Her main hindrance, she suffered fatigue and vertigo. She labored to maintain her balance as she followed numerous curves until she approached a dead-end. Teddie tamped down her panic. A dinging sound caught her attention. She turned and heaved a relieved sigh. Elevators were located across the hallway.

Without hesitation, she rushed over and pressed the down button. Tugging her dead cell phone out of her jeans rear pocket, she leaned against the wall and pretended to study the screen while she waited.

A voice blared over the loudspeaker. "Attention visitors."

A startled Teddie flinched. Mentally, she demanded the elevator to hurry.

"Davis Medical Center visiting hours are over in five minutes," the announcer broadcasted. "Thank you, and have a pleasant evening."

Double knots formed inside her stomach. Would she make it out without getting caught? Thus far, passages stayed empty. The elevator doors opened. Teddie took a step and froze.

Two healthcare types stood inside the car. They were in deep in a conversation and didn't seem to notice her. Ducking her head, she yanked her hat further over her face and strolled inside.

She remained forward so her back faced them. In no time, she reached the first floor. A gurgle of laughter slipped from her lips as she spotted an automatic sliding doorway, leading outside.

Freedom waited mere feet away. She wandered into the vestibule. Twenty-four inches, and she'd fade into the night.

"Attention personal." The PA blasted again, this time the speaker sounded more ominous. "We will be going into a soft lockdown until further notice. A soft lockdown is now in progress."

Chapter 25

Teddie crossed the threshold instants before she heard the exit automatically latched. Outside, she hugged the wall and hid among the shadows as she sought a chance to flee.

Security personnel had rushed out of every aperture as soon as the broadcaster made the announcement. They scoured the surrounding borders noiselessly searching. Teddie remained in her spot and silently viewed the commotion, surprised no one bothered to check close to the building's walls. Gradually, the uniforms spread beyond the facilities and evaporated into blackness.

Now what? She had to do something. Except any advancement left her exposed. Video recorders were mounted on the hospital's eves. So far, she hadn't stirred enough to be captured on film, but cameras would record her image if she weren't careful. Plus, the guards would return at some point.

Either way, she couldn't stay here. She had two choices. Run or backtrack.

Sidling around the corner, she advanced on tiptoe, her eyes peeled to make sure she steered away from uniforms and video surveillance.

A vacant truck next to a curb caught her attention. She could make a dash across the parking lot and hole up in the bed. It must be almost nine-thirty, the owners should show up soon.

Decision time.

Teddie skimmed to her left and then right. No one lurked nearby. Checking the cameras, she took off, sprinting to the trucks rear end. She hunkered low, peeking above the rim to study the area again.

Good so far.

Grabbing the edges, Teddie lifted a foot onto the running board and hoisted over the tailgate, just as two guards rounded opposite corners. She dove to the bottom, landing on her stomach. Flattened against the grimy truck-bed, she laid still and listened.

Their boot heels smacked against the asphalt, shuffling nearer. Teddie braced, wishing she wore darker clothing.

"Anything?" one inquired.

"Naw," the other replied. "Bet it's another false alarm."

"My thoughts, too." A pause proceeded. "Break time. Let's check and see if the coffee's fresh."

Their footsteps ricocheted, fading further until she no longer heard them. The evening became eerily quiet. Remaining still, she listened for anything odd, but only hums of night creatures and an occasional car speeding down the main street sounded.

Noise dynamics altered within an instant. Voices rang boisterously, coming from the direction of the building, and advanced her way. Teddie stained to hear. Two males, but not guards. Younger.

Their chatter continued even after they arrived at the truck. Doors opened and closed. Within seconds, the motor roared. Tires squealed as they sped out of the lot onto a single lane, leading away from the facility.

The road was full of curves and bends, Teddie had to grip the flanks to avoid being hurled out.

They traveled the highway about ten miles when their speed slowed. The driver pointed the nose onto a graveled road and once again hit the gas. The wide tires kicked up clouds of dust and an occasional rock exploded inside the truck's bed. Pot holes were frequent, although the driver didn't bother to dodge the ruts. The constant bouncing sent Teddie sailing in the air and gravity counteracted by slamming her down, hard enough to rattle her jaw. Her hat flew off her head and disappeared into the darkness.

They turned onto a sandy path. The vehicle rocked back and forth as if confined amidst a tidal wave. Teddie felt nauseous but silently conceded queasy was an improvement over airborne. Finally, they skidded to a halt. The engine was turned off, doors clicked ajar, and clapped shut as footsteps pounded the earth.

"Damn, Chase," howled one of the riders. "Marshall looked awful, didn't he?"

"Tell me, Daniel," the other retorted. "Face's cut up like someone took a steak knife to him, and did you see his teeth?"

"Teach him not to drink and drive."

The duo shared a chuckle. "Maybe he's educated, but we're not."

"Let's toast to our fallen man's honor."

"You brought beer?"

"Yeah, I did, jerk."

"Awesome possum. Let's roll. And don't call me jerk."

The youngsters dug into the backseat to retrieve their beverages and quickly vanished, not once examining their truck bed for possible stowaways. Their prattle interlaced with laughter continued as they partied further away.

Teddie peered above the frame. Except for their distant voices, she was alone. She sat and cast an eye over the region. They'd driven her into a thickly treed piece of land, undoubtedly a teen haunt. Gentle breezes exhaled amid the trees as the moist tang of sea filled her nostrils.

In the forest, next to water. She might be anywhere near the outskirts of Jacob's Cove. She threw a leg across the back and jumped to the ground. Silently, she circled to the passenger side and gently pulled the door handle.

"Yes," she whispered as it gave way.

A rapid exploration of the cab's insides produced a small flashlight. She slid the control to on, nodded as the diminutive bulb beamed, then eased the door shut.

Unsure of her next step, she wandered around the truck. Her only other option was to campout, but she lacked equipment.

She preferred not to hang around here. Maneuvering past dense trees and clusters of brush, Teddie scrounged to locate a trail, using the tiny sliver of light to front her. Scents of dirt and cedar fumigated as insects noisily twittered off key, bringing the night to life. A random wail howled above the winds and provided a trace of unwanted eeriness.

Her stolen flashlight didn't give off much light. Although the moon soared overhead, foliage took over and shaded her view, obstructing her ability to discover a decent trail. After what seemed like hours, she emerged out of the woodlands, coming upon a glistening cove.

She trekked the inlet's border. The night had calmed, and the lone sound was her shoes crackling beneath grassy firth. Extremely tired, she rested while she admired the silvery glow, shimmering across the water. It had been a long time since she viewed the cove during the night hours, but the beauty hadn't changed.

A loud snap shattered behind her. She hesitated and flickered a glance across the surroundings. Nothing. She started to walk again but abruptly stopped. Hair on the back of her neck stood on end. Another odd noise rustled in the middle of the stillness.

Instincts told her, she had company. Without a thought, she broke into a run, racing toward a line of trees. Fingertips grazed her skin shadowed by a large, warm hand clinching her forearm, and hauled backward. The light flew from her grasp. Her heart whammed into her ribcage as a scream jammed inside her throat.

Her captor twirled her to face them, using added force.

"I might've known," said a raspy voice.

Teddie suspended her struggle and squinted as her eyes adjusted to the dimness. "Drew?"

One of the last people she wanted or expected to run into.

"Who else? Now, why are you out roaming the woods at night?"

"I needed some fresh air," she responded coldly, wiggling out of his gasp.

"I thought you were still in the hospital."

"They released me."

"When?" Drew moved farther into the moonlight. His expression was irritated, which matched the harshness in his intonation.

Clamping her mouth closed, Teddie stomped away.

"Teddie?" Drew trailed her, keeping close behind. "Why aren't you in the hospital?"

"The staff and my sister insist on keeping me in a coma. I happen to wake up on accident. I declared myself healed and checked myself out."

"You checked yourself out? When did you get a medical degree? Thought your profession was singing?"

Teddie snapped an angry scowl his way although he probably couldn't see it. "Did you follow me? Because I'm not going back to that prison disguised as a clinic."

"No, I did not follow you." He spun and wandered into a dim cavity located amongst a tree grove. "What's your plan now that you've escaped?" he queried from the darkness. "That's what happened, right? They don't know you've left?"

She stared at the ocean.

"Okay, fine. Don't tell me. Come over here and sit. You probably need rest."

Her first thought was to tell him to go to hell, but she was tired, and a breather might not be a bad idea. She tracked his steps into the gloom until an outline of a tent materialized. Drew already relaxed on a log.

She paced farther in and sank to the ground, far away from him, sitting on a layer of pine needles carpeting the terrain.

"How did you breakout?"

She lobbed another heated glare. Not information

she intended on sharing, since she may need to repeat her actions later.

He laughed at her avoidance. "Fine. Keep your little secret, but you might ought to consider returning."

"Why would I after I went to such trouble to leave."

"Ah, you're confessing. You may want to go back because the world knows you've been hospitalized. You won't find a place to hide."

"You know what? I don't care."

"You're mad at me because of my part in your intervention."

"No, more like furious. You betrayed me."

"I'm sorry you're hurt, but you needed medical assistance, and you refused to get help."

"I'm not a doctor, but you are?" Teddie cut a glare at him. "Thanks for the blindside."

"I didn't arrange anything."

"You didn't contact my sisters and Nash to put together a trap?"

"Yes and no. I did call your sisters to tell them you were having major hallucinations and about the empty medicine bottle. But Aubrey was the mediation organizer. Seriously, you think I'd invite Nash Sewell?"

"You were still involved."

"Because I was worried. You were saying some crazy shit."

"You can choose not to believe me, but everything I said, happened. One day you'll say you're sorry for your participation."

"If it gets to that point, I will fall down on my knees and beg your forgiveness. Until then, you ought to be under a doctor's supervision."

"I disagree, and I reject the idea of going back."

"You never said where you're planning to go?"

"Why are you camping?" Teddie challenged.

"For now, this is my home." Drew raked his fingers through his hair. "I'm living here till I can relocate."

"You moved out your house?"

"Kinda. Evie threw me out." He flashed a smile. "I didn't fight her much."

A minor elation erupted, and Teddie momentarily forgot she was mad.

"She'll be ready to fight me after the divorce papers are delivered."

"You're no longer married?"

"Nope. I'm a free man. I warned her, but she didn't believe me."

"I thought you planned to hold off."

"Changed my mind."

Teddie met Drew's gaze, trying to keep the moment in perspective. "Wow, I'm stunned. What's next for you?"

"As soon I can get details settled with my cousin about the business, I'm heading to east Texas. My dad has a sister firm, and since he and Mom are getting older, they could use extra help."

"You won't do anything with your music if you move there. Your talent will die."

"Bars are everywhere, and I can still write songs. People in that type of venue appreciate artists more, anyway."

She disagreed but let his comment slide. "What about Savannah?"

"She has to let me know what she expects. Does

she just want meet, or is she more interested in a father-daughter relationship?" He raised a shoulder. "She and I need to talk."

Teddie scanned the perimeters anxious for a subject change. Even in the dark, she detected a familiarity about his campsite. Then it dawned on her. She eyed Drew, elevating her brows. "Are we…?"

"At our old hangout. Kind of a special place." He twisted to her and grinned. "For me, anyway."

Teddie suppressed a smile. "I treasure our time here, too."

The location sat on the border of what once was Drew's family property. Situated on the water, full of pines and tall weeds, he discovered his sanctuary when he first came to Jacob's Cove as a teenager. He introduced Teddie to his retreat not long after they began to date.

"Lots of memories here," he murmured.

Her pulse fluttered, but Teddie didn't respond. This wasn't a good time to journey down memory lane.

He gestured toward his shelter, wisely sidestepping the old days. "Bedroll's inside. Food too, if you're hungry."

Teddie studied the moon floating high in the sky, suspicious of his sudden compliance. "I refuse to return the hospital if that's your idea," she vowed in a soft timbre. "I need to stay hidden until I find a ride to getaway."

"To go where? I'll remind you again, you're famous, and your face is plastered on the internet, TV gossip shows, and magazine covers. It's not like you can vanish or hide. Someone will recognize you."

"I've managed anonymity in the past. I'll do it

again."

"You managed because you had support." He glimpsed at her sideways. "You're by yourself, now."

"You won't help me."

"Teddie." He drew her name out. "There's nothing in this world I wouldn't do for you, but the problems you're dealing with," he paused, rising to his feet. Treading to her, he extended a hand. "Let's get some sleep and talk more tomorrow."

Teddie ignored his offer. "I'm not receptive to your negations. My minds made up."

Stooping forward, he circled his fingers around her wrist, and tugged. "Come on. We'll figure this out in the morning."

Her wrist went limp. "If you intend to convince me to go back to that place, this conversation is over."

Without a word, he freed her arm, snatched the ends of his shirt, and jerked it over his head.

Teddie's eyes widened. "What are you doing?"

"Going to bed." He tossed the tee aside. His features were blank, but a wicked twinkle entered his eyes. "Been a long day, and I'm washing off before I turn in."

She gulped as she drank in the perfect contours of his bare chest and broad shoulders. Her gaze drifted back to his face. Their eyes locked.

His lips curved up, slow and easy. "What's on your mind?"

Teddie struggled to speak as seventeen years of pent up desire promptly devoured her.

His worn jeans top button unsnapped and the zipper parted. The pants slid to his ankles, exposing a pair of muscular legs.

The interior of Teddie's mouth moistened.

He stepped out of his jeans, kicked them off, and strolled to the water's edge. There, his boxers dropped to the ground. With a glance over his shoulder, he knowingly smirked and dove into the inlet.

Chapter 26

Her annoyance diminished, and her heart assaulted her ribcage. Desire quivered and propelled as heat saturated her belly. The warmth spiraled downward, settling into the apex of her core, intensifying her hunger.

His skin glistened in the pale moonlight as he dolphined among the pond's ripples. He paddled to the bank and lay on his stomach, his firm backside visible in the shifting moonbeams.

Propped on his elbows, he beamed knowingly. "Enjoying the show?"

She didn't reply, unable to tear her eyes away from the liquid drops shimmering down his pecs.

"Come on, Teddie. What's so captivating?" His naughty grin didn't waver. "You keep ogling the cove, like you're absorbed with the view. Something interest you?"

She gulped. "I was just…thinking."

"About what? Anything you'd like to share?"

"I don't remember."

"Maybe you need to clear your head."

She slightly smiled. "According to you, and the rest of the world."

"The water's great. You should come in."

"I didn't bring a suit. I'd have to go without clothes, and I'm not comfortable with the scenario.

Unless, you plan to leave and let me bathe alone."

He chuckled. "Not a chance."

"There you go. We shouldn't even consider the thought, and you know why."

His eyes twinkled in the moonlight as he challenged her. "I do?" he taunted, daring her to accept.

"The universe and *you,* say I'm crazy, so I'm not inclined to swim with you."

"You worry too much about things that aren't important."

"My sanity isn't important?"

"You're cute when you're irrational."

"I'm not. Besides, I'm not understanding where you are in your marriage. Are you officially done or just in the process? Unless a judge's signature is on the paperwork, you're legally married."

"Legal, schmegal. We're over. I made sure we're through."

He pushed off the ground and squatted, exposing his entire frontal region. Teddie groaned. This man may've put her through hell, but physically he was sheer perfection.

Splashing drops across his forearms and torso, he washed off, then hopped to his feet and unabashedly strolled past Teddie into his camp. Moments later, he returned wearing a pair of blue running shorts, and carried a manila envelope.

"Here." He unwound a string holding the flap in place. "A judge signed off on my divorce yesterday. My marriage is over." He removed the papers and extended them.

Teddie accepted the documents and read. The words were blurred and hard to examine in the dimness, but the moon beamed enough light to comprehend the meaning. Drew was no longer married.

She lifted her head and stared into his eyes. The pages tumbled from her grasp. Drew bent and netted the stack before hitting the ground. He tossed them inside the tent.

He shot her another wicked grin. "We used to have fun skinny dipping."

A small smile warmed her lips as she studied her shoes.

"We always had a good time together. Writing songs, playing the crowds, sneaking off to make our own private excitement."

"I don't need a reminder, Drew. I haven't forgotten a minute."

"Maybe we ought to make new memories or a one time for old times."

She shook her head. "I can't. We can't."

"Fine. You win," he conceded. "Go for a swim. You'll sleep better than you have in months, after. I'll wait here." He held up a hand. "Promise."

"You'll watch me, swim? Naked?"

"A sacrifice, I know, but I'm willing to make it."

She scanned the pond. Aches she developed from her trip, throbbed. The idea of a soak was inviting. "I don't need you to babysit me."

"What if you get a cramp or caught in an undertow and need me to rescue you?"

"I'm a strong swimmer and cramps never bothered me."

She peered at the alluring pool again and rose to her feet. Drew stepped closer. Pure masculinity radiated off his bare skin. She fought the urge to trace her fingertips across his muscles, but if she stroked him, she'd lose the battle, and attack.

His gaze traveled the contours of her figure, taking his time at each curve. Shivers of heat swathed her. Teddie glanced at his face. His smirk indicated he was aware of the temptation he aroused.

The memory of the intervention, her hospital visit, and his part in putting her there brought her to her senses. She backed away. "Forget it. You're not charming your way into my jeans. Especially after you helped initiate my stay in a psych ward."

"I understand why you're upset, and I'm the cause."

"How'd you feel if you were me?"

"Like you. Hurt and deceived." He observed her, his face displayed sadness. "I didn't intend for the outcome to end the way it did. I never wanted you committed."

Teddie took off her jacket. "But you didn't stop them?"

"Not my call, although I did try. Aubrey and I argued long after you'd been admitted. I was told since I wasn't family, I had no say." His face flushed. "Apparently, being the father to one of your children doesn't qualify as a relation."

"I won't go back."

"So you said."

"You think I should."

"I'd feel better if you were under a doctor's care, but it's your choice, and not my main issue."

"Your main issue?"

Drew walked to her and brushed a soft kiss across her cheek. "We're both available for the first time in seventeen years. I want to make the dream I've held onto, come true."

"What's your dream?"

"To spend the rest of my life with you."

She withdrew out of his range. "Even if I'm a loony tune?"

"I love you. I always have. Your tune doesn't matter to me. My feelings will never change."

He reached for her, but she ducked to avoid him. She shook her head and smacked a palm onto his damp chest. Heat seared her skin.

She couldn't withdraw.

He seized her shoulders and squeezed. "Let this happen."

A large, cool hand slid to her backbone to seal the gap between them. A hissed escaped as his nakedness seared past her clothing and into her flesh.

This time, she couldn't tell him no.

His head dropped to lightly caress her mouth with his. Fingers plunged into the softness of her hair, their kisses instantly became urgent, each greedily consuming the other. Angling his hips, he surged his swollen erection into the junction of her thighs, delivering her an indisputable message. He intended to have her.

She molded her breasts to his chest. Without breaking apart, they sank to the ground, their fiery tongues entangled as he laid her back. His knee nudged and urged her legs to open to fit his solid length into her jeans. Nestling closer, he nibbled her neck and nipped up to her earlobe.

Powerless to delay any longer, Teddie prodded him away, sat up, and bunched the bottom of her t-shirt and tugged it over her head, flinging it aside. She stretched toward the rear to unhook her bra.

"Let me help you."

Before she protested, he twisted her around. Fiery pressure grazed her skin as he unhurriedly mastered the fasteners. Deft fingers traced over her silky shoulders, lowering the straps down her arms until her upper torso was completely nude.

He turned her to face him, taking his time to visually devour her. His eyes sparkled in delight. Like a kid in a toy store, he couldn't keep away and skimmed his fingertips, teasing her nipples into taut points.

Teddie emitted an uncontrollable shudder as his gentle swirls flourished into wild strokes. Ravenously, he lowered his head and claimed her mouth once more. Fingers continued to massage each mound, taking time out to knead her rosy peaks. Without warning, he broke free and glided his tongue over her neck trailing to her chest, eagerly clutching his lips onto a nipple with a forceful draw.

She arched and groaned while he surrounded her breast with his mouth and sucked hard, while cupping the other into his palm. He shifted to suckle the other side, showering her breasts with his attentiveness.

Unable to wait any longer, she clasped her knuckles behind his neck, bringing his face to hers and captured his mouth. He spread her legs wider and settled over her body. He thrust his rock hardness into her moistening denims.

Her calves bound around and squeeze his middle as she instinctively elevated, brazenly shoving her core into his firmness, wishing her pants would magically vanish. She needed him to enter her and if it didn't take place soon, she feared she'd burst.

He felt the same. Abruptly, he rolled away, long enough to undo and peeled off her blue jeans and panties. He cupped her labia as she opened farther to give him total access. Positioning his fingers, he slipped his fingertips into her wet, tender folds, while his thumb located her sensitive spot above.

Teddie breathed in and held it. Her muscles tensed, her tremble contrasted against his feathery caress. The building force within her was incredible. Screams long to escape. She yearned for him, needing him in her this instant.

"Drew," she panted. "Now."

"Not yet," he teased. Then he took her fist and guided her to the top button of his shorts. Without further instruction, Teddie urged his fly to divide, and eased them downward.

"I need some attention, too."

Her fingers coiled around his throbbing cock and pulsed. He released a soft exhale. His breathing grew choppy as she pumped. He remained conscious enough to reposition his hand smoothly back into her center, re-launching two fingers inside her clit.

Fortunately, it didn't take long, before he flattened her on her back. Teddie gripped his biceps and elevated her lower body, impatient for his insertion. Braced above her, Drew sank down and, pierced into her. Her interior muscles constricted, embracing his intrusion. But he didn't stir.

"Drew?" Teddie gasped.

"I need a moment," he rasped, tracing a fingertip across her jawline. "If I move, everything will be over, and that's not what we want."

"No, we don't."

Slowly, he began to shift. He swept his lips across hers and completely submerged into her once more. He expelled a long moan, plunging deeper. Their mutual hunger ignited and flowed, their entwined bodies pulsed, grinding in a rhythmic dance.

A turbulent explosion stirred. Teddie's spine arced as she raised her hips and froze. The world faded. Squeezing him tight, she threw back her head, shut her eyes, murmuring a quiet cry as she hauled him to her. She buried her face into his chest and shuddered against him.

A sigh discharged, and she relaxed.

Drew breathed a satisfied noise and crumpled on top of her. Both lay still. The only sound was their panting breaths. Finally, he rolled off her, gathering her in his arms. She curled next to him as they lay content, in a sleepy haze.

"I missed you," he murmured.

"I missed you, too."

"Do you know how long I imagined this?"

"I can guess."

"It doesn't seem like anything's different." Drew nuzzled her ear. "Just as if you went on vacation, and now you're here with me."

"Right," she agreed attempting to keep the doubt out of her tone. "I've come home."

Chapter 27

Daniel tottered along the rocky coastline, his arms held straight out to the side. Tilting to the left, he caught himself before he toppled into the mud.

"Watch it," warned a laughing Chase.

"Nothing to watch. I'm great." Daniel dragged his sneakers in the frothy spray. "Correction. I'm better'n great. I'm drunnnnk."

"Still, you oughta be careful. Sinkholes are scattered along the cove. People are swallowed up and *never seen again.*"

"Stock 'em with a lifetime supply of Bud, n' I won't care." Daniel displayed a partial-filled can. "Didya see Marshall's teeth?"

"How could I miss 'em? You think he'll get fake ones?"

"Oh man, how much would that suck." He swigged his beverage and swallowed loud. "What time is it?"

"You worried Breena or her deputies will find you're out after curfew." Chase chuckled. "Drunk off your ass?"

"Nope. Don't care if Breena or her dumbutties see me." Daniel tilted his drink upward and planted his foot onto the shifting sands. The ground gave way where he stepped. He slipped and stumbled, splashing into shallow seawater. His beer sailed out of his grasp. "What the fuck?"

Chase howled. "How wasted are you, dude? Or did you drop into a sinkhole?"

Daniel jabbed his hand into the water. "Shit," he shrieked. Instantly sober, he crab-crawled onto land, and leaped to his feet, ogling the dark object. "You got a light on your phone?"

"What happened to yours?"

"Do you have a fucken' flashlight on your phone?" Daniel shouted.

Chase's hand glided to his rear pocket and plucked out his cell. "Chill, man. I made up the shit about the sinkholes."

Daniel pointed to a mound washed onto the coastline. "Shine it there."

"Why the attitude, man? You trip over a dead body?"

"I think so."

"No way. Bet it's just a whale or dolphin."

"Giant fish don't grow hair, man."

Chase advanced, pointed the dim glow where his friend indicated. "Holy crappola."

The two teens glanced at each another, and then they gawked at the motionless form partly submerged on the sand.

"In-fucking-sane."

"What'll we do?" Chase squeezed his phone, still directing the ray across the lifeless body.

"Alert the sheriff, I guess."

"And let 'em find out we're drinking? You fucking nuts? Breena's always hunting to find a reason to ride my ass. I'm not givin' her another one. She'll toss my butt in jail…" Chase hesitated. "She's gonna blame us for this, isn't she?"

Daniel shrugged. "Probably."

"Hell, I don't want to be hauled off to the slammer."

"Don't call, then." Daniel backed away. He gathered his soaked t-shirt and twisted the water from the material.

"Not cool, jerk."

"I don't give a shit. All I want is alcohol and ditch these wet clothes. Rinse the death smell off me."

"We can't just walk away." Chase aimed a forefinger toward the body. "Something's very wrong, here."

"They're dead, and I stink. So yeah. Something's wrong on both counts."

Chase scanned the quiet bay. "Remember that singer claimed she witnessed someone die at the Phoenix. I wonder if this is that person."

"Don't know, don't care. I just wanna get the fuck outta here."

Chase shined the beam closer. "But this's history. A bonified homicide." He chuckled. "Ha. Made a rhyme."

"Chase, your imaginations shifted into overdrive, plus you drank too much. I'd wager that's this person's problem, too. They either fell off a cliff or tripped and hit their head and drowned." Daniel slowed to swipe up the can he'd lost earlier. "Murdered, *sheesh*. Nobody's killed in Jacob's Cove."

"Check the face, man. It's all screwed up. I mean, can you even tell who this is?"

"I can't, and I don't care to."

"You're not even a bit curious?"

"No, Chase, apparently dead bodies don't hold the

same fascination for me as they do you." Daniel shook his head. "And no one's been murdered, so quit talking about it."

"I disagree, but you're too shitfaced to argue."

"True." Daniel flung his empty into the sea and rotated away. "But I'm finding a new spot to party. One that isn't a graveyard."

"You want to leave?"

"Chase, my friend. My idea of fun isn't hanging with the dead. Ever. I'm gone."

"Shit." Chase waded amid the mild breakers, until attaining the beach, then he hurried to catch Daniel. "I'll call the cops. Let 'em know anonymously. They won't take me seriously if I'm the one doing the reporting."

"You do that," Daniel expressed. "Hey Chase. Did you see Marshall's teeth?"

****

"Can you believe this?" Evie stormed into Nash's office and slapped a stack of stapled papers onto his desk.

"What's *this*?"

"*This* came in my mail."

Nash frowned. "Again, what is this?"

"My divorce decree. My asshole attorney sent the packet here. To my work." Evie huffed. "In a certified envelope. Drew ended our marriage without me knowing. And I just set up an interview with a reporter to tell all. Lot of good that'll do me."

Nash expelled a smoke cloud and stabbing his smoldering cigar into an ashtray placed nearby. He retrieved Evie's paperwork and studied. "Drew warned you." He chuckled, laying her forms aside.

Seething, Evie's pale skin transformed to a deep crimson as the interiors of her chest tensed. This man was the love of her life, and she assumed he'd stay by her side, yet he considered it amusing her husband tricked her.

"You think this is funny?"

"Not the circumstances, but I do find it humorous Drew actually carried out his plan. I didn't figure he had the balls to follow through."

"Well, he evidently does." Evie leaned upon the corner edge of Nash's desk. "Bastard."

"Perhaps. But the documents appear legit and legal."

"My law team's incompetent." She orbited a chair and sank into the seat. Nash didn't respond. He lifted his brows, glimpsed at her, then resumed his work. "Should I still go through with the interview?"

"No, you should've abandoned the idea once Breena revealed those photos of us."

"But if the public's aware—"

"Evie, no. You attempt this stunt, yours and my entanglement will become known. It's in both our interest to leave the situation alone. Drew did you a favor by ending your nuptials swiftly and *quietly*."

"Without notice."

"He informed you of his intentions two years ago."

"I'm not ready to enter singlehood."

"Too late, I'm afraid." Nash shot an odd glance in her direction. "Isn't there a fundraiser this evening?"

"I just found out I'm divorced. I'm not in a foundation-y kind of mood."

"I'm sorry, Evie, I truly am. Now, if you'll excuse me, I must go back to work."

"Excuse you?" Her internal hackles rose. Nash had been awfully unavailable, lately. Almost as if he were dodging her. She wouldn't consent to his blatant dismissal. "I came to tell you my dilemma, hoping you'd provide a speedy solution."

"And I gave you one. We've completed our conversation, and I have stacks of reports requiring my immediate attention."

"I've hardly seen you all week. You haven't phoned nor did you respond to my calls."

"I replied to your texts messages."

"In one-word responses." Her eyes narrowed suspiciously. "What's going on?"

Nash's jaw stiffened. "I'm dealing with my own issues and don't have time to dally in your trivial disputes."

"My matters are far from trivial."

"Compared to mine, they are." He pulled the upper drawer ajar, removed another cigar, and positioned it between his lips. A lighter laid within arm's reach. He snatched and flicked, floating the flame beneath until the fire took hold. After inhaling several puffs, he blew out a feather of smoke and then laid his stogie in the corner of his ashtray. "My wife knows about us."

Evie gasped. "Did Breena notify her? Or Drew? He's behind the pictures by the way."

"I suspected he was. As for Celia, I'm not sure who informed her. She won't talk to me." He bowed his head. "She will, however, text and she advised me she'd become aware of our—friendship, and she has issued me an ultimatum." His eyes bore into Evie's. "Leave you or she'll leave me."

A ripple of excitement veered through Evie. She

and Nash would finally publicly unite. "Get ready. Once the word spreads you're single, Jacob's Cove's casserole brigade will be parading in, blabbing their fake condolences, and wave their newest, homemade mac and cheese concoctions under your nose."

"Casserole brigade?"

"Unattached women. Competition is fierce. They'll bake tasty delights, do your laundry, clean your house, and comfort you in your time of need. Eventually, you'll have a lineup of potentials, and you'll be expected to choose the one."

"The one?"

"The next Mrs. Doctor Sewell." She drove a thumb into her chest. "Only, I'm first in line. Even though I don't cook." She giggled. "At least, not in the kitchen."

"We need to talk, Evie." He fidgeted as if to find the words. "I'm considering relocating. Away from Jacob's Cove."

Evie's exhilaration nosedived.

"Celia and I decided to make a new start. In another city."

"Oh, you have? Just where does that leave us?"

He peeked at her, his face uncertain. "At an impasse?"

"At a dead end, you mean."

"I fear so." His bland expression altered to miserable, while his tone lowered to solemn. "My intuition isn't strong as a woman's, but I'm worried you and I are near exposure, and I don't want to embarrass Celia."

"So, I take the fall by myself?"

"Your choice. You can disappear, too."

"Only if I chose to leave, I'll go my way and you

and Celia will go the other. You're not extending an invitation for me to accompany you."

"The experience was wonderful, our time together, superb, but this is life, Evie. Our relationship ran its course and reached its conclusion."

"Especially after your wife found you out and can jerk the financial rug from under your feet."

"It isn't the money. Celia's discovery forced me to reevaluate my life. I feel we need to make a new start."

"Without me," she restated, wanting him to squirm.

"Reluctantly yes, Evie. Without you."

Evie stood and smoothed her palms across her skirt. "I suppose we're done."

"I appreciate your understanding."

She rambled toward the exit.

"I'll never forget you."

Evie had stretched an arm toward the knob, freezing at his final words. She turned around. Getting dumped twice within hours was enough to incite rebellion. But his abandonment didn't provoke her agitation. No, the definitive blow was the obvious relief that dominated his features.

"Do you need anything else, Evie?"

A Bacchantes vase filled with fresh flowers decorated a lightweight stand next to the doorway. Celia had purchased the pricey adornment and insisted housekeeping switch flowers every other day.

Evie smiled, tracing a fingertip across a shiny, emerald leaf. "No. I'm just experiencing a *slight* touch of rage."

She swung her foot to kick one of the table legs, tipping it off balance. Blossoms, urn, and support collapsed. Glass exploded and water expanded, saturating the floor.

"Oh, yes," she yelled, adding a fist pump. "That helped."

"Evie." Nash vacated his seat and bolted. His hands were thrust ahead to protect his body as he circled the desk and scurried to her. "Let's be reasonable…"

Utilizing the spear of her stilt-like high heel, she wagged the toe of her shoe back and forth, grounding buds into the tiles.

"I am behaving reasonable," she maintained through clenched teeth. "You're lucky the vase wasn't your head."

He slanted forward and attempted to grab her, but she reacted quickly and ducked. She rushed to a massive credenza situated on a far wall and straight-armed across the base. Family photos and their expensive frames slammed down hard. More glass tinkled and splintered.

"You made me a promise, now your wife knows, and you go running back to her with your tail between your legs. You're a coward, Nash Sewell."

"She'll take away my children."

Books soared from the shelves. Loud thumps echoed as they collided with the wall, then clapped loudly as they plummeted to the ground.

"Evie. Stop. The cleaning crew will complain about the mess."

"I don't give a rat's ass about the cleaning crew."

She reared back, ready to lob another hardcover, but Nash snatched her wrist and seized the volume from her grip. "You're acting like a mad woman."

She wrangled out of his clutches, grabbed another

thick edition, and chucked it at another one of Celia's special treasured lamps.

"I am a *mad* woman."

Nash's arms encircled her, wrapping her in a secure embrace. "Evie, settle down."

Evie braced and fought his hold, unable to break free.

"You're right," she wheezed. "I'll quit."

Nash released her and examined the room.

"Sorry, Nash. I went a bit crazy." She adjusted her blouse. "It's all good, now."

"Unfortunately, my belongings are not. You wrecked my office." He marched to the door and jerked it open. "Goodbye, Evie."

Evie sidestepped broken glass and other damaged items as she walked to the exit. He was dismissing her, like she was yesterday's garbage. Had he not learned anything in the past five minutes?

She paused at the doorway to fluff her hair, then tapped one of his framed diploma's hanging on the wall, enough to disengage the mount from its support. It shimmied down emitting a low rumble against the sheetrock, hooking the remaining pictures so they all crashed to the floor.

Evie's hands flew to her cheeks. "Oh my, Nash." She sported a wicked smile. "I guess the crazy wasn't gone, after all."

Chapter 28

"We should create a plan." Teddie gave her shoestring an exaggerated yank as she finished tying her sneaker.

Drew shot a grin her way as he slipped his jeans over his hips, working to secure his zipper. "A plan to do what?"

"To prove I'm not insane or addle-brained because of prescription drug use."

"Any ideas?"

"Maybe." She scrambled to her feet. "Due to my hospital visit, I was away from my parents' house a long time. I hired a service to scour the interiors. Hopefully, they did what I paid them to do."

Drew transferred his attention to the rippling cove ahead. Morning mist hovered above the wavy surface as the vapors elevated and faded into nothingness. Kinda like this this conversation. "I'm lost. I don't understand how a clean house will substantiate your wellness."

"If the workers completed their job, I can move forward with my concept." She stopped and inhaled as if she were ready to make a huge announcement. "I want to install video cameras on the inside and outside of the property."

"Why, exactly?"

Teddie regarded him anxiously. "I'm wondering if

someone is setting me up."

"Setting you up?" He found a dried leaf and crunched it between his fingers. "As in somebody's giving you the drugs without your knowledge?"

She gave a hesitant nod.

"You ingested a lot of pills, Teddie. Too many can cause hallucinations. You can't rule yourself out."

Her face flushed pink, but her jaw tightened with certainty. "Except, I didn't intentionally take any medications." He opened his mouth to protest, but she didn't give him an opportunity to speak. "Hear me out. Exhaustion's been coming on a while, but I didn't require anything extra. I got along fine without using the pain killers prescribed. My nightmares are the norm and have been since my parents died, but the images, sounds, and smells didn't start until my return to Jacob's Cove."

Drew peered through a tiny clearing and studied the flawless, azure sky above. He struggled to sort through her logic. "You're dealing with a lot. Entwined with your tiredness, you might've gone over the edge without realizing it."

His theory was met with a span of silence. Only a trickle of water, disturbed the quiet, and later an animal darted inside the brush, rustling dry leaves, and plopped into the water.

"You won't consider the possibility, will you?"

He observed her. A soft, but cool wind swept among the pines and lifted her long hair off her shoulders, and his attention temporarily deviated. The lovely sight had him thinking about tangible fantasies of her naked and beneath him, like he had her all night.

A buzzing insect invading his ear snapped him

back to reality.

Not the time to venture there.

Drew didn't agree an unseen force wanted to harm her, but he had to keep her moving until she accepted her problem.

"Okay, Teddie. Say you're right. How? Who?"

"I can't answer you," Teddie finally confessed. "But I'm standing by what I believe. You won't change my mind. Somebody is messing with my head, which is why I will purchase the cameras and hire an installer. I intend to trap whoever is trying to ruin me."

He wouldn't win this one. She made her decision and would stick to her beliefs until validation was shoved under her stubborn nose. He peeked at her. And maybe not even then.

"Every movement in your house will be recorded. What happens if you manage to obtain evidence? You can't confront this individual."

She knelt to flatten the sleeping bag and rolled it up. "Why not?"

"If another person is drugging you, then they're a threat. You attempt to catch them in action, your circumstances become more dangerous."

The realization across her face almost broke him. Her focus was so centered on proving she wasn't an addict, other possibilities hadn't occurred to her. If her speculations were true, she had a frightening enemy.

"I never thought about that, but you're right."

"Yes, I am. If someone's sneaking you mickeys, they aren't doing it for fun. They mean to hurt you or do you and your career major damage." Drew paused as an ominous chill ran across his spine. "Their intent might be to shut you down. For good."

Scrambling to her feet, she dusted her denimed knees. "I've been subjected to fanatics and stalkers since I became famous, but it's never been this serious."

"Crazies have followed you in the past? Did you document every intrusion?"

"Threats are part of the biz. And yes, Aubrey and the police keep records of them all."

"All?"

"Stalkers, disgruntled fans, even a few competitors."

Drew's heart went rigid, nearly stopping. He never considered someone off balanced shadowing Teddie, but the scenario arose often with many celebrities, and the prospect just became very real.

"I'm acquainted with a guy who stocks surveillance material. I can do the instillations. You'd run a risk if you employed a stranger who might not care about your safety and spill to reporters about the work he's done."

A small smile tugged at her lips as her face brightened.

"Let's drive into town find food, because I'm sure you're starving, and once our bellies are filled, we'll drop by his store."

"I hope this will work."

"Me too. If we discover you're right, we'll contact and show the data to Breena. Let her handle the trouble."

Teddie leaped and flung herself into his arms, melding her body into his. Every nerve ending yearned as his desires saturated him. Heated cravings loomed, threatening to overpower and strip them both naked, and allow nature to take control.

Only sex was not an option.

He fought to clear his head while his mind struggled with his libido. Disengaging, Drew moved out of temptations range.

He aimed a glimpse toward Teddie. "We have lots of work ahead. We ought to head out."

She stepped in front of him, blocking his way.

"What's the matter?"

"We need to talk. About last night."

He moaned internally. Their evening was a dream come true, and he detested the upcoming discussion, dissecting the why's, when's, and whatever's and ruin the whole night. But if she wanted to talk, then they'd talk.

"What about it?" he asked, not trying to keep the stiffness out of his tone.

"Our relationship took an interesting turn."

"I suppose interesting is a good expression, although I'd say it did more of a U-turn."

Tilting nearer, she skated her hands across his chest. "I wouldn't mind another turnaround before we go." She flashed a seductive smile and backed away, interlacing their fingers. "One more time?"

Drew relaxed and grinned back, taking her into his arms. "How can I say no?"

Thirty minutes later, they traveled the forest, both content and a bit groggy. A hint of late morning sunshine spiked and penetrated the tree-line. A warm glow infiltrated the thickness as a comforted calmness lay silent across the timbered terrain.

Drew's truck appeared far too soon.

"You almost hid it," she marveled as they

approached his mud splattered vehicle.

"I did my best." Two fingers slid into his front pocket to extract a key.

She stood and flickered an uncertain smile. "Can I ask you a question?"

Drew rotated and leaned against the door. "Go ahead."

"We're about to re-enter the real world. What happens, now? Between us."

Unable to resist, he pulled her to him and orbited her around and pinned her to the pickup's side. He buried his face into the softness of her hair. "Whatever happens, I'm here for you. Know that."

"But where are *we* going?"

"Wherever you choose." He nuzzled her velvety mane and moved his lips to trail her jawline until he captured her mouth with his. A tiny moan seeped. Smoothing his hands around her waist, he strengthened his embrace as the kiss deepened. Their bodies meshed closer, desperate to become one, one more time.

He drew away and scouted the woodlands. "How 'bout we can find an empty spot in those trees so we can lie down."

She nodded eagerly. "We only need space for one."

"I like the way you think."

Click. "Gotcha."

They sprang apart. Drew hitched a breath and slowly revolved toward the noise. He froze as his stomach took a plunge off a high dive.

A guy holding a camera stood five feet away.

Teddie released a surprised gasp. Drew's gaze remained glued to the equipment, but he managed a slight motion to the rear as an indication to Teddie to move farther behind him.

"You're Drew Millard, aren't you?" the newcomer inquired.

"None of your business."

"You don't have to tell me. I already know."

Teddie swerved around Drew and marched to the unwelcomed guest. "Hello, Rodney."

Rodney nodded. "Nice to see you, Teddie. You don't seem in as bad of shape as the world's saying."

"What are you doing here?"

"You don't really need to ask, do you?"

"You're wanting a story. Forget it. I don't do random interviews."

"You don't gotta say a word. I got all the info I need."

"Sad way to make a living," Drew stated.

Rodney's eyes narrowed. "You think? Every media outlet is offering top dollar to any photographer who manages to shoot the first pics since her escape with you."

"How much is top dollar?" Teddie inquired.

"Fifty grand." Rodney shifted to reposition his camera. "That's good money, and I'm hurting. Haven't gotten a decent shot all year."

Drew seethed at the bottom feeder who sought to earn money off Teddie and others like her, misfortune. Exposing one's personal life, without confirmed details was not okay in his book, and he craved to pommel the guy. But he took his cue from Teddie, doing his best to preserve his calm.

"I understand your quandary, Rodney," Drew chimed. "But on the flipside, I can't let you peddle those pictures to the highest bidder."

"Who's gonna stop me?"

"I am." Drew straightened his frame and crossed his arms over his chest. "This is private property, and you interrupted a private moment."

"Privacy doesn't matter much to me. I'm after the cash, and I'll do whatever it takes to get it." A malicious expression spread across his face as he turned to Teddie. "I'd like to tell you I'm sorry, but I'm delinquent on child support payments, and landlords just increased my rent. It's a survival thing."

"I understand," Teddie sympathized.

"Doubt it. You're loaded. You got no idea how hard it is to hustle a buck in this business."

Teddie placed a palm on Rodney's arm. "What if you earned the income another way? Perhaps by utilizing a more ethical approach?"

Rodney frowned.

"I'll give you an exclusive. Photographs and all." Teddie threw a sharp glare at Drew. "If you let us leave, now."

"Teddie, no," Drew protested, not fond of the course this conversation was taking.

"An exclusive, eh?" Rodney raised the baseball cap he wore to scratch what was left of his graying hair. "Tempting." He refitted his hat, then wiped the sweat off his brow. "But how can I be sure you'll keep your word? We don't got a formal contract."

"And there's no way to draw one up." She briefly pondered. "What if we make arrangements to meet tomorrow? I'll answer any question within reason, and you can snap as many photos as you please. I'll also bring a contract we'll both sign. Another perk, I'm acquainted with every big-time magazine editor and publishing house in the business. Once you're satisfied, I'll email them to inform them you're in possession of the one, true Teddie Donavan story, with prints. Your article will be worth a fortune."

"And if you don't show?"

"If I don't follow through, you can market the pictures you've taken." She smiled charmingly. "Does that sweeten the pot?"

"A little, but you never gave me the time of day, before, so I'm not sure I'm buying what you're selling." He fiddled with his lens. "I could just put out what I have, collect the fee now, and move on."

"Teddie has a ton of attorneys," Drew advised. "You may net enough change to jingle in your pocket today, but she'll sue your ass. You'll never get another paying gig again."

"Not scared of lawyers, dude, plus there are tons of ways to duck lawsuits."

Drew stepped closer to Rodney. "Let me make this simple. Take Teddie's kind offer and forget you saw us."

Rodney jerked at his sparsely, whiskered chin. "Not many choices."

"Your other option is, or else."

"Or else what?

Drew's blood simmered as he glowered at the grinning scumbag. "I don't think you want to find out."

"Threats, dude?" Rodney chuckled. "Just keep yapping. Every word goes in my piece. Don't gotta be official, either." The deliberate smirk on the guy's face begged to be erased. "Dirt sells. The dirtier, the better."

Without thinking, Drew dipped a shoulder and caught their intruder in the chest. Rodney's camera sailed out of his hands. The older, overweight guy fumbled as he strained to grasp his 35mm whirling in the air. The gear suspended a moment and then dropped, landing hard.

Rodney hurled toward Drew. "You son of a bitch."

Instinctively, Drew balled a fist and propelled his arm forward. Rodney's head snapped backward. Blood spewed in every direction. The man toppled to the ground, smacking the surface. He hit his head and knocked him out, cold.

"Great, Drew." Teddie gestured at their unconscious visitor "This will not help me."

"Yeah well, it was him or me, and I preferred it be him." Shaking his punching hand, Drew walked to where Rodney had fallen. He bent and touched his neck. "Still breathing, dammit."

"I suppose that's a positive."

"You and I have a different idea of positive." He stepped over Rodney and swiped up the camera, careful to avoid Teddie's scowl. She'd attempt to redirect him, and he'd made his decision. Bypassing her, he strolled toward a wooded area. "Get into the truck. Don't move until I come back."

"Where are you going?"

"Get inside my truck, Teddie. And don't ask questions."

Chapter 29

Drew directed his truck onto the graveled driveway of Teddie's home. He switched off the engine, removed the key, and boosted the handle.

He glimpsed toward the passenger side before exiting. "What's wrong? You're unnaturally quiet. In fact, you've hardly said a word since we left the woods."

She lifted the lever. "I'm fine."

He stepped outside his pickup, studying the low, dark clouds swirling within the atmosphere. A span of foreshadowed grumbles announced their presents with raucous hostility.

Thunderstorms had riddled the region the past three days. Luckily, the weather stayed clear last night when he and Teddie slept outdoors, but the ominous grayness blanketing the eastern skies indicated the conclusion of mild conditions.

"Do you believe we made a smart decision leaving him? Rodney?" Teddie cut a scowling glance at Drew, then she examined the whirling vapors overhead. "Thunderclouds look mean. Like they're ready to bust. He still may be unconscious and could suffer serious injuries or worse if the cove floods."

Drew stretched and snatched a bag filled with recording equipment and walked to the rear to fetch his tools. Teddie seized another sack and held their meal, snuggling two drinks between her forearm and chest.

Arms loaded, they hurried to seek shelter inside the house. Drew placed the gear on the side table, and wiped his feet on the mat, while Teddie swept past him, carrying their sustenance and cups into the main room. She spread the food onto the coffee table and sank onto the sofa.

Drew sat down next to her. "Us leaving Rodney in the storm bothers you?"

She didn't respond but peeked out of the window. Curtains of rain began to gush inciting large, hard drops to smack the glass.

"I had to find a way to stop him, Teddie. Sleazes like him would sell naked photos of his mother if paid enough. Don't worry. We left hours ago. He's long gone, I'm sure." He snuck a French fry out of their shared jumbo pack and chuckled. "Hopefully with a hell of a headache."

"Rodney's physical state isn't my concern. I mean, it is, but not in the way you think."

"What are you saying?"

"I'm disturbed you punched him to get your point across instead of reasoning with him."

"He wouldn't quit. Would you rather him keep hassling us?" Anxiety tightened in his chest. He should've known this exchange was imminent. Teddie never advocated violence when he defended her in school or during a bar fight.

"I'd *rather* we talk about something else."

"Okaaay," Drew countered, baffled. He searched his brain, attempting to uncover a neutral topic. "Hey, your cleaning crew did a great job. The place almost shimmers."

Teddie surveyed the premises. "It's a huge improvement."

He sniffed the air. "Smells better, too. Wonder how they got rid of the mustiness."

"Airing and lots of scrubbing."

He unfolded his hamburger's wrapping. "Let's eat, so we can install your video recorders."

"Will it take long?"

"There are quite a few to mount. Obviously, we can only set up indoor kits."

A knock pounded on the door.

Alarmed, Drew eyed Teddie, who stared back.

She tore her gaze away and glanced at the doorway. "No one knows we're here, right?"

"We took the backroads into town and used the video store's rear entrance. We were the only vehicle in the drive-through when buying lunch."

Loud rumbles bounced directly above. Teddie looked up at the ceiling. "Can't imagine anyone would want to be out in this nastiness."

Their visitor knocked again.

Drew laid his burger aside and stood. "Might as well end the suspense." He walked to the window and peered out. "Shit."

"What's wrong?"

"Sheriff's car is parked in the drive."

"Breena?" Teddie's voice hitched. "Why is she here?"

"Not sure." Drew traipsed to the doorway and twisted the knob. "Guess we're about to find out."

A dripping Breena strolled inside, not waiting for an invitation. A deputy shadowed behind. Both stomped their feet on the hardwood, shedding water off their slick, black boots.

She entered the living room, removing a hood attached to her dripping raincoat. "Sorry to interrupt your lunch, but we need to chat."

Drew returned to his seat. "Problem?"

"Rodney Guthrie? Name ring a bell?"

Teddie discontinued eating, but Drew ate as if Breena hadn't spoken. He shook his head, stuffing his mouth full of fries. "Nope."

"Come on, Drew. You met him earlier. Cold cocked him and messed up his face?"

"Oh, him. Can't say we really know each other, but I guess you could call us acquainted."

Breena tossed a paper over his half-eaten lunch. "He's filed an assault charge against you."

"What's this?"

"A warrant to arrest you."

"Told you," Teddie taunted softly.

Still chewing, Drew pushed his food away, lifted the document, and read. He should've seen this coming, but he didn't believe the man had big enough balls to accuse him.

Apparently, he was wrong.

"Come on, Breena." Drew threw down the warrant. He picked up his drink, captured his straw with his lips and pulled, then swallowed hard. "The guys below a maggot."

"Not the issue. He said you struck him without provocation. Is that true?"

"No. He harassed Teddie. I protected her."

Breena squinted at Teddie. "Did he try to harm her physically and you reacted?"

"Not at first. We tried to be nice. He rejected the

idea of compliance, so I showed him a way to be more submissive." Teddie cleared her throat. "In a manner of speaking."

"So, you became violent?"

"I prefer the term assertive. I eliminated his resources to continue his project, he charged at me, so I, um, obstructed his advancement."

"You admit to striking him?"

Drew kept silent. He confessed in a roundabout way and wouldn't complicate the matters acknowledging he decked the guy. Only his avoiding a confession wasn't significant.

Breena was an upstanding law-woman. She was here to do her job. If Rodney brought charges against him, she'd follow procedure, and detain him. His lawyer and the district attorney would duke out the specifics, later.

The sheriff bent in half to insure he viewed her dissatisfaction. "Did you also break his camera and dump it into the cove?"

Teddie gasped. "You did what?"

Drew made a face, pleading for her to stay silent. "Don't help me."

"If you destroyed his equipment, then it's your responsibility to replace whatever you ruined." Breena straightened. "I hate to do this. I'm sure Mr. Guthrie got what he deserved, but"—she looked at her partner—"Cuffs and Miranda."

Drew refused to rise. "Dammit, Breena, come on. Don't take me in because some idiot trespassed on private property to take pictures. Isn't there an invasion of privacy law?"

"You're welcome to file suit against him, but it

won't change the outcome of this situation." Breena's phone buzzed. She yanked it out of her pocket, checked the readout, and then replaced it. "Stand up, Drew. This'll go down nasty, but it's your own doing. Be a big boy and take your medicine."

"Can I call Abel?"

"Protocol. We'll take you into town and book you, first. You can contact Abel after."

Teddie leaped to her feet. "Does he have to go to jail?"

"We'll hold him until he's bonded out. It can take up to seventy-two hours before his honor sets an amount," Breena explained. "Move it, Drew. I don't have all day. Another emergency's been called in, and I need to hurry."

A reluctant Drew stood on his feet, turned, and put his hands behind his back. The deputy jerked his arms in alignment. Cold bracelets encircled his wrists, trailed with a decisive click.

His rights were read.

"I'll grab a raincoat." Teddie circled the table and ran toward the stairs. "I can post bond if the judge will decide on a total today."

"Just hold on a minute." Breena snapped up a palm. "I brought help for a reason."

Teddie halted, confused. "I'm under arrest, too?"

"She didn't do anything," Drew protested as his fear welled.

Teddie couldn't manage a jail visit, nor would her career, even if she never set foot inside a cell. He wasn't in the position to assist her, but he'd battle the world to make sure they didn't include her on this little trip.

"Teddie, you're not in trouble with us, per say," Breena clarified. "But you did escape the hospital."

"I released myself."

"Not officially."

"Fine, after Drew's arraignment, I'll head over and sign the necessary forms."

Breena shook her head. "Won't work."

"Why not?"

"When you were admitted, you gave Aubrey power of attorney. Until your doctor declares you well and discharges you, she makes your decisions."

"I don't have a say in what happens to me?"

"Unfortunately, not at this time."

"But you can see I'm fine, Breena."

"My opinion doesn't matter, Teddie. Aubrey has the final word. She wants you sent back to the institution." A crack of thunder exploded and shook the house. "And we're here to make sure that happens."

Chapter 30

"Maybe Teddie Donavon isn't crazy after all."

Breena squinted at the unrecognizable female positioned along the shoreline. Her skin was blanched except for a series of pronounced red splotches dotted across exposed areas. Her hands had wrinkled, the fingers unnaturally knotted after spending a lengthy period submerged into the sea's frigid depths.

"Nobody should be found in such a horrible way," she said in a soft tone to no one.

A forensic team had arrived and lined yellow tape around the gruesome scene's parameters. They'd scattered, their faces stoic as they meticulously collected evidence off the rocky beach. A lone photographer squatted next to the deceased, snapping photos at every angle.

Breena kept out of their way but continued to observe the victim. Two questions hammered her thoughts. Who was this poor woman, and was she the one Teddie Donavon witnessed helped off the pier last weekend?

She circled to face the medical examiner in hopes of obtaining a tiny idea. "Is it too early to tell if marks are on her head, Marty? Like a sign, she may've bumped it or was hit?"

"Nothing I can distinguish, right off. Doesn't mean there aren't any, but head injuries are perplexing at a glance. Especially if the person's been submersed a long time. Wounds occurred prior to immersing will seep after an extensive soak and isn't visible to the naked eye. We also must take in account the gashes we do find could've happened when swift currents dragged her across the ocean's bottom."

The sun was dipping below the horizon and the earlier intense rain triggered a cool breeze to waft off the deep. The duel elements created the unseasonably cold evening.

Breena tugged at her jacket to protect herself against the strong winds. "You believe she's been dead a while?"

"Yep." Marty indicated at the dead woman's neck. "Barnacles attached to her skin, and marine animals nibbled the flesh off her ears and other extremities." He removed a handkerchief and swiped it across his forehead. "Glad I don't do this every day." He took out a recorder and spoke into the speaker. "Subject was discovered floating face up in shallow water. Hands were unclenched, suggesting the victim died before falling into the ocean."

A deputy who just entered the scene, advanced. "I guess that call last night wasn't a hoax."

The coroner toggled off his device and stared at Breena with a startled expression. "Call?"

"A little after midnight an unidentified kid phoned saying they stumbled across a body, but they couldn't pinpoint the location."

"No detective work required to identify the caller. Had to be Chase or Daniel. The line of empty beer cans strung along the shore are a dead giveaway." The newcomer glimpsed at the woman and discharged a lame chuckle. "No pun intended."

"My feelings too." Breena nodded in agreement. "Problem is, you can never tell if those two are for real. They're known pranksters. My first thought was those brats got wind of Teddie's claim and decided to inflate the report as a joke."

"You investigated anyway?" Marty surmised.

"Right. I sent Andre here and two others to scour the coast, particularly near the Phoenix, but thus far they found nada."

"Any idea who this is?" Andre asked in almost a whisper.

"Skin's too discolored to tell. I can't stomach getting much closer to make an educated guess." Breena's attention transferred to the cadaver. "Don't suppose there's a clue as to an exact time of death, Marty?"

"Not until I do a complete autopsy. I'll need to perform one, quickly. The corpse will rapidly deteriorate now it's been subjected to oxygen."

Andre pointed downward. "Is this the spot where she went in?"

"I wondered that too," Breena uttered. "I had the state police bring in equipment to drag the vicinity surrounding the pavilion after a crime was reported. They didn't find anything."

"Not sure. Bodies usually sink shortly after passing and emerge later in the same region. Refloat varies on water temperature. Rains made the sea colder, keeping her under. I'm guessing the storms carried her here. We're lucky she resurfaced. Sometimes they'll remain on the bottom suspended in a state of decomposition until disintegrated."

"Wait a minute." Breena motioned at his recorder. "When you were recording the specifics, you said she was dead before she went into the water. So, she didn't drown?"

"Drowning isn't pretty. Victims will struggle to live. They grasp at whatever is within arm's length to keep from being pulled under. Typically, you'll find plants, twigs, or other foreign objects in their fist. I'm not making an assertion until I investigate further, but her hands are empty. I'd unofficially rule this casualty as suspicious."

The photographer stood and gestured. "Hey Marty. Did you notice the leather strap draped across the victim? Is that a purse?"

Breena and Andre stepped nearer as the examiner hovered over the woman. A blue strip blended in with her dress, crisscrossing a shoulder to her waist, almost unnoticeable.

Marty sloshed to the other side and bent to search underneath her. Carefully, he slid a secured bag around her torso. "Must've slipped behind her. I can't cut it away just yet, but I'll check for identification. Perhaps we can learn who this lady once was." He opened the flap, dug inside, and confiscated a wallet.

He looked at the I.D. and splashed to Breena. With grim features, he held the credentials face-high for her to view.

"Even if you haven't made an official ruling, I'm deeming this death as a probable homicide."

"I'm inclined to agree, but nothing's formal yet." Marty waved at attendants, who had parked an ambulance beyond the rocks. "Bring it, guys. We're ready to transport."

The men grabbed their gear. With much difficulty, they wheeled the gurney across the bumpy strand. Marty moved away once they approached but maintained control, while directing them.

"Careful when transporting her," he cautioned. "Specifically, the hands. Degloving's a real possibility."

Breena frowned. "Degloving?"

"Skin will slip off the hands and feet if we're not cautious when moving." He held out the wallet and nodded toward his case of tools. "Snap on a glove and take this. You'll want to find out if anyone's seen her recently."

Breena walked to the kit, retrieved a rubber glove, and then took the wallet from Marty. She studied the photograph and shook her head. She sure didn't see this coming.

Within minutes, the unit zipped her in the body-bag, hoisted onto the stretcher, and guided the corpse to the waiting emergency vehicle. The crew slowly rolled over the shores' rough patches. Once they cleared the uneven terrain, they pushed the gurney into the ambulance and slammed the hatches. Noiseless lights whirled as the van sped away.

Marty gazed at walkers standing past the site. They kept their hands tucked into warmup jackets. Their heads were bowed, obviously shaken.

Andre did a side nod. "Bet those two wished they'd never left home."

"Never fun to stumble across someone dead." Breena turned to the duo and signaled. "You two can take off. I've got your info and will contact you later." She said to Andre, "We need to locate Celia Sewell."

"Dr. Sewell's wife?"

"I want to visit with her. If she's unavailable, Nash'll do. And it's got to happen ASAP."

Andre threw a thumb in the direction the EMS van disappeared. "That's Celia Sewell?"

"We won't know until Marty's autopsy is concluded or we confirm she's alive, but I'd say it's likely. I need the information yesterday, Andre."

Without another word, Andre hurried toward his county sedan.

"My gut kept nudging me, telling me something's been wrong since Teddie claimed she saw someone murdered." Breena clutched her abdomen. "My stomach's rolling now."

"Do you believe Dr. Sewell's involved?" Marty sounded surprised by the suggestion. "Why would he kill his wife?"

"Oh, he has his reasons," Breena revealed in a grave tone. "Millions of reasons."

Chapter 31

Nash's head raised at the sound of his office door opening.

"Nash?" Aubrey peeked around the edge. "Are you busy?"

"Aubrey. I'm never too busy for you. Come in." He swiftly rose and circled his desk. Zigzagging past the disarray, he hurried and embraced his former girlfriend. "How wonderful to see you. We didn't get to visit the other evening."

Aubrey accepted his hug. "Yes, what a terrible night. Again, I appreciate you taking the time to lend your expertise. I'm so relieved my sister's receiving the help she needs."

"How is Teddie? I've been preoccupied the past few days and haven't had the opportunity to check on her. She's better, I assume?"

"Doctors want her sedated so she'll rest and let her body rejuvenate."

"Fantastic."

"Yes, well…"

"Something wrong?"

"Due to an oversight, the saline and medication emptied in her IV, and she awakened. I'm not sure how, but she managed to escape."

Nash's expression flattened. "I presume Drew Millard interfered?"

"No, he didn't help her, but she went straight to him, which almost surprised me since he participated in having her committed. Anyway, they were found at my parents' house. I had to make a hard decision and readmit her. Dr. Ramey prefers to keep her under and give her more time to recuperate."

"He's the best. I imagine the decision to recommit her was difficult, but I'm glad you listened. How long is her expected stay?"

"We don't have a timeline. Once we know, I'll arrange transport to Nashville. We've already pre-admitted her into Tennessee's top recovery facility. She'll have intense therapy and be kept away from Drew's influence."

"He's a savage, but in this case, I'd say he thought he was helping."

"Oh, he helped her, all right."

"Be fair, Aubrey. Drew called you to alert you of her decline. She chose to leave the facility. You aren't certain he didn't try to convince her to return to the clinic. I'm not a huge fan of Drew Millard, but I do believe he truly loves your sister and is driven to do right by her."

"I suppose." Aubrey exhaled. "My main objection to Teddie and Drew's interactions is she doesn't need romantic entanglements right now. And didn't I hear he officially divorced Evie, like two days ago? He requires down time, too."

"Yes"—Nash's gaze wandered the room—"a split with Evie can be taxing."

Aubrey's brows knitted as she surveyed his untidy office.

Nash shadowed her visual inspection. "An upset

colleague had a small meltdown. Cleaning crews are on their way."

"Small meltdown? More like major explosion."

"Childish behavior due to unhappy news." He shrugged. "What's done is done. Other issues are occupying my mind." He paused. "Celia left me."

She gave him a sympathetic look. "How are you?"

"We're dealing with the shock."

"I'm sure times are tough. The children? Did you tell them?"

"Bits. I instructed Nanny to take them to Mother's so Celia and I can work through our problems."

"Celia's contacted you?"

"Only via text." He positioned a hand onto her spine and guided her to a chair, motioning for her to sit. "She won't return my calls nor will she respond when I phone her."

"Do you know where she is?"

"She won't tell me that, either."

Aubrey blinked, appearing speechless. "Nash, I am sorry. I'm grateful you put your personal matters aside to take care of my family. But truthfully, I can't blame Celia." Her face revealed her dismay. "Evie St. John? I mean, really?"

"The past lacks forgiveness, but nonetheless, I confessed my transgressions and promised Celia I'd never see Evie again." Nash strolled behind his desk and sat. "Let me clarify. Yes, Evie and I had a romance. I received word from Celia. She knew of my infidelity and threatened to divorce me. I pleaded with her, and she's agreed to talk."

"You cherish her, I can see that, so why sleep with another woman and put your marriage in jeopardy?"

"We're like so many others who've been together a long period. We grew stale. Evidently not thinking with my brain, I strayed. Not a respectable excuse, but I do love my wife. I'll do what she wants to save my marriage."

Aubrey only nodded.

"Change of subject if you don't mind."

"Not at all."

"I'm sad you're departing so soon. Your reappearance is a pleasant surprise, although I was shocked you decided to revisit Jacob's Cove after your prolonged absence."

"I can't say the trip's been enjoyable, but it fared much better than last time." She fidgeted nervously. "Such an emotional time. Mama and Daddy's funeral."

"They cross my mind every day." He opened his drawer and retrieved a cigar. "I hold myself responsible in their deaths." He idly posited it between his lips and lit the tip. Inhaling deeply, he removed the stogie and blew a stream of smoke. "You hold me responsible, too."

A shaky smile touched her lips. "Kinda hard not to. You were entangled in the predicament and didn't do anything to stop it."

"I was young, Aubrey. I made mistakes. I never meant…" The chair groaned as he reclined. "I bear so many regrets."

"I understand, the fallout wasn't your goal, but your inadvertent actions hurt a lot of people. My sisters and I still suffer because of the aftereffects. Especially Teddie."

"Then why come back? Obviously, you haven't resolved your anger."

"Teddie came to Jacob's Cove to find peace." She smiled a jaded smile. "I should emulate her, only I'm not there yet. I'm working on forgiving."

"As I labor to forgive, too." He took a long drag, then placed the cigar on the ashtray's edge, and gazed at the thread of smoke dancing at the end. "By Teddie's reaction toward me, I'm guessing you never revealed what you knew. You suffered alone."

"I've wrestled with what I should do. Both Teddie and Raven question if our mom had another man on the side or if Daddy dreamed the whole affair." Her features displayed the guilt she felt "I'd create lots of complications if I owned up after so many years."

"To tell them your mother was involved with someone else?"

She nodded.

"Yet, you're here to reconcile your internal conflict."

A knock on the door waylaid their conversation. Not waiting until Nash answered, Breena poked her head inside. "Sorry to interrupt, Nash, but you and I need to chat." She glimpsed at Aubrey. "Alone."

He took a final puff of his stogie and smashed it into the ashtray. "Whatever you say can be said in front of Aubrey. We're old friends, as you're aware."

She fully emerged into the room and frowned at the disorder. "Dumped Evie, didya?"

"Obvious, isn't it?"

Breena squinted toward Aubrey. "I'm thinking your presence isn't a good idea, but never mind. The information indirectly affects you. Maybe I should talk to you, first." She turned to fully faced Aubrey. "A body was discovered. I'm not privy to details yet, but

I'm ninety-nine percent convinced this is the person Teddie witnessed murdered on the pavilion."

"You found someone at the Phoenix?" Aubrey's forehead creased. "I drove past. I didn't notice any commotion."

"Storms drove the corpse onto the beach. The weather also instigated strong currents to carry it a ways and kept it below the surface, or so we think. Anyway, back to your sister. I'm unfamiliar with the particulars of her illness, but you might rethink keeping her holed up in that asylum."

"I will, thank you, Breena. Her doctor and I will discuss this latest update. And I'll tell her, too. She'll be ecstatic to learn the incident isn't a part of her nightmare."

Breena looked at Nash. "Now, your turn. I need to speak to Celia, ASAP."

"Celia?" Nash's skin paled. "She's… I don't know where she is, Breena. She found out about Evie and me, and she refuses to come home."

"The two of you've spoken?"

"Not spoken, per say. Only through text messages."

"When was the last one?"

"Earlier today."

"Give me your cell, Nash."

"Why?"

"So we can trace the tower frequencies and locate the area she's contacting you from."

"I'm not grasping, Breena. Why are you so desperate to talk to Celia?"

"Let me explain further. The body washed ashore belongs to a woman. Her appearance is rough after being submerged for a lengthy stretch. We can't tell who she is. We did, however, find a handbag on her person and inside a driver's license." Breena directed her gaze toward Nash and held it steady. "Celia's driver's license."

"You're not saying…no, that's not possible. She's texted me."

"We didn't find any electronic apparatuses, Nash. Those messages were transmitted from somewhere else, which is why I need to confiscate your cell."

Nash jumped to his feet, confused. "Is my wife dead or not?"

"Nothing's substantiated. Marty's performing a quickie autopsy because of the corpse's condition. He's calling in favors, urging connections to put a rush on the results. You can say no, but I'd like you to go to the morgue. The remains aren't recognizable, but it'd be a big help if you can tell us if the clothes or purse are Celia's."

A white-faced Nash sat back down and laid his head on his desk.

"Nash?"

Nash nodded and stood again but was visibly unsteady.

"In the meantime." Breena extended her palm. "The phone."

He didn't argue and relinquished his device.

"Hopefully, we'll have an official verification soon. If there's an indication of foul play, we'll need complete access to your home and office."

"Foul play?" The sadness on Nash's face transformed into alarm. "You think I killed Celia?"

"Spouse is the first person we investigate. Just

want my ducks in a row when the word comes."

"Why on earth would I murder Celia?"

Breena almost smiled. "Only you'd know that, Nash. But you were having a fling, and Celia's worth a fortune. The kind of fortune that makes even a doctor's earnings seem paltry. Wealth you wouldn't acquire in a mere settlement."

She gave the room another onceover. "Wife discovers your lady friend, and you speed back to her with your tail between your legs. But wait, she intended to divorce you. Only way to obtain Celia's money is if she's dead. Sounds like a solid motive to me. Speculation. I might be stranded in left field minus a catcher's mitt." She walked to the exit. "You're needed at the morgue. Go ahead and swing by my office, after."

"May I take a moment?"

"Take several. Just don't leave town."

"Nash, this is awful," Aubrey comforted after Breena departed. "Are you okay?"

"I'm not sure what I feel. I hope in my heart it's not her, but Breena seems almost positive."

"Breena's been in law enforcement a long time. She goes by her instincts, but she could be wrong."

"But if Celia was killed, they'll accuse me."

"Breena is messing with your head, hoping to trick you into incriminating yourself and make her job easier. I wouldn't say a word without an attorney present." A coldness developed in Aubrey's look and speared into him. "Makes me wonder, though."

"Wonder what?"

"If history hasn't repeated itself."

"You're suggesting?"

"You were sleeping with my mother when you and I were a couple. My father realized what you were up to and shot them, both. You and Evie have been doin' the deed even though you and Celia are still married, and now, officials believe she's dead. Not exactly the same, but close enough to be considered a coincidence." The corners of her mouth lifted maliciously as the blue in her eyes darkened. "Or is it more?"

Chapter 32

"I refuse to let you medicate me." Teddie sat on the bed, her legs crisscrossed, her arms doubled tightly over her chest. "You're not keeping me unconscious, especially without my permission."

A man who claimed to be her doctor stood next to a plastic saline bag attached to a stand, holding a needle connected to a tube.

"Ms. Donavan," the physician stated in a stern tone. "You passed out on arrival last week and hit your head. X-rays showed trauma. I suggested putting you in an induced coma to allow the swelling in your brain to go down."

This was the first she heard of her fainting or bumping her head when she first entered the facility. Did he tell the truth, or was he manipulating her? Her gut told her it was the latter, and she trusted her instincts a lot more than she did this quack.

He grabbed her wrist, attempting to undo her folded arms. "We're only doing what's best for you."

"Stay away from me." She jerked, wrangling from his grasp, and scooted backward until her spine touched the headboard. "You're the one who's insane. You're drugging me, yet you swear I'm addicted to prescription drugs."

"We will wean you off a little at a time."

"No, you won't. I refused to continue these

unnecessary treatments."

"You require medical care, and your sister agrees. She makes your decisions until further notice."

This argument began the moment she re-entered the facility. Although coerced into her room, she refused to change into the mandatory hospital gown nor would she allow anyone to put a finger on her.

"Aubrey might call the shots, but her control is only temporary. I still sign her paycheck, and the money will stop if she continues this tyranny."

"Your family's discords are not our concern, Ms. Donavan."

No, they weren't worried if she cut off Aubrey's cash flow or how upset she was the sheriff hauled her back to the medical center. Still, her sister overstepped major boundaries, and the second Teddie was able, she'd summon her legal team and strip away Aubrey's authority.

Teddie drew her arms closer. "You may as well leave, because you're not getting near me."

"Ms. Donavan," the doctor sighed.

"Get out," she screamed.

He shook his head at the nurse, who stood in the doorway, and hung the drip over the rack, stomping out the door.

Teddie pointed at the nurse. "Forgot your guard dog."

The woman threw her a nasty glare, slamming the door behind her.

She scrambled off the bed and hurried to the exit. Cracking the door, she peeked past the gap then quickly jumped away, backing into the wall.

"Damn."

Two uniforms stood on either side of her doorway and eliminated an escape route. She left the set of gargoyles and settled onto the mattress, studying the long drapes concealing the window.

"Hmmm, possibly?"

Easing off the bed, Teddie walked to the curtains and ran her fingers across the coarse material. She shoved the heavy shades aside, exposing a windowpane, large enough for her to fit through. "This'll work."

****

Evie leaned on the pavilion's rail, staring at the dimming sky. A ferocious wind blew off the water, pushing the waves high enough to brush the pier's underbelly. Black vapors loomed and vibrated, while veins of gold shattered the gloom.

Evie wasn't interested in an incoming storm. Or anything in life. Nash had dumped her. She'd also received word her superiors demanded a meeting. No need to ask why. Her and Nash's affair had been leaked, and her bosses would probably terminate for moral cause.

She had nothing. No man, no job, and everyone would desert her.

Glancing at the revolving clouds, she pushed off the banister. "Time to regroup," she said aloud.

"Talking to yourself?" A chuckle followed the jeer. "Jacob's Cove water must contain toxins and turn everyone looney."

Evie stiffened. "Whoopee, another Donavan."

"I knew you'd be thrilled to see me."

"Why are you here, Aubrey?"

"To watch the storm and breathe." Aubrey

sauntered to the barrier and stood by Evie. "Had a rough morning."

"Poor you."

She tilted and gazed at the squally waters. "By the way you look, your day hasn't gone smoothly, either."

"I don't want to talk about it."

"Bet I can make you smile."

Evie's lips pressed tight as her eyes tapered. No one could make her happy, specifically Aubrey Donavan.

"Don't believe me?" Aubrey's expression brightened. "Your ex-husband? Remember him? He's been arrested and is sitting in jail."

Fingers sprayed across Evie's chest as her mouth gaped. She strained to keep the shakiness out of her vocal cords when she spoke. "Drew's in jail? What'd he do?"

"He was hanging out with my sister. A photographer interrupted them. Apparently Drew took exception to having their space invaded and cold-cocked the guy."

Evie tossed her head back and released a loud laugh. "You win. You gave me the best news I've had in a long time."

"He's not your only former who's had a run-in with the law today."

Evie's face went solemn. "Who?"

Aubrey's lips lifted. "Nash. He's in hot water. Scalding hot, and he's sinking fast."

Evie blinked, still baffled.

"I see you're uninformed." She edged closer. "Let me fill you in. Teddie is dealing with issues, but she isn't all crazy. Someone was discovered on the beach, dead." She paused for effect. As if on cue, a boom resonated above them. "Authorities believe the body belongs to Celia Sewell."

Evie gasped. "You're kidding. And she was murdered?"

"Nothing's confirmed, but that's what's speculated."

"How's Nash involved?"

"Investigators always look at spouses first. Breena demanded he meet her at her office for questioning. I'd say the good doctor's having a worse day than you."

Another rumble exploded overhead. Tiny drops began to spill out of the sky.

Evie moved away from the guardrail and slid a hand into her pocket. She extracted her cell phone. "I received a call from the sheriff's office earlier, but I didn't answer." She glanced at the screen. "They left a voicemail." She put the phone to her ear and listened. "It's Nash. He needs me."

"Sure, he does."

Evie spun toward the sheriff's building. "I have to go."

Aubrey moved to block Evie, holding up a palm. "Have you lost your mind? That man used you. He played you for a fool, and you're rushing to save him?"

"I love him."

"Uggg." Aubrey rolled her eyes. "You're as insane as everybody else in this town."

Evie frowned. Why would it bother Aubrey if she supported Nash? Unless…Aubrey wanted to be his girlfriend, again. Perhaps she still loved him, and she wanted to be the one to rescue him.

"Move, Aubrey." Aubrey stayed put. "This isn't a

request. You need to get over the past and accept Nash no longer wants you." She pushed her thumb into her breastbone. "He wants me."

"What are you talking about?"

"Your feelings for Nash. You're still in love with him."

"Oh my gosh."

"Don't deny it. But he's free to choose, and he chose me. Get it?"

"Who cares who he chooses? Nash Sewell hurt a lot of people. It's time he pays for his crimes, and I intend to see he does just that." Aubrey closed in on Evie. Glowering, she poked her finger into Evie's upper chest. "You will not budge from this spot, and you will not help Nash. If you so much as try, I *will* stop you. Get it?"

Chapter 33

Teddie shunted the curtains farther apart and scooted a chair closer to the window. She planted a foot into the seat and boosted up, then curled her fingertips, grasping the window's quarter-inch ridge. She gave it a hard tug. The opening refused to budge.

Frustrated, she folded to inspect the window's bottom rim. A generous quantity of caulk had been spread around the edges, obviously to prevent patients from doing what she attempted, escape.

Releasing an aggravated breath, she stood upright and considered her options. Easy. Leave or not stay in this hellhole. She repositioned and tried again, receiving the same outcome.

Okay, her flight wouldn't be as easy as her first. Standing back, she studied her problem. If the window refused to open, her next option was to shatter the pane.

She turned to scan her room. Nothing. Objects were either plastic, lightweight, or bolted to the floor. Dejected, she stared down, looking at her boots. Heavy boots, Breena suggested she change into before moving into the earlier downpour. If one was thrown hard enough, the glass would fracture.

She placed her toe behind her heel and slipped a foot out of the shaft. She grabbed the top, reared back to fling, and froze. Two guards waited outside. Surely, they'd hear smashing glass, or she may trip an alarm.

Breakage might also include sharp slivers and rip her to shreds when she exited. On the contrary, if she desired to flee, she had to take the risk. She stretched backward clutching the footwear like a football, then held still, biting back a scream.

A grinning face stood on the other side of the window.

"Drew?" Her arm sagged, allowing her boot to dangle between her fingers. "Did Breena let you go?"

He snapped a forefinger across his lips. Beaming, he produced a miniature gun like tool, holding it high so she could see.

She shrugged with a bland smile, not knowing what he showed her.

He placed the instrument's blade to the glass and began to etch, operating slow and meticulous. Teddie watched as he performed his handiwork, periodically glimpsing at the doorway, hoping nobody would come check on her.

After what seemed like forever, Drew put the cutout on the ground. He leaned in and outstretched his arms. "Hurry."

She clutched onto him as he hoisted her over, swinging her to the grass. Teddie searched the upper eves trying to spot cameras and stay out of the probing lenses view.

"Don't worry." Drew pocketed his cutter and jumped off a small, stepladder he'd brought. "I've done lots of work at this facility. I know every nook. I snuck inside, stole a uniform, and disabled the cameras after I located your room. Security's communicating with tech support now."

Without another word, he rushed her across the

parking lot, in between a pair of convenience stores, down a dark ally, and to a deserted street. Cracks of thunder rumbled again as they scurried down the block. Tiers of rough clouds had gathered and coated the eastern corner of the sky. Another storm brewed.

He motioned to his pickup. "I'm over here."

Drew shut his door the second the rain started to pour. Large droplets smacked the windshield. He waited until the gusher decreased and pulled onto the road.

"Thanks for springing me," Teddie told him meekly.

"You don't belong in there."

Her stomach summersaulted. "You believe me?"

"Hikers came across a body lying on the beach."

"Seriously?" Teddie's heart bumped. "When? Who was it? Are they sure the person was murdered?"

"Whoa, you're rattling off too many questions. Give me a minute." Drew braked to maneuver an ample flow of water. "A couple stumbled upon the corpse adjacent to where we camped the same time Breena hauled us to our perspective prisons."

"How did it get way over there?"

"Speculation is forceful currents from the storm moved it. To answer your other questions, no, the victim hasn't been positively IDed, but they suspect it's Celia Sewell."

Teddie gasped an, "oh no."

"It hasn't been confirmed the death's a homicide, but they're thinking it's your mystery murder."

"Any possible suspects?"

"Nash."

Stunned, Teddie's lips tightened. "That's rather

shocking. You certainly are privy to a good deal of information."

"You learn a lot sitting in a jail cell."

"Right. Did you bust out, too?"

"Nope. Posted bail. His honor didn't set the bond too high, and I could afford to pay." He clicked on his turn signal to change lanes. "So, which way?"

Teddie curled her bottom lip underneath her teeth. She didn't think any further than leaving the hospital. "I'm not sure, but I need to go somewhere. Staying in Jacob's Cove isn't an option," she faltered. "Home, maybe? To Nashville. I can regroup, regain prospective, and try to understand what's happened here."

"Sounds rational."

"Plus, I have access to my legal team. Aubrey can't interfere."

"Yeah, I don't get her."

"Me neither. She's always been overprotective, but this time she's overstepped. I intend to take her power away."

"Not sure why you gave it to her in the first place."

"I signed it over to her during my admittance into the hospital."

"Not ethical."

"She thought she was helping me."

He grunted and gave her a side glance. "So, you want to go to the airport?"

"I have to pack and alert my pilot to ready the plane." She peeked outside to inspect the turbulent skis. "I hope this weather passes, soon."

"Towers will keep the planes grounded, if it doesn't."

Teddie frowned in Drew's direction. Did she catch

a hitch in his voice? Was it there because she meant to leave him?

A few days ago, she suggested he come to Tennessee, but he declined, telling her he was moving back to Texas. Except their relationship had altered since. He formally split with Evie, and they'd rekindled their romance last night.

Should she ask him again?

She took a deep breath. "I suggested repeatedly you come to Nashville with me, and you've always said no. But things have changed. Maybe your mind has, too?" Another inhale. "Should I tell the pilot to prepare for one passenger? Or two?"

****

Nash folded a handful of tissues and dabbed his temples as Breena sat at her desk, speaking on the telephone. "Appreciate you, Marty. Oh, and Marty. Pass on a bucket load of kudos to your colleagues. Tell 'em we're grateful for the quick results." She hung up, her expression grim. "It's official."

He nodded. "I'm not surprised. The purse and clothes were hers."

"Sorry about your loss, Nash."

He gazed at her through reddened eyes. "Are you? You summoned me so you can grill me about her death. I had nothing to do with her dying, and this is a waste of my time. I need to be at home comforting our children. My family should be allowed to grieve in private, devoid of frivolous accusations. Organize her memorial service." He crushed the wad of tissue in his fist and lobbed it into the trashcan. "Instead, I'm here."

"Protocol, Nash."

"Yes, I'm aware of your procedures. Investigate

the husband first."

"Then let's investigate, so you can act as Celia's grieving husband." She shuffled a stack of papers to the side, opened a folder, and selected a pen. "First, let's discuss yours and Evie Millard's affair."

"Evie and I are no longer involved."

"Right. Celia threatened to divorce you if you continued sleeping with Evie."

Nash's head bobbed.

"But she only warned you through a text message, correct? She never made the demand in person?"

"No, she never told me face to face."

Her forehead creased as she wrote. "Celia's cell." She peered at Nash "I mentioned earlier we didn't notice any electronic devices on her. Now, it may've gotten lost in the sea, but I don't believe she sent messages while under water."

"I can't explain any of it."

"I can shed a little light on the mystery. Cell tower transmitted both phones pinged near your office building. I find that a tiny bit strange, since your wife's body wallowed in the deep."

"Should I call an attorney?"

"Your choice. As of now, we're fact gathering. You're not under arrest, and you're free to terminate this interview at any time. However, we will address the topic again in an official capacity. You might contact a lawyer to keep on tap."

"Will you interrogate others?"

"Drew was on the pier, although I can't imagine why he'd want Celia dead. Now Evie's a different story, and we'll look at her closely. I'm sure there's more." She nodded at her phone. "Did you want to speak to an attorney before we go on?"

"Not yet, but I may choose to not reply to your inquiries."

"Your prerogative." She checked her notes. "Let's talk about your finances."

Nash straightened in his chair, his face instantly shrouded in crimson. "Let's not." He leaped to his feet and sprinted toward the doorway.

"You earn a hefty salary, Doctor. A substantial amount, compared to the rest of Cove residents."

Nash extended a hand toward the doorknob.

"Except you're broke."

He halted.

"Beyond broke, Nash, you're ass-deep in debt. Tax liens, judgements, and several triple-digit credit card balances left unpaid."

He deliberately turned to face her. "You unearthed that report in record speed."

"Pulling credit and checking bank statements are standard in an inquiry. The process doesn't take long."

"Much shorter time than finding my poor wife."

"You never reported her missing. I find that off, too."

"I thought we'd split up. There's no way I could've known otherwise. No one in town was aware either."

"They are now. Few homicides occur in Jacob's Cove. This is the first in seventeen years, and while the fine Cove citizens are upset, they want to assist in solving the crime. I'm receiving more help than I can handle."

"How fortunate."

"Understand you're a gambler." Her eyes narrowed. "Who knew?"

He didn't react.

"I also found out you won't inherit Celia's money, which is a huge blow, since she had enough to settle your debts. You could still play the ponies quite a while, but she left it to your kids." She snatched an oversized fountain drink, shook the ice, and drew a long sip. "You can count that in your favor. No use killing for money you can't touch."

He gradually returned to his seat. "Then you should have your answers."

"But," she glanced at him, again, "there are life insurance policies."

"I purchased them years ago. Celia bought coverage on me, as well."

"Disbursements on her is much larger than the payout on you."

"Yes, but last I heard, that's not a crime."

"No, it isn't, Nash, but it is unusual. The wife normally receives the greater sum, but I suppose in Celia's case, she wouldn't require as much if you were to die first. But she beat you. As it is, you're primed to be paid a buttload of money. You can repay your bookie and still have plenty." She retrieved a document and smiled. "Quite a motive, if you asked me."

Nash rose out of his chair. "Unless you're prepared to arrest me, I'm finished."

"You've made the call about a payoff date, too. Only hours after poor Celia was discovered and prior to positive identification. Tells me you might've known she was gone before we did." Breena dropped the paperwork on her desk. "If the insurance company hasn't already informed you, they'll wait until we conclude this investigation before they reconcile."

Nash spun away, propelling her office door ajar, and quickly zigzagged past the desks, almost sprinting toward the outlet.

"Hang around, Nash," she shouted. "We're bringing in FBI. They'll want to talk to you."

Chapter 34

A satisfied smile settled on Teddie's face as she watched Drew's pickup disappear into a blanket of dirt. Once their belongings were packed, they'd meet at the rental agency to turn in her car, then fly to Tennessee.

His decisive yes to her invitation had her almost school-girl giddy. A major factor was to get to know their daughter, but Teddie also fit into the equation.

A rumble above averted her attention away from Drew's vanishing truck. Enraged clouds loomed beyond the cliffs. Streaks of light shimmered against the darkness.

Spinning, Teddie headed into the house. The latest storm was catching up, and she preferred to get on her way before the downpour hit.

Inside, she cleared the staircase and sprinted down the hallway into her room. She grabbed the small suitcase her helpful siblings left and placed it on the bed. It didn't take long to load her possessions, since most had already been shipped.

Thunderous booms grew closer and rattled the old house. The sheers covering her window, lifted, and flapped as gusting winds howled. She tossed in her last piece of clothing and zipped the bag. Grabbing the handle, she hurried back down the hall, then skidded to a halt.

Her blood turned cold.

The door to her parents' room was open, again. Music box tinkles intermixed with roars of thunder. She abandoned her luggage and creeped toward the sound. Palm on the door, she pushed gently and eased it farther ajar. Peeking past the edge, she inhaled her mother's fragrance.

She sidled farther in. Nothing gave the impression of being amiss, but her instincts had jumped to high alert. Evil lurked near. She rushed to the dresser, jerked the sheet off, and slammed the box shut, keeping her trembling hand on the lid.

She breathed in.

The perfumed scent grew stronger.

"You slipped by the guards and escaped again."

Teddie jumped as she peered behind. She frowned. "What are you doing here?"

"Finding you."

"You're not taking me back. I won't go."

"You don't have a say, Teddie. I have power of attorney, and you will go."

"No, Aubrey. I'm leaving for Nashville. The plane's fueled and ready. You can hitch a ride or find your own way. Either way, I won't go back to that quack or that hospital."

"We're trying to help you, Teddie."

"I don't know what you're doing, but it doesn't feel like help."

"You're my sister, and I'm devoted to you. Trust me, I'm only watching out for your interest."

"I appreciate you, I do, but I'm okay." Teddie narrowed the distance between them, positioning her palms upon Aubrey's shoulders. "You've wanted to leave since we arrived. I'm done here. Let's go home."

"I'm so relieved to hear you say that. Yes, I can't wait until our lives are back to normal."

"Glad we agree." Teddie dropped her hands and started to move, but she paused. "Are you wearing Mama's perfume?"

A peculiar smile warmed Aubrey's lips. Teddie's gaze shimmied to Aubrey's hands.

Cautiously, she nodded at the object her sister gripped. "What are you doing with that?"

"Remembering," she replied dreamingly.

"Remembering what?"

"That day." Her expression appeared serine, but her features seemed different. Her eyes had gone cold and blank as if her soul deserted her. "The day they died."

"How can you remember? You weren't here."

"But I was."

"I don't understand, Aubrey."

"Yes, you do. You just don't want to accept what you know."

"What I…"

Teddie's mind was abruptly trapped in a reverse vortex, reliving her nightmare. Only she was wide awake. The entire scene replayed, ending with her younger self tearing inside and hearing her own terrified screams. Her conscious shifted her back into real time.

Teddie stared. A flash of chills shivered across her spine. "It was you, not Mama. You and Daddy yelled at each other. Mama was already…"

"Dead."

"I'm confused. Why didn't you stop him?"

"Teddie, you're not getting this at all." Aubrey

squeezed the gun she held between her hands. "Daddy didn't shoot her."

Teddie stopped to think. "You did. You murdered her," she choked, grasping what she now knew as the truth. "Why?"

"She was having an affair with Nash Sewell."

"Mom and Nash? No. You dated him."

"I was crazy about him, but he loved *her*."

Still in disbelief, Teddie grappled to process it all. "Mama, Nash? What happened?"

"I came home after Nash ended our relationship."

"I thought you broke it off."

"Their deaths made headlines. As an up and coming physician, he didn't want his name tied to the story, so he stayed quiet."

"Did Mom admit she and Nash were together?"

Aubrey's fingers tightened on the firearm. "I confronted her."

"What did she say?"

"That's life, and I should grow up. Then she told me to go away. She was meeting Nash later, and she had to get ready. I was so mad. Dad stored his .45 in his sock drawer. She went into the bathroom and while she was changing, I found it. She laughed when she saw it and called me a silly, little girl." Aubrey smiled as if still pleased with the outcome. "Her last words."

Teddie stomach coiled as she struggled to keep her revulsion at bay. "And Dad?"

"He'd gotten home after I killed her. We fought, too. He wanted to notify the police. I didn't want him to."

"So, you shot him?"

"When the chance arose, I planted the .45 on his

temple, and pulled the trigger, twice. Then I positioned his Colt in his hand to make it seem like he did it. I was hiding in the closet when you walked in. You spoke my name, so you saw me. I assumed you heard my voice during our argument, but you've blocked the memory. Except your nightmare kept hanging around."

Teddie gazed at Aubrey, striving to comprehend. "You tried to make me believe I'd gone insane. The smells, sounds"—Teddie pointed at metal piece between her sister's grip—"the handgun on the bed. Sending me to a mental facility? Why'd you do that?"

"I didn't want you to remember."

"The medication? Did you give me drugs?"

"In your vitamins. I also leaked your substance abuse problems to the press."

Teddie's head swam, unsure her legs would hold her. How could her own flesh and blood, a person she adored, do such horrible things to her and even worse to others?

She had to keep Aubrey talking until she figured out what to do. "Lucky I saw Celia die. Fit right into your plans, huh?"

"I didn't intend for you to witness Celia's swan dive."

"What do you mean, you didn't…?" Awareness punched Teddie square in her gut. "You shoved Celia into the ocean?"

"I followed you that night. Celia tailed Nash. We met on the pavilion by coincidence. She knew about him and Evie. Celia said Nash's true love was Mother, and how glad she was Daddy killed her. That annoyed me. I mean, Mom may've been a first-class bitch, but she's still my mother. We argued and then…oops."

Aubrey smiled again. "You know the rest."

"Is there anyone else?"

"Sadly, Evie Millard passed away earlier today. Nash's prepared to take the fall for Celia's passing, and Evie wanted to save him."

Teddie eyes tapered. "You're setting up Nash?"

"Celia lost her phone before she involuntarily exited the pier. I retrieved it, read her messages, and tracked her calls. Besides being a philanderer, Nash also has gambling troubles. She threatened to divorce him if he didn't end his affair with Evie and get help for his gaming. Apparently, Celia already cut off the money train. I continued the conversation as Celia, and then I planted the cell in his desk so Breena could find it after Celia's body washed ashore."

"What about Evie? Does anyone realize she's gone?"

"I phoned 911 and informed them I discovered a despondent Evie by the Phoenix, and how she talked about ending it all. I tried to prevent her from jumping, but she hurdled the rail and leaped to her death before I could stop her."

"So many people are dead, and you're the cause. And you are hell bent on destroying me, my career, and my life. I can't fathom."

"You're my meal ticket, I'd never destroy you. I only wanted you to quit trying to make sense of your nightmare." She directed the weapon at Teddie's forehead. "Unfortunately, now that you know, I can't allow you live."

"How do you plan to explain me dying?"

"Suicide, in the room where your beloved parents took their final breaths. No one will be surprised, given your mental instability. You will make your mark in music history."

"You're reporting two suicides the same day? Breena will view that as suspicious."

"Not me." She raised the revolver and slowly tugged the striker back. "Drew's going to find you. He'll call it in."

"Aubrey, no!" Drew exploded into the room.

Teddie shrieked as he volleyed into the air toward Aubrey. Aubrey whirled around and pulled the trigger. Blasts echoed, shattering Teddie's eardrums as gunpowder saturated the room. Drew's body jerked, then shuddered and collapsed.

Teddie dashed to him, kneeling by his side. Blood soaked the front of his shirt, his eyes fluttered. His skin whitened and breathing shallowed.

Teddie glared at Aubrey. "What did you do?"

Aubrey re-positioned the pistol, directing it toward Teddie's head. "Murder/suicide in the exact spot, seventeen years apart. What a great ballad." Aubrey's voice sank low as her thumb twitched on the hammer. "Too bad you won't be around to sing it."

Teddie leaned back and balanced on her elbows. She kicked her leg high, her foot connecting with Aubrey's wrist. The revolver dislodged from her hand, flying overhead, and landing on the far side of the room. A pop resonated. Once more, scents of cordite inundated the space.

Teddie scrambled to her feet and raced to the location where the hardware rested. Aubrey headed in the same direction. They arrived simultaneously, both wrestled to the floor, seizing the gun.

"Drop it, now!" Breena burst inside, her weapon

drawn. Two deputies entered in behind her. Teddie and Aubrey froze. The sheriff waved her own gun. "Put the shooter on the ground."

"She's trying to kill herself and accidently shot Drew." Aubrey rushed as they lowered the .45.

Breena stepped to where Drew lay hemorrhaging. She placed two fingers onto the side of his neck. She straightened and spoke to the men. "Heart's beating, but barely. Call 911." She squinted at Drew again. "Hope they're not too late."

Sanctioning one of her men to attend to Drew, she walked to the women and swept up the firearm.

Her eyes bore into Aubrey. "Figured you be here. We recovered Evie Millard." Breena gripped Aubrey's upper arm and yanked her to her feet. "Alive. And she's telling a very interesting story. Let's take a trip downtown and chat."

A deputy moved in front of a protesting Aubrey holding a pair of steeled cuffs. Quickly, he spun and shackled her, then led her away.

Nothing after registered. Teddie crawled to sit by Drew. His skin appeared swallower, his chest hardly moved. She positioned her hands over his wound and applied pressure to keep more blood from seeping.

"Help's on the way, Teddie," Breena said in a soft voice.

Teddie combatted her tears, studying his paled, but calm face. She feared he'd given in and was content to fade to whatever waited on the other side. "It doesn't look good, does it?"

"No, Teddie. It doesn't."

Chapter 35

Teddie dragged a fist across her cheeks, wiping away the flow of tears, while she stared at Drew's colorless face. Her weeping wasn't just because of his predicament, but for every sad occurrence that recently transpired.

Drew flashed a weak smile. "Enough crying, already. It's over."

She nodded, minus a conviction. Teddie had remained by Drew's side until help arrived. The paramedics quickly stabilized him the best they could, and then they whisked him away. "You lost so much blood. I didn't think the ambulance would ever arrive, and when they finally showed, the EMTs wouldn't allow me to ride along. I discovered later you flat-lined, and they had to resuscitate twice. You nearly died because of me."

"You didn't shoot me. Your sister did." Drew wiggled a hand from underneath the sheet. A grimace spread across his face as he reached to clasp her palm. "You're not responsible for what Aubrey did."

"I feel like I am. If I hadn't returned to Jacob's Cove, Celia would still be alive, and you wouldn't be lying here."

"No worries. Doc says it's gonna take time, but I'll fully recover."

"I'm happy you will. I just hope we can

emotionally recuperate."

Drew elevated his head an inch off the pillow. "Teddie, we'll survive this." A corner of his lip upturned. "We may require a hell of a lot of psychoanalysis, but we'll be great if we stick together."

Teddie released a quivered laugh and squeezed his hand she clutched between hers. "We'll help each other."

"We will. Now I need my doctor's okay to leave this antiseptic smelling hell. I'm ready to head to Nashville."

"Our trip's been postponed. You just had a major operation. You had a bullet lodged into your chest, very close to your heart, and it took hours to remove."

"I know, but I'm ready to go," Drew complained.

"We will, once your physician gives the okay. I spoke to Raven, and she'll contact contractors and physicians about constructing an area for in-house physical therapy when we can move you."

"How did Raven take the news about Aubrey?"

"The way you'd expect."

Teddie and a stunned Raven had a lengthy conversation while Teddie waited for Drew to awaken in recovery. Neither were sure how one accepted a close family member was a cold-blooded murderer. They couldn't understand how Aubrey's twisted brain worked.

They did agree to finance her care, providing she followed their hired attorney's instructions; confess and be institutionalized. If she chose a different route, she'd figure it out on her own. Either way, she'd be locked up the rest of her life, and they never wanted to see Aubrey again.

"You're awfully quiet. Are you all right?" Drew mumbled.

"Just a lot on my mind."

"I can imagine." He grinned sadly. "Or maybe I can't."

"Whether you can or can't, you don't need to."

"You aren't going to fill me in on the details of the inquiry?"

"Aubrey denied everything. Regardless of her disclaimer, she's been transferred to county lockup, waiting in a heavily guarded cell for arraignment. The investigation's still in progress, but too many facts are stacked against her. Breena guessed a judge would set the bail high, if at all.

Authorities found Celia's phone in Nash's drawer where Aubrey told me she stashed it. Evie also gave a formal statement, and you will too, once doctors deem you healthy enough. My vitamins were sent to a lab to run tests. Breena's also mentioned exhuming my dad's body for a proper autopsy, but I can't focus on that."

"Shitload of info." Drew hacked a dry cough. Her grip tightened around his hand. "Calm down. Doc said drainage tube in my chest may cause congestion."

Teddie's lips curved. "I brought you a surprise. Would you like it now or are you too tired?"

"Exhausted, but if you're gonna shower me with gifts, I'll stay awake."

She freed her hand from his and walked to the door. "A special visitor's come to see you." She peeked through the doorway and spoke outside. "He's awake."

Her grin widened as she turned back to him. A beautiful teen strolled into the room. She stopped beside Teddie.

Drew's head lifted. "Savannah?"

Teddie seized their daughter's arm and led her to his bed. "I phoned Jarod. He and Savannah hopped the first plane to fly to the U.S. She wanted to be here and greet you when you woke up." She glanced at Savannah. "This is your dad, Drew. Drew, Savannah."

Savannah gave a shy smile. "Hi, Daddy."

Drew's eyes watered. "You two are the only medicine I need."

"Don't get used to lounging in bed," Teddie teased. "Your girls plan to make some music, and we require a first-class guitarist to accompany us."

"I'm definitely on the mend." His bright expression transformed into serious as his gaze settled onto Teddie. "Love you, Teddie. Always have, you know."

"Back at you." She sank down next to him, slipped her arm across his stomach, and gently laid her head on his shoulder. "Right, back at you."

A word from the author…

Debra is a home-grown Texas girl who loves to write romance/suspense with a bit of steam and a love fun.

She is also the adoring mother of two children, Stephen and Hannah, and the equally adoring mother-in-law to their spouses, Astrid and Ryan.

Besides writing, Debra stays busy teaching special education at a local elementary school. At home, she fosters homeless dogs for the Humane Society, and she is a shelter volunteer.

During her spare time, she enjoys the beach, painting, photography, travel, and a tasty plate of Tex Mex at her favorite cantina.

Debra began writing in 2004 and currently has three books published with The Wild Rose Press. She is an active member of the Central Texas Romance Writers of America Chapter and has served as secretary of the group for many years.

Visit www.debjupe.com to find out more.

Thank you for purchasing
this publication of The Wild Rose Press, Inc.

If you enjoyed the story, we would appreciate your
letting others know by leaving a review.

For other wonderful stories,
please visit our on-line bookstore at
www.thewildrosepress.com.

For questions or more information
contact us at
info@thewildrosepress.com.

The Wild Rose Press, Inc.
www.thewildrosepress.com

Stay current with The Wild Rose Press, Inc.

Like us on Facebook

https://www.facebook.com/TheWildRosePress

And Follow us on Twitter
https://twitter.com/WildRosePress